The Perfidious

Parrot

Also by Janwillem van de Wetering

FICTION
The Grijpstra–de Gier series:

Outsider in Amsterdam
Tumbleweed
The Corpse on the Dike
Death of a Hawker
The Japanese Corpse
The Blond Baboon
The Maine Massacre
The Mind-Murders
The Streetbird
The Rattle-Rat
Hard Rain
Just a Corpse at Twilight
The Hollow-Eyed Angel

OTHER
Inspector Saito's Small Satori
The Butterfly Hunter
Bliss and Bluster
Murder by Remote Control
Seesaw Millions

NONFICTION
The Empty Mirror
A Glimpse of Nothingness
Robert van Gulik: His Life, His Work

CHILDREN'S BOOKS
Hugh Pine
Huge Pine and the Good Place
Huge Pine and Something Else
Little Owl

The Perfidious

Parrot

Janwillem van de Wetering

Copyright © 1997 by Janwillem van de Wetering

Published by

Soho Press, Inc.
853 Broadway
New York NY 10003

Library of Congress Cataloging-in-Publication Data
Van de Wetering, Janwillem, 1931–
    The perfidious parrot / Janwillem van de Wetering.
       p.   cm.
    ISBN 1-56947-102-9
    I. Title.
    PS3572.A4292P47   1997
    813'.54—dc21   97-2548
                                                           CIP

10 9 8 7 6 5 4 3 2 1

Author's Note

This tale is based on imagination. We all know that the Military only misbehaves while under orders. Helicopters most likely thrive on salt air. Rotterdam, Holland (I was born there) is beautiful and filled with pleasant people. How could the Amsterdam Police (I served with them for seven years) possibly be corrupt?

For my (I wish I could shimmy like my) sister Toos

1

RIDDLED BY BULLETS ON THE HIGH SEAS

"You want stiffs?" Carl Ambagt asked in a singsong voice while he shot linen cuffs from beneath the sleeves of his cashmere blazer. "Listen, Mr. Detective, if you need corpses before you can get going, Dad and I will give you corpses. No problem." The visitor gestured magnanimously, as if giving away precious objects. "No charge, free, they're all yours. Stiffs galore."

Private detective Henk Grijpstra didn't care for visitors. He looked over the head of this one who kept talking in a high penetrating voice. The open window offered a view of budding elm leaves and bright red gables on the other side of Amsterdam's Straight Tree Ditch. He prayed. He wanted an elm branch to enter the window, grab the visitor and *Whop,* into the canal. After that, nothing but ducks quacking. Life goes on.

A fellow forty years old. A short fellow. Grijpstra didn't care for short forty-year-old fellows, and this one was arrogant, with the musical Rotterdam way of talking, each sentence ending on a lilting tone. "Right?" The endless Rotterdam question.

Beat the short forty-year-old fellow to death.

Visitor, visitation.

It irritated Grijpstra that he still thought in religious terms. Whatever you learn while young can be practiced throughout life, says the Dutch proverb. Learn young, be stuck forever, Grijpstra thought.

If there were a Lord would He grant a Grijpstra prayer?

Fuck this fellow, Grijpstra prayed. Lord?

Grijpstra constrained his wishful thinking. He was from Amsterdam, the capital, the spiritual heart of Holland, the center, the creative core of the Netherlands.

Rotterdam, Holland's second city, is considered—by Amsterdam—to be a working town. But that's all right. Rotterdam is tolerated by Amsterdam, providing the upstart town keeps its distance. Some people work, that's okay, there's nothing wrong with work, if someone needs to do it, that's perfectly fine—good luck to the working folks of Rotterdam. But let them stay home, not bother their betters with useless and repetitive information that lilts at the end.

"Right?"

Grijpstra's hands, invisible behind a stack of empty folders on his desk top, groped about for something to hold on to. The antique desk was a present from Grijpstra's former chief. The commissaris had used the desk as a fortress from whence he defended his privacy. Since his retirement, at age sixty-five, the commissaris's defenses had been leveled. Detective-Adjutant Grijpstra retired too, ahead of time in his case. Sergeant-Detective de Gier quit as well, to help Grijpstra do nothing, well, at least do very little. The partners of *Detection G&G Incorporated* preferred peace and quiet in their spacious offices.

"Several corpses, Mr. Ambagt?" Grijpstra asked, *sotto voce*.

"Ah well, just one I'm really sure of," Ambagt said contritely—but arrogantly again, Grijpstra thought, as if the little asshole was proud of his assholery, jeez.

Ambagt was sitting comfortably, in the luxurious brown leather easy chair reserved for clients. This client did not seem impressed by the vast room under its high ceiling, supported by ancient hand-hewn beams. Even Grijpstra himself did not impress this intruder from the lower spheres and the detective *was* impressive: big, burly, wide in the chest, with steel gray brushed-up hair, bouncy thick eyebrows, a wrestler dressed up for the occasion. There Mr. Grijpstra presented himself to an annoying world, in a three-piece tailored suit, complete with watch chain. The silver tie, with a design of small turtles, a present from Katrien, the commissaris's wife, upon the start of his new career, accentuated solid elegance. The superior clothes enhanced the intelligence of faded blue eyes in what Nellie, Grijpstra's new wife, liked to call a "rugged countenance."

"Not counting the missing persons," Carl Ambagt semi-shouted, happy to add to the misery. "All we found was a befuddled Captain Souza, and a dead sailor, Michiel. Otherwise not a single soul." Ambagt dropped his voice, to indicate tragedy. "Me and Dad were just in time, the tanker was about to land herself on rocks. Right?"

"Right on rocks, not right on rocks?" Grijpstra asked, bewildered by the Rotterdam way of questioning reality. "Yes or no?"

"No. Right?"

"And the missing persons?" Grijpstra asked.

"Let me explain, right?" Carl Ambagt asked.

Carl Ambagt handled an imaginary machine pistol and imitated spraying deadly bullets.

"This tanker of yours . . ." Grijpstra said.

". . . the supertanker *Sibylle* was robbed of its contents. The cargo was pirated," Ambagt said. "Do you have any idea how much money we are talking about?"

Grijpstra looked detached. His visitor didn't have to know that the image of a crewless gigantic tanker, illegally drained of a valuable cargo, fascinated Grijpstra. In his long career with the department of Serious Crime of the Amsterdam Municipal Police such an immense felony had never come his way. He envisioned the steel vessel, a quiet ghost ship towering above tropical seas. Ambagt had told him the location: the Caribbean. The event had taken place close to the semi-Dutch isle of St. Maarten (its north half is French). Grijpstra didn't know any tropical islands personally but he now saw pictures, a collage of impressions taken from TV and magazine advertising: golden beaches, waving palm fronds, and several swimming, sunning, ball-playing young women. He was there too, hands behind his back, his contemplative eyes shaded by the wide brim of a straw hat. "Panama Jack" Grijpstra. Grunting pleasurably, the daydreamer observes brown and black breasts, legs and buttocks. How about his new wife, Nellie—wouldn't she be jealous? Not at all, Nellie has just joined the picture. There she is on a surfboard, subtly pink all over. What a winner, this ex-model Nellie, nominated once to become Miss Holland, chosen Number Two because of too ample breasts. The other beach ladies, however, are attractive too, performing seductively on the golden sand, almost struck by the pirated supertanker *Sibylle*. A charming multicolored collection. Strange, really, Grijpstra thought, once you start traveling, racism doesn't work too well. Out there the minority is a majority. Object becomes subject. Relativity wipes out the racist view. Good thing he didn't consider himself to be racist. Didn't know what the attitude meant really.

"The chartered supertanker *Sibylle*," the short fellow said. "Never invest in those suckers, they leak. Giant rustbuckets, that's all they are. But we do use our own crews. You may be thinking *accident* now, right? Wrong. The sailor, Michiel, was riddled by bullets."

"You don't say." Grijpstra's voice stayed flat, touched by just a little compassionate vibration. A bleeding corpse, missing mates. This client talked trouble.

"Quite a bit of wind," Ambagt was saying, "we had a problem with our spinning top. A heaving deck doesn't make for easy landings."

"Spinning top?"

"Helicopter," Carl said.

"The alleged piracy of a supertanker, involving murder, close to St. Maarten, in the Antilles, in the Caribbean Sea," Grijpstra summed up. "You landed your helicopter on the vessel and noted evidence of foul play."

Carl Ambagt stared beyond Grijpstra's bulk. "Ah yes."

Grijpstra noted signs of what could be true emotion while his visitor relived painful moments.

"On the bridge," Carl Ambagt said, "was Michiel's body. All innocent-like. Nice looking young chap too." Carl Ambagt took a Polaroid from his wallet. He studied the picture. "Michiel, the sailor, in his blue banded T-shirt. Named for our famous buccaneer admiral, Michiel de Ruyter. Remember him from the history books? Seventeenth century. Beat the bloody British time and again. Burned a British war fleet right at home, on the Thames. A great strategist. Dad has studied him, you know. Dad likes strategy—it's made us rich and famous."

"I have never heard of you," Grijpstra said.

"You have now," Ambagt said. "Here. Look at Michiel's body."

"What are all these holes?" Grijpstra shuddered. "Was your sailor tortured?"

"Gulls," Carl Ambagt whispered. "You know that seagulls like carrion? They pick at dead bodies. We saw it from the sky, me and Dad—red shreds of Michiel's flesh, within an oval of white gulls. Like an eye. Red pupil, white oval. Pecking seagulls. The whole thing was like an eye that stared at us. The eye of the raped *Sibylle*."

Grijpstra pushed the photograph away. "You mentioned Captain Souza. Captain of the ship?"

"He was there," Carl Ambagt said. "Master Guzberto Souza, down in his cabin." Ambagt's smile was crooked. "Drunk out of his mind."

"Not dead."

"As if." Carl Ambagt nodded. "Between balls and fucking."

"Beg pardon?"

"Jenever. Our famous national brands. Dutch gin." Carl spelled the brand names. *"Bols. Focking."* Ambagt shook his head. "That's what fueled our captain. Kept him going while watching porno. That was his other thing, T&A on video. The never-ending show."

"The captain informed you of the crime committed?"

"Captain Souza never noticed."

"Not even the shooting?"

"Delirious," Carl Ambagt said. "So what do you expect? A black man from Aruba. Dad hired Souza. I did say 'Daaaaad, what are you doing, Daaaaad? Right?' But it was too late. Dad and Guz, drinking themselves silly." Carl checked his manicured nails. "Try and get between *that* situation."

"This took place in St. Maarten?"

"Aruba." Carl pointed at an imaginary map. "More to the left and down below, west, off Venezuela. But Dutch, of course. Amazing. Why do we hold on to those money-losing islands?"

Grijpstra pushed the Polaroid back. He wondered why he was encouraging his visitation by asking questions. Had he forgotten that Detection G&G was a *fata morgana*? A mere front? That the nameplate on the gable meant nothing? Sure, something: a hoax. Put up to fool the tax inspector. Behold this beautiful gable, Mr. Tax Man. Note the varnished front door, the polished bricks, the recently repainted woodwork, the blossoming geraniums in the window planters—will you just look at the stone steps, worn smooth by clients' trampling feet. Yes, sir, we work here and earn good money, our wealth has a legitimate source. Okay, Mr. Tax Man? Now keep going, old fart.

However, no work was done behind this splendid gable at one of Amsterdam's show canals, Straight Tree Ditch.

How the hell could all this have happened? Grijpstra screamed when the ghostly hand of his conscience grabbed him during nightmares. How could he, a stolid public servant, and that faithful cooperator, de Gier, have stumbled into this demonic trap together?

It had happened. Three years ago. There, one bad day, Adjutant Grijpstra and Sergeant de Gier, of the municipal police, were doing their job in a ramshackle hovel in Blood Alley, Inner City, Amsterdam. De Gier forced a door. Rats scrambled about their feet. They entered a small room filled with empty bottles and porno posters. There was the sweetish foul smell of rotting food. The kitchen was an open dump. In the basement de Gier kicked his way through more refuse. An amateurishly built brick wall aroused suspicion. De Gier pushed it over with his foot. Behind the wall, in plastic bags, a treasure in small banknotes had served as rats' nests. They counted the treasure. There was just over a million in undamaged notes.

So what does one do, being—as the police manual has it—"engaged in the correct exercise of your public service"? You hand in the loot, straight into the hands of your own superiors, at Headquarters, Moose Canal. Decent and admirable folks, all ladies and gents, in uniform, gold- and silver-braided. The superiors address you in well modulated tones. "Good job, Adjutant. That's right, put it down there, Sergeant. All this goes straight to the Country's Coffers. No, that's all right, that will be a little job *we* would like to perform. On your behalf, colleagues. And thanks again, indeed. Enjoy the rest of your public service today, Adjutant, Sergeant."

Then what do you notice? That superiors are inferior. That the authorities, so far respected by your dumb selves, are taking holidays in the Pacific, Fiji, the Marquesas, out-of-the-way places, out of an ordinary citizen's reach. New cars appear in

POLICE PARKING ONLY spots. There is revelry around the pleasure area of Leyden Square, Amsterdam. There are intimate meetings in the royal suites of the Amstel and l'Europe Hotels. Champagne pops and slurred voices make fun of the abysmal, abominable adjutant and his silly, stupid sergeant.

Haha! Hoho!

So to whom do you complain?

Your own chief has rheumatic troubles that keep him in his hot tub—he is about to retire anyway. The Chief Constable is in serious therapy, the Minister of Justice has been issued a golden parachute while preparing himself to walk the plank.

However, luck is with the lucky (Grijpstra grinned sadly). It turns out, that in the same ramshackle hovel in the same Blood Alley, by the same adjutant and detective-sergeant, another treasure is found. The second treasure is a multiple of the first. This time high denomination notes—hundreds, thousands—are stacked neatly in closed metal containers.

The detectives hesitantly open more lids. Could this be true? Swedish five thousand crown banknotes? American hundred dollar bills in ribbon-tied packages of one hundred? Even a few bars of gold?

"Oh dear." De Gier had wanted to bandy about the most horrifying curses. The words, none of them able to represent the seriousness of the situation, had stuck in his throat.

Grijpstra mumbled, "Dear me."

Nobody was informed of the reason for these exclamations. Well, sure, the commissaris heard, he would have found out anyway—why try to be clever?

"We're going to keep the money, sir," Grijpstra said.

"We will also resign," de Gier said. The commissaris said he was happy that they could make such a weighty decision themselves and that he would like to help invest the loot. "Grab some of the cash for your immediate necessities and bring me the rest. I'm good with numbers."

The commissaris, in his old model Citroën, drove the money to the independent duchy of Luxembourg and opened an investment account in the name Grijpstra and/or de Gier with permission to sign on behalf of these beneficiaries—any transaction, any amount. The bank director thought the arrangement was unusual but, hey, who was he to refuse a sizable deposit?

It was all a matter of trust, of course.

The predictable hardly ever happens but the unexpected, invariably, does. For de Gier that truth emerged from a stale fortune cookie. Grijpstra heard it from a brown skinned man with magnetic eyes and a white goatee. "It always turns out different," the street guru told him.

It did. Instead of graying gently while working hard to serve the community, Grijpstra—suddenly unemployed and wealthy—aged quickly while suffering anxiety attacks. Ulcers gnawed. Gums rotted. Veins varicosed. He regained his health after marrying his free-sex friend, Nellie. Nellie said she had known all along that this marriage would happen. "Whores," Nellie said, "don't have to bullshit, so we're close to Truth."

Grijpstra emptied out his rented apartment at the Leathermakers Canal and moved in with Nellie at Straight Tree Ditch.

Nellie owned her building outright. It contained a small bar, the ONE ON ONE, in the basement. "Hotel Nellie" occupied all of the four stories and there was a messy loft on top.

The unpredicted change closed the basement, moved Detection G&G Inc. into the first two floors, made luxurious living quarters for Mr. & Mrs. Grijpstra on the next two floors and had de Gier—back from New Guinea and a sojourn in Maine in the USA—strip and refurbish the loft as an indoor garden cum camping ground.

"Things change," the commissaris said at the housewarming party that he and his wife, Katrien, attended. "Fortune cookies and street gurus speak the truth." He also quoted an obscure Dutch medieval poet who had versified on the theme that things are not what they appear to be. "Nothing but change is constant."

Apart from the treasure-finders themselves, only the commissaris knew where all the money came from. Three Surinam-based drug dealers knew too, but they were found dead in Paramaribo, their hometown on the South American coast.

"But Henkieluvvie," Nellie said. "Where did you get it?"

Grijpstra claimed that her building's expensive restoration had been paid for from his savings plus a bank loan to be repaid from the future income of Detection G&G Inc. "Everything just dandy and hup ho," Grijpstra said. De Gier confirmed that statement. The commissaris nodded affirmation. Nothing to worry about. Nellie was not to worry her beautiful blonde head.

"Sure," Nellie said, preferring the present lucrative arrangement to giggling with and being bruised by paying and often out-of-control clients. Pacific Rim business gents, she had been specializing lately. Her selection paid better, but often played rough.

No more being a long-legged playpen dolly, Nellie thought. No more following patrol car-radio orders when you are ready for a smoked eel sandwich and whipped-cream coffee, Grijpstra thought.

No more administering, correcting and enforcing, de Gier thought.

"Released from the straightjacket," the commissaris said. He used his grandfather's smile. "And how are you going to get through the days, Henk and Rinus? No more 'sir'ing me. I am Jan."

"Doing nothing, sir," Grijpstra said, citing his laziness.

De Gier agreed, citing his philosophical search for meaning that would require meditation. He even explained: "To see where I get to when I care nothing about nothing."

The commissaris deemed the plan to be good but advised his former assistants to find some occupation. His wife agreed. "Emptiness filled with wealth creates camel-sized vermin," Katrien said, quoting an ancient Dutch proverb. She claimed to know what she was talking about. Having inherited money that her husband helped her invest, Katrien—weighed down by wealth she had no use for—had needed therapy. "Stay busy," Katrien said. "Do something you like doing."

"If you can't make it, fake it," the commissaris said. "Start a business, hang out a shingle."

Thus the birth of Detection G&G Inc.

Some jobs turned up. There was an insurance investigation, referred by a former police colleague, the recently promoted Simon Cardozo. There was a missing girl tourist to be located. Also a pension for the widow of a hashish dealer to be arranged with the dealers's association. Three cases in one year. Minimal income, maximal spare time. Grijpstra painted dead ducks; de Gier carefully pried attractive looking weeds from between the inner city's cobblestones and grew them in artful planters he created from plywood found floating in canals. He arranged his wildflower and herbal garden in Nellie's loft. He looked up the weeds in a picture book he found at an Old Man's Gate stall. He lay about in a hammock amidst his plantation of bladderwort, crimson clover and marsh bellflower, thought about clever Zen sayings and read Nietzsche in German.

"What are you *doing*?" Grijpstra asked at times, when, fleeing Nellie's TV, he found de Gier staring at the floor, from above twisted legs, or bent over books.

De Gier liked to answer with oriental silence or Nietzsche-quotes in German.

"What do your exercises or books deal with?" Grijpstra asked once. "With nothing, okay? With the nothing that the Lord created things from and that still shines through."

"I don't really get it," de Gier admitted.

They also liked to make music together, in a jazz cellar at the Endless Prayer Alley, Grijpstra on drums, de Gier behind his mini-trumpet. Leisurely. "Leisure" was the key. Cool. Relaxed.

We won't be busy.

The one who agreed to join de Gier "in doing by not doing," after finding the second Blood Alley treasure, was Free Grijpstra. There were, however, other Grijpstras.

Busy Grijpstra, run to earth by oil-tanker-charterer Carl Ambagt, noted Free Grijpstra's objection to Carl's proposal. There was a conflict there. Continue daily relaxation or dip into some exciting action maybe?

Piracy near the Netherlands Antilles? Busy Grijpstra liked that.

Free Grijpstra was fading. Busy Grijpstra took over. Busy Grijpstra regressed to a modus operandi learned during some twenty years of daily police work. Busy Grijpstra noted that the client, albeit unsympathetic, appeared to be energetic and intelligent. Carl, although short, had wide shoulders and, inside the blazer's sleeves, bulging muscles. Sporting type? A gymnast? Weightlifting maybe. Ambagt's flannel trousers had been neatly pressed. His shirt was made to measure, out of bleached linen. Its collar, in keeping with the current fashion, was buttoned down. The silk necktie, printed or maybe handpainted with— Grijpstra put on his glasses—the image of a nude woman, glowed under a massive golden pin shaped like an erect penis. Unsympathetic, intelligent, energetic, short, flashy fellow in his early forties.

While showing the complainant in, Grijpstra had noted Ambagt's pigskin half boots, and while shaking hands he'd noticed a platinum bangle and a watch decorated with jewels. Rich little fellow. Powerful little fellow.

Complainant was still being emotional. "Poor sailor Michiel, riddled with bullets." Ambagt wrung his small childlike hands. "That's what you get when assholes use arms." Ambagt's gold fillings sparkled. He spoke easily, forgot to use his Rotterdam accent, added fewer question marks, toned down his arrogance.

"Action movie. There's something for you, Mr. Detective. Last time we talked to Captain Souza he gave the tanker's position as just south of Saba. After that we lost contact. Got us all worried, started up the old chopper-top, flew off, nosed about everywhere. Me and Dad in the chopper. Went back twice to refuel. Helicopters don't fly far you know. Looked about for hours we did, checked out all the islands, starting at St. Maarten, all the way down to Barbuda, then Antigua; we counted off the French, the British, the Dutch Antilles, choppered back north again, right up to Anguilla. At last, there she was, the old hulk. Drifted away from Saba, got herself tucked between Nevis and St. Kitts. You have to be careful there, lots of reefs and rocks and what have you. Had to put down the chopper on that little rear deck. You should have seen me and Dad, sliding about on the *Sibylle*. A real situation. Had to get that huge unwieldy tanker away from the reefs; steering all that bulk isn't easy you know, even if I do have captain's papers. There was a stretch where we didn't have half a fathom under her keel. Fortunately the old cow was empty. High as a church tower and last time we'd seen her she was up to her chin in water. So where, for fuck's sake, was her cargo?" Ambagt dried off his forehead with a silk handkerchief that he had unfolded angrily. "Nothing moved on board except two cats racing about like crazy. We heard them yowl as soon as we switched off the chopper's engine."

Grijpstra was distracted. "You caught the cats?"

"Found them a home on St. Maarten," Carl said. "They weren't much fun in the chopper. Dad wanted to toss them."

"And you had been on St. Maarten?" Grijpstra asked. "You and your father happened to be flying about in your helicopter?"

"We were *sailing* about," corrected Ambagt, "and the chopper comes with our ship. The tanker, the *Sibylle* was coming from Iran." Ambagt held a finger upon his lips. "A secret, yes? On her way to Cuba. Nobody is supposed to know that either, yes?"

"What's with the secrets?" Grijpstra asked.

"Uncle Sam just hates that route." Ambagt kept smiling now, winking between bits of sentences. "Iran, that's sheiks blowing up kindergartens . . . Castro is bad for American health too . . . the USA blockades Cuba's supply route . . . only little fellows like us can sneak through . . . international waters . . . me and Dad don't subscribe to anything . . . anonymous is the word . . . used to be South Africa that was blocked oil-wise . . . Ambagt & Son used to sell them Russian oil . . . that South Africa is niggerland now, dirt poor niggers won't let you make a profit. . . ."

"Your and your father are smugglers of crude oil?"

"Free traders," Ambagt said.

"Is your chopper-equipped ship a tanker, too?" Grijpstra asked.

"NononoNO." Ambagt waved defensively. The Rotterdam accent returned. "Our *Admiraal Rodney* is a FEADship. FEAD like in *First Export Association of Dutch Shipbuilders.* Yessirree. Seaworthy super luxury." He looked at Grijpstra. "Designed for superspenders like me and Dad. For the cat's meow. For the crème de la crème. For the upper layer of the crust of an otherwise negligible humanity, Mr. Detective. Right?"

"Ah," Grijpstra said.

"Be impressed," Carl Ambagt said. "Who else owns a FEADship? The sultan of Borneo, richest man in the world. Some movie moguls, a merger billionaire or two. Freddie Heineken, maybe. The Chief Samurai of Mitsutomo. You know who does not own a FEADship? The Dutch queen. She can't afford one."

How terrible, Grijpstra thought, to be really wealthy. Like himself for instance. Fortunately he did not have to tell anyone. Ambagt did—why else would he keep winking and raising his tiny voice? Grijpstra felt increasing shivers. "Yes, Mr. Ambagt, so you live on a houseboat."

"Palatial motorized vessel."

"Tax free?" Grijpstra asked.

Ambagt slapped his thigh. "Not one penny for the Dutch authorities. Our yacht flies the Liberian flag. Ever heard of Liberia, where American slaves were transported and freed so that they could keep slaves themselves?"

"And your sailboat touched the island of St. Maarten and . . ."

"Power boat," Ambagt said. "Thirty million dollars worth. Gold and marble interiors. Very silent engines. Hot and cold water. Giant microwave oven. Direct TV-dish with five umpteen times umpteen channels. Twenty-four-hour suite service."

"My *my*," Grijpstra said.

"And yes, indeedy," Carl Ambagt said. "We were visiting St. Maarten. We often do. *There* is an island that allows for pleasure. The authorities like to come on board for drinks before having us share their joys ashore. Me and Dad, from our master suites on the *Rodney*, were talking to the *Sibylle* when we lost our connection. The tanker was south of St. Eustatius then, about to cross to Cuba."

"You said south of Saba, just now."

"No matter," Ambagt said. "Saba, St. Eustatius, St. Maarten—three pimples on the same ass. So me and Dad were sipping piña colada and nibbling caviar on toast and Dad is cell-phoning the *Sibylle*, like twice every day and nothing doing, yes, right, a canned voice talking bull."

"Answering machine?"

"Satellite," Ambagt said. "So Dad goes to the bridge of the

Rodney and tries the radio and still nothing doing. Our business capital is afloat on that dumb tanker. Uninsured. So let's have a look, Dad says. We couldn't get off straightaway for the chopper had a problem. Moisture in the engine, she never liked sea air. And the *Rodney* herself was low on fuel."

"And because you couldn't make contact you feared something bad happened to your chartered tanker?"

"Yes," Carl said angrily. "Yesyesyesyes."

"Do you fly the helicopter yourself?"

"Who else?" Ambagt asked. "Dad drinks. He reacts slowly. He doesn't get the dials. Besides, Dad is pre-puter."

Grijpstra looked surprised.

"Computers?" Ambagt asked. He looked about the room. "Hey, you're pre-puter too? How can this be? Where is your 'puter?"

"Upstairs," Grijpstra said. Nice big one, Grijpstra thought, with speakers. Nellie could work it—handled the mysterious machine's modem, its rom and ram, showed color photos on the monitor, printed the photos in color too, used it for video clips. Played games. Computer completer.

"It'd better be there," Ambagt said. "We may need your databank of befriended bad guys. Your file on judges craving sex with kids. Your list of cross-dressing prosecutors. Your notes on the private lives of colleagues from yesteryear when you still slaved in the service." He slowly lowered an eyelid. "Haha, Mr. Detective. We know you know the ins and outs so Dad and I don't mind slipping you big banknotes." He gestured widely. "I know what you're up to, Fats. I'm offering just what you need. With this case you can show some real earnings to the Tax Man." Carl smiled. "Right?"

Grijpstra growled.

Ambagt looked frightened. "You okay?"

"One moment here," Grijpstra said. "Just one doggone moment before we continue this conversation, Little Feller. How did you find me? Tell me, right now."

Grijpstra got up ponderously.

"Hey," Ambagt said shrilly. "We're going to stay nice, right? You and your partner are free men too, am I right?" He gestured wildly. "Get it? Why I came here? Right? Sartre, you know? *Condamné à la liberté?* Condemned to freedom? Isn't that what you are too? You and Sergeant de Gier, the hero? Ever since you found your treasure you don't care a damn about anything neither? Like me and Dad? Adjusting to being freely afloat in the lawless void? God-less?"

Grijpstra sat down. There He was again, the Lord, or was it the non-Lord, or was there a Difference? Same Difference? And there was His Non-Law again too, or was it His Non-Law Neither? Befuddled by too many negatives Grijpstra groped.

"So what about this Sarter?" Grijpstra asked.

Carl hastened to explain. "That we, by a provable absence of a creator taking an interest in the right or wrong of our existence, are condemned to be free. Alas." Carl grinned helpfully. "Alas, perhaps? Maybe being left alone is not that unfortunate after all? Perhaps we can put our newfound liberty to some use? Me and Dad enjoy our newfound freedom on our yacht, right? You and your former sergeant do the same in this building, right? Aren't we birds of a feather? Free creatures of splendid plumage?"

Grijpstra grabbed his phone. "Rinus, mind coming down a

second? Put on your gloves. I have a wise-ass here who needs beating."

Ambagt rose slowly.

The long fluted barrel of Grijpstra's weapon, quickly retrieved from his desk's top drawer, pointed at Ambagt's forehead.

Ambagt sat down slowly.

2

A Wise-Ass Threatened

Ex-Sergeant-Detective de Gier entered the executive office of Detection G&G Inc. Athletically, of course, Grijpstra thought bitterly. De Gier would never perform in an ordinary manner. Always the bouncy gait, always the wide swinging shoulders, the proudly raised square chin, the hawk-like nose, the large sensitive eyes, the heroic mustache, the brushed-up curly hair.

Grijpstra introduced henchman to victim: "My partner detective, Rinus de Gier. Carl Ambagt, alleged piracy victim, a native of Rotterdam, a tax-free dweller on an international houseboat."

"A speaker of nothing but the truth," Ambagt said. "Me and Dad live on the *Rodney*. A type of luxury yacht built in this country. King Saud of Arabia owns a FEADship. We do too."

De Gier held up a pair of leather gloves. "And why, dear sir, do I have to beat you?"

{ *21* }

"Dear sir accuses us of owning an illegally obtained treasure," Grijpstra said.

"Dear sir accuses nobody of nothing whatsoever," Carl Ambagt said.

Grijpstra frowned furiously. "You're with the Tax Department, aren't you, fink?"

De Gier frowned too. "Entrapment isn't legal in your game, fink." He flexed muscles. "I am good at judo."

Ambagt said he wasn't bad at boxing.

"Shall we?" de Gier thought, making gracious movements with his gloved hands.

They should not, Ambagt said, because surely de Gier would be better at judo than he himself was at boxing. He asked for permission to reach for his wallet without being beaten or threatened. He just wanted to show some ID.

"Here with the wallet," Grijpstra said.

Grijpstra emptied the snake-leather pocketbook. He studied the credit cards, the passport, an American driving license, a photograph of a uniformed naval officer with sideburns and a large purple nose ("Dad," Carl Ambagt said), a wad of hundred dollar bills, assorted Dutch banknotes, a laminated playing card-sized drawing of a skeleton in a dress, riding a horse. "Mexican Magic," Ambagt said. "Female death imagery is supposed to be lucky. Ever been to Mexico? Not yet? Me and Dad visit there all the time, Yucatán mostly, the peninsula pointing at Cuba, right? Ever heard of a Dutch Government Tax Inspector knowing his way about the Yucatán peninsula, right?"

"Proof?" de Gier asked.

"How do I prove I know the Yucatán?" Ambagt asked.

"Mexicans speak Spanish," Grijpstra said. "Speak Spanish, dear sir."

De Gier danced about the room, feinting at Ambagt's head.

"A través de los siglos," Carl Ambagt said, *"por la nada del mundo, yo, sin sueño, buscàndote, el paraiso perdido."*

De Gier sat on the other visitor's chair. "That's what most of us are doing, all right."

"What are most of us doing?" Grijpstra asked.

"Throughout the centuries," de Gier said, "dealing with the world's lack of substance . . ."

"Por la nada del mundo," Carl Ambagt said dreamily, "Nicely put, right? *'Nada'* doesn't just mean 'insubstantiality' you know, but indicates an illusion, an appearance of the earthly bullshit we keep creating for ourselves, insisting that it would be reality . . ."

". . . and I," de Gier continued translating, "restlessly, keep searching for . . ."

". . . for 'paradise lost,' " Ambagt said, "meaning truth in this case, the beautiful essence of being that forever, *a través de los siglos,* is beyond our reach."

"A tax inspection poem," Grijpstra said. "Only a tax inspector can think up such endless misery, dear sir. Beat the shit out of him, Rinus, I knew he was no good."

"A poem indeed," Ambagt said. "Later, the poet will face a bouquet of shadows, *un boquete de sombras,* and quiet folks standing up in their graves, and a bunch of sad birds, *aves tristes,* trying to sing with dried-out voices, *cantos petrificados* . . . a work of art by Alberti," Ambagt sighed. "No Mexican but a Spanish poet. I found his work in a Puerto Juarez bookstore, however, on the Yucatán, magic land of the Mayas." He addressed Grijpstra. "Isn't Spanish the most beautiful language ever?" He addressed de Gier. "So where did you learn the lingo, eh?"

De Gier looked past Ambagt's head.

"In his loft planted with weeds," Grijpstra said gruffly. "Upstairs, in this house. De Gier absorbs foreign languages between sneezeweed and purple fringed orchid. And yourself, you fickle fellow?"

"I started learning Spanish at Erasmus University, I completed my studies being bedded by Mexican lady-whores." Carl Ambagt laughed. "An ideal program."

"Erasmus University is exclusive," Grijpstra said. "Isn't your background rather humble?"

Ambagt blushed. "You noticed?"

"Answer the question," Grijpstra shouted.

"I got a scholarship," Ambagt said. "I am a genius as you must have noticed." He patted his own shoulder. "Number One on the admission exam. Once in, I did well but I truly excelled in Spanish. But school was boring. I dropped out. Dad had started up the car business by then and I had to help out with the inventory. The teachers were glad to see me go." He smiled. "Lot of jealousy, you know. Not only was my intellect superior to theirs but I was driving a Jaguar, visiting the better brothels."

"Kicked out of Holland's most prestigious university of commerce," Grijpstra nodded. "Came to a bad end. As was to be expected."

Ambagt raised his hands. "Whatever you want to call it, but what else is an end but a fresh start, right, Fats? So what? Right?"

"So I don't believe you, you asshole," Grijpstra shouted while hitting his desk top. "So you like visiting brothels do you? So that's how you got to know this house. You came after Nellie. The ONE ON ONE bar. You noticed the new sign. You decided to check out the present situation."

"Confess," de Gier said kindly. "If you do maybe I won't beat you."

Ambagt looked surprised. "This place was a dive?" He looked about him, noticing mahogany wainscotting, a portrait—in oils—of a magnificently bearded constabulary captain in a lace collar over a velvet tunic, orchids in a Chinese vase on the wide windowsill, a leather bound encyclopedia in twenty-four volumes, a medieval crossbow decorating a white plaster wall. "One wouldn't think so." He pointed at empty wall space. "Why don't you hang a Rembrandt etching? You guys are loaded."

Bad Detective de Gier brandished his gloved hands.

Good Detective Grijpstra smiled kindly. "Now, dear. Who recommended us? Tell us."

Ambagt let that pass. He was here to do business. He offered a million, a hundred thousand up front to cover expenses, if Detection G&G Inc. would recover, in any which way the firm cared to do that, one uninsured cargo of crude oil, lost due to piracy of the *Sibylle*.

Grijpstra's egos battled. Busy Grijpstra lost.

"No," said Free Grijpstra.

"You're not serious," Ambagt said.

"Yes," said Free Grijpstra.

"Me and Dad," Carl said, "we're talking *dollars*." He looked at de Gier. "Same green shit you see in movies. Franklin himself, smiling at you ten thousand times. Ten thousand times one hundred dollars. What say? You'll do it, right?"

"Not right," de Gier said.

Carl snarled. "Now look here." He showed de Gier his small fists. "What if I visited Mr. Tax Man some time soon? I can do that without getting hurt myself. Me and Dad are not registered in this stupid country. The tax man can't get me and Dad but he sure as hell can get you. What is the source of your income, he'll ask. And what will you say? Earnings, what earnings? And you live here. You have this building. Mr. Tax Man just loves nicely restored buildings. Impound. Auction. You and Fats do some time in jail. I won't even send cookies."

It was quiet in the vast room.

"Right?" Ambagt asked. "One million? With one hundred thousand up front for expenses?"

"Go visit Mr. Tax Man," Grijpstra said.

De Gier rubbed his gloved hands softly. "You do that, dear."

3

THE LADY LIKES TO STRIP

In a billiard café for Men Only—
Run Alley, Inner City of Amsterdam, between Prince and
Gentlemen Canals—Grijpstra and de Gier met, that very
evening, with two colleagues from the good old days.

Constables First Class Karate and Ketchup, both short of
stature, both dressed in leather, wearing tight pants and calf-
high neo-Nazi boots—Ketchup long-haired with beard and
mustache, Karate shaven, skin-headed, lightly powdered and
delicately made-up, said they had no idea what recommenda-
tion Grijpstra and de Gier might mean.

Grijpstra was quiet between the dry ticking sounds made by
his billiard cue hitting ivory balls. He was making a nice
sequence, too nice for de Gier to match. Grijpstra's success was
upsetting de Gier who, long ago, had stopped banging his own
cue on the floor as applause.

De Gier was quiet too. He had, after smiling coldly at his

guests, accused Ketchup and Karate of meddling. "You know we are retired. So why send us that fink?"

"What fink, Sergeant?"

"The little whippersnapper from St. Maarten," de Gier said. "You two corrupt cops maintain a holiday house in the Caribbean. You met the despicable loudmouth Carl Ambagt in some bar. Blah blah and yackety-yack and then he pops up in our very own office. Trying to make us an offer we can't refuse."

"Forty-year-old fink," Grijpstra said. "Talks bullshit. Tits and ass on his necktie. Polished nails. Works out. Overwhelms in Spanish. Learned wheeling and dealing at Erasmus University, Rotterdam, of all towns. How the hell did you two dare to . . ."

"Who?" Ketchup asked.

"What?" Karate asked.

That was when they started playing billiards. Karate, being even shorter than Ketchup, also being a guest, got the first shot. His white ball hit three sides, then nothing. Ketchup's shot turned out badly too. De Gier, inspired by a jazz improvisation on Miles Davis's "So What," performed by a black pianist on the baby grand in the back of the café, slid gracefully around the billiard table. The balls clicked lightly, he overreached, he missed. Now, with Grijpstra in charge, the clicking kept on. Another point. Another point.

The pianist paused. It was 12 A.M., time to go home, but the café filled up with quiet men. The men bowed toward the bar before sitting down. A lady behind the bar, statuesque and firmly shaped, polished glasses. The lady was dressed in red velvet, the neck of her gown was open down to well below the navel. Louis Armstrong blew "Basin Street Blues" out of a late model CD-playing juke box, activated by the pianist who had paused in his playing. Colored lights flashed while Louis Armstrong played complicated, yet fluent, trumpet phrases.

"You," Karate said, "want to know if we know a fellow. We know all kinds of fellows. This fellow wouldn't by chance resemble the comic character, Tin Tin?"

"Now that you mention it," de Gier said. "Exactly. Tin Tin."

Grijpstra agreed. "Short-haired. Blond. Silly looking."

"Let me see now," Ketchup said. "A native of Rotterdam? Lives with his aged father on an ocean going yacht, of a type known as a FEADship? With a motorized cream stirrer tied to her rear deck? We would not be discussing the *Admiraal Rodney*?"

Grijpstra broke his self-imposed silence. He looked up. "*That* fellow."

"*That* fellow we don't know," Ketchup said.

"But we do understand that you think that we think that *that* fellow is the one we referred to your office," Karate said.

"Because of our alleged state of corruption," Ketchup said, "and because he made a criminal impression."

"Of the uncatchable type," Karate said. "Because we are supposed to be hunting that type."

"But not catching," Ketchup said, "because we, as new-modish law enforcers working pursuant to present police instructions, prefer to let them get away."

"Knowing," Karate said, "that they will lead us to other criminal contacts."

"Who, once identified," Ketchup said, "will lead us, yet again, to other criminal contacts."

"Who we won't catch either," Karate said, "knowing that, once again, they will bring us into contact with other criminals."

"Who we won't . . ."

Grijpstra interrupted his billiard series. "CUT THAT OUT!" he shouted, threatening his guests with his cue.

"This former almost over-correct adjutant-detective, now an escapee from public service," Ketchup said, speaking slowly, softly and articulately, and addressing Karate, "this finder of illegal treasure, and his fellow-escapee, who we once knew as a heroic detective-sergeant, think that we, as an exception to the rank and file of ex-colleagues, have swung down too far . . . as they call it . . ."

". . . so," continued Karate, equally softly and articulately, "if suddenly a suspect client appears in their make-belief office, a fink in his forties who doesn't want to tell who sent him, then . . ."

". . . we have to be the senders," Ketchup said.

"Bah," said Grijpstra, who, missing his ball, almost tore the billiard table's cloth. The lady behind the bar leaned in Grijpstra's direction while looking at him through the glass that she had just polished. She had large, now almost completely visible, perfectly shaped breasts. The glass framed and enlarged her staring eye.

Grijpstra, hit by the stare, stepped back. "Sorry, darling."

"Maybe you better sit down," de Gier said, pulling up a chair.

"You are real good at anything you deign to put your hand

to," Karate said Grijpstra. "Including billiards. Do you know that I truly admire you?"

"If," Ketchup said, "you hadn't commanded us while you were still serving the public, Karate and I would have reached abject depths. You were our example. You have no idea how much we miss you. Except for Inspector Cardozo, all our present superiors are total assholes."

"I," Karate said, "would call them brown paper bags filled with foul farts."

"You know what makes this worse," Grijpstra said, flattered and annoyed, "is that Carl Ambagt does indeed resemble Tin Tin. I refused to see that. Nellie and I have the Tin Tin comics complete."

"How come you chose us?" de Gier asked. "The *Yellow Pages* are filled with detectives."

"Not with those who can do big things," Karate told Grijpstra. "Only you can do that. And de Gier is so gutsy."

"The sergeant speaks big languages and pulls big punches," Ketchup said.

"But de Gier is a little too quick on the uptake," Karate told Grijpstra, "while you, on the other hand, are nicely heavy, slow, old-fashioned, drag your feet splendidly."

"But you're insistent," Ketchup said.

"Reasonable and solid," Karate said.

"You know how to push ahead," Ketchup said.

"And when," Karate said.

"An expert."

"And the commissaris backs you both."

"A pirated pumped-dry supertanker is too big for us."

"Me and Ketchup have neither fore- nor hindsight," Karate said, "we're only good in action."

"And we don't mind helping out," Ketchup said.

"You say something, Rinus," Grijpstra said.

De Gier, watching the barlady's breasts and listening, simultaneously, to Louis Armstrong's version of "I Wish I Could Shimmy Like My Sister Kate," asked "What?"

"Ketchup said we wouldn't mind stepping in if required," Karate said.

"You know," de Gier told Ketchup and Karate, "sometimes, while in my hammock among the weeds, I think about you two. I see you then as devilish henchmen, figures out of a Hieronymus Bosch painting, disgusting worms with broken eggs for heads that ghostlike ants crawl from, black-winged bats rising from a smoking chimney, turds gone bad in a transparent pot being filled by a shackled boorish retard."

"No kidding?" Karate asked.

"I thought we were just us." Ketchup blushed. "You're serious, sergeant? We're creatures shaped by a genius like Bosch?"

The lady brought drinks, beer for the corrupt constables, sodas for the retired detectives. She also brought cigars. Ketchup and Karate lit up, nonsmokers de Gier and Grijpstra, after some hesitation, lit up too. Everybody's eyes slid along the lady's cleavage. The lady, smiling dreamily, took her time biting off cigar ends with perfect teeth, striking long matches, offering flames, blowing out flames. The cleavage stayed poised. Grijpstra wondered how that could be for a cleavage is nothing, empty space, it does not exist. How can emptiness be poised?

"You're getting a cut," de Gier said to the constables after the lady had moved to another table. Grijpstra now saw her back. The long gown was slit. She had smooth calves and her thighs flowed up gradually, creamy-white, untouched, virgin ladylike territory. That such beauty was allowed! Grijpstra thought.

Ten percent commission on what de Gier and Grijpstra would collect was offered by Ambagt & Son Inc. to Ketchup and Karate. The constables admitted to it, why not? But once again de Gier had been too quick, too jumpy, grabbing hold of the first motivation that happened to pop up. Did de Gier really think that greed mattered here? Did Ketchup and Karate really need a hundred thousand dollars? For what? Money makes things serious so they had named a figure, but profit was not an issue here. They already owned everything. Their cottage on St. Maarten. Their apartment facing the Amstel River in Amsterdam. The car of all cars. A flat-bottomed sailboat on Holland's Inland Sea. Two Harley Davidsons on St. Maarten. Even the evil of the situation did not, basically, interest these corrupt cops. Sometimes evil did matter, they admitted to that too— there was a fascination in trying to figure out just how bad things could get on a rapidly worsening planet. So, yes, there was money, and violence and whatever the shadowside offers but what mattered ul-ti-ma-te-ly was, Ketchup explained, what the commissaris always called the 'joy of living fully'. If there was a possibility of doing a really good job here, within their own expertise, a challenge to their training, Karate explained, speaking clearly and without being interrupted by Ketchup— for the couple had invested in a good relationship together, so why spoil it—what really mattered was just to do a good job.

JANWILLEM VAN DE WETERING

"You are called Ketchup because you like to see blood," de Gier said, "and you are called Karate because you like to split the enemy into two."

Ketchup said that this was just the surface, little things on the side, quirks and eddies; their true characters were pure.

An example of what they liked to achieve? Very well. Take the barlady here for instance, take this facility where they happened to meet right now, billiard balls and jazz, a space filling up right now with quiet men. Here was an example of what Ketchup and Karate had helped to bring about.

The lady, before she bought the bar, was—in her little house with the big show window in Long Street—happy. She lived alone. She craved solitude for she was autistic. She could not bear being touched but she did like sexual togetherness abstractly, give and take, at a distance.

What did the autistic-but-sexy lady do? She undressed every evening in her living room, street level, no curtains. She undressed slowly, dreamily, in front of a Biedermeyer couch, covered with blue velvet, between palm trees in copper pots, against a backdrop of an empty off-white wall. No decorations on that wall for she herself was the decoration. She exhibited her own nude shape to quiet men, standing quietly in the Long Street outside.

Grijpstra nodded his appreciation. "What kind of lighting?"

"Two candles," Karate said, "in giant brass holders."

"Church candles," Ketchup said.

De Gier watched the barlady. The barlady, leaning toward him, watched a horizon, well beyond the wall.

"But she does notice you," Karate said kindly.

The café was filling up slowly, with old-fashioned gents and artistic types and young ones, some with shaven skulls, some with hair all over. The male audience bent down slowly, lips pursed, ready to sip syrupy ice-cold jenever from high-stemmed tulip shaped glasses, filled to the rim.

"Taking off the head." A Dutch solemn custom.

The pianist played again, "Around Midnight" by Thelonious Monk, but 12 P.M. was long gone.

"Great," Grijpstra said.

Yes indeed, the constables said, but the way the lady did it in her house in Long Street could no longer be tolerated, of course. Long Street filled up every night, with row upon row of quiet men. Traffic became a problem. Plain-looking neighbor women dropped flowerpots on the frozen figures below but the audience kept coming. Some men wore old-fashioned army helmets, decorated with the Dutch lion in bronze; others wore cooking pots with folded towels inside.

The ugly neighbor ladies phoned the police.

The lady, questioned by Constables First Class Ketchup and Karate—saluting politely and excusing their intrusion—promised to install curtains. She did, but the problem persisted for the curtains were transparent. The performance, vaguer now, became more interesting to the quiet men outside.

"Obscuring sometimes intensifies," de Gier said.

Sure, and the improved performance caused more trouble. Gridlock became complete. The neighbor women dropped bigger pots.

They kept phoning the police.

A solution was searched for. As the commissaris often said, the constables knew that solutions are formed by fitting problems into each other. Find the perfect fit. There was this empty billiard café that could, any moment now, be invaded by squatters.

"You bought this café?" de Gier asked.

Just for a moment, the constables said. They bought it at the time to help out an aged and retiring owner who wanted to enter a home serving the special food he craved. No regular fare. Extras cost money. Indonesian food, red hot sambal, grilled pork on wooden sticks, noodle soup, sushi, no porridge if you please, no kale, hold the mashed potatoes.

"You profited by selling the old gourmet's café to the undressing lady?" Grijpstra asked.

Who cares for profit? the constables asked rhetorically, although they were pleased to note that the lady had not been poor.

"She is now?" de Gier asked.

She was making up the difference, and her outlay of capital bought her considerable pleasure. The lady now performed in her own business, for a paying audience, and had good living quarters upstairs.

"Is she going to step out of that dress soon?" Grijpstra asked.

She would step out of everything. Karate pointed to a balcony under which the pianist now played "Stella by Starlight." The stripping lady's bedroom was behind the balcony. She would climb the stairs soon, slowly, and take her time on the little balcony.

The silent men tensed. The pianist played Monk's "Goodbye." The audience got up quietly and arranged its chairs into two parallel crescents. The men looked up quietly at the still empty balcony. The barlady sleepwalked graciously, across the café, up the stairs. The pianist kept playing. A long Goodbye.

"Deep Goodbye," Karate said.

The constables whispered proudly, while the lady stepped out of her slip dreamily, absentmindedly rolled down her stockings—knowing that she was alone—turned and bent her beautiful body, caressed her breasts and thighs, and, finally, slowly, ever so slowly, retreated into her boudoir . . . no, she had forgotten something, what could it be? Had she forgotten what she had forgotten? Oh well, gracefully she turned—while the silent men sighed their thanks—kept turning, slipped into her boudoir.

The empty balcony was dark.

There was no applause for this was not a real happening—she didn't know they were there, they didn't really know they were there either.

"So didn't we combine this nicely?" Karate asked. "Empty café at Run Alley, illegal undressing at Long Street?"

"And now, once again, we prove our skill at combining," Ketchup said.

"A ghost tanker pirated between Caribbean islands," Karate said.

"Two unemployed super detection agents," Ketchup said.

"Goodbye," breathed the pianist into his microphone.

The silent men left the café quietly.

Grijpstra left too much money on the table and joined the silent men. De Gier got up too.

"So you're going to do this?" Karate asked.

De Gier laughed. "Never."

4

Assaulted By Skeletons

The early morning was beautifully clear. Just an hour before sunrise de Gier strode down Run Alley, turned into Skin Alley, turned left onto Singel Canal's eastern quay and aimed for Stulp Church and ancient *Hekel Veld*—Torture Field surrounding Stulp Church—that venerable God-serving building.

Grijpstra had taken off without waiting for de Gier in his gleaming new Full Size Fourwheel drive. U.S. made. Airbags. Tax deductible driving cost: 77 cents per kilometer. Eight cylinders. "Get in, win the war," the salesman said proudly. "Superpower, sir. Makes the little guys run."

"Whose side are you on?" said the commissaris, who had come along to watch Grijpstra spend big money.

The salesman wasn't sure. Depressed by the Nearing End he himself rode a bike now. He admired clients like daredevil Grijpstra, polluting the country, clogging narrow streets, being out for Self only. "Drive this monster away, sir. Ignore silly cyclists."

De Gier wondered if he had offended Grijpstra. Was Grijpstra eager to give in now? Was he, de Gier, playing spoilsport? But what about their wondrous plan of never ever working, growing noxious weeds, enjoying anarchy, playing atonal jazz, and ignoring a terminally dark life by reading weird shit?

Outcast de Gier felt lonely, depressed.

A lugubrious atmosphere pervaded the dark mouths of quiet alleys. Nobody but bad folks, crazy people—freaks would be about in the inner city.

It's a good thing I am out of this, de Gier thought. That was all he aimed for, outness. Banished to the loft, between his potted alien nipplewort and hairy lettuce. Refusing to be part of anything. Avoiding the pain of belonging.

What, de Gier thought, can happen to what isn't?

Karate and Ketchup passed him at speed, cheering the lone pedestrian from their Dodge Viper GTS, eight liter, ten cylinder, 450 PK. The red convertible, as it came from an unexplainable source, was known as the "Wondrous Wagon." The constables touched their noses with their thumbs and wiggled their pinkies.

Definitely on the outs—left behind by his final friend, made fun of by perverts—de Gier felt threatened.

Maybe it hadn't been such a good idea to call up the spirit of Hieronymus Bosch. Bosch pictures were magical. Invoking Bosch might mean doom and damnation.

Doom and damnation started with a slow *zuffing* sound emerging from Hell Alley. The alley's shadows moved closer. Like in Bosch's pictures, horror was built up from known, harmless parts. The vacuum cleaner-like *zuffing* made de Gier look up. Anyone cleaning house at two in the morning? No, but it was okay, the sound came from a slowly approaching moped. What could possibly be wrong with a moped-riding lady, or a dog in a basket on the luggage carrier of said moped? Well, certainly, it was rather odd that both woman and mongrel wore identical straw hats, decorated with gaudy felt flowers. Realistically wilting felt flowers. The woman's face was painted white, with a big red mouth that made sucking noises. She stopped and got off the moped. "Coming along, dearie?"

The dog's body was skin on bones. Its slavering head was pure hyena. It growled and drooled. The moped lady suggested discount oral sex.

"No, thank you."

"I didn't really want to do it anyway," the woman shrieked, astride her moped again. The dog stared at de Gier in consternation. Did de Gier *know* what exquisite pleasures he was missing?

The moped, whose rear light, between the trees lining the quay in the before-sunrise darkness, gleamed correctly, had covered a block before de Gier could move again.

He shouldn't have smoked the cigar offered by the stripping lady. He hadn't smoked for a while and the burst of raw nicotine must have hit him square in the stomach. The sound of softly splashing waves made de Gier nauseous. How could the canal splash when there was no wind? De Gier stepped between parked cars, held on to a tree and bent down to the water. What was going on here? A swan pulled her sinuous neck from her wings. Swan and de Gier saw the cause of the splashing simultaneously. In the midst of the canal a rowboat moved in a furious circle, making waves.

"Hello?" de Gier called.

The rowboat stopped circling and approached him, rear end first. The rower, cursing himself rhythmically, pushed his oars. The reversing rowboat closed in on swan and de Gier.

" 'Hello' what, if you please?" The thin man wore a threadbare dufflecoat. Its hood had been pulled halfway down the rower's face. A sharp chin and an oversized equally sharp nose stuck out of the gap between hood and collar.

"Why are you cursing yourself?" de Gier asked.

The rower seemed to expect that question. "My meditations have maddened me, sir."

"You are a monk?" de Gier asked.

The monkish snout pointed at a heavy book, bound in yellow plastic, that contrasted with the tarred wood of the boat. The boatman's voice sounded flat, like that of a teacher holding forth in a dark room on a sunny afternoon while the class waits for the bell. "Praying doesn't help, I move in circles." The fox-like face looked frightened. The rower pulled in his oars. "My solution is to damn the self rather than pray to the non-self." The monk folded his hands while his head bent back. "Damn *me*, by God."

The night-rower crossed himself, taking his time, while repeating the curse.

The rower said that he was a linguist, had earned a Ph.D. in Netherlandic Language and Literature, before joining his order. He claimed to be the first to understand Holland's most popular and forceful curse, the Dutch self-malediction. God damn me. God *verdom* me. His thesis had been titled "Of the Mystic

Qualities of Netherlandic Cursing." Once again the Low Countries proved their superiority. There had been windmill and dikes, the invention of book printing, the microscope, euthanasia, and now there was true insight into a superior, so far not essentially understood, linguistic habit of damning the guilty self. That's right, the ego. The British/American god-damn*it* was the curse of denial, of trying to blame some unnamed third party for the suffering of living. German *Gottverdammt* showed even more ignorance, aggravated by fear. Germans wouldn't even mention the source of their pain, that, by intoning the destructive mantra, they were trying to get rid of. "It's *me* that did it," the monk said solemnly, "it's *me* that I want damned deep into hell, not *it*, not the *other*."

The swan flew off, flapping its angel's wings in loud protest.

"Fly back to heaven, Angel," the monk shouted sadly. "You are guiltless. I am not. I have to curse my way out. You enter through the front gate. I'll sneak in through the servant's entrance."

He pushed his oars into their locks, waved at the fleeing bird, started up his cursing again and rowed off at speed.

A vision?

Had the lady stripper drugged him? De Gier remembered the rowing monk from a Hieronymus Bosch triptych. The left panel shows a heavenly scene. On top, a barefoot God wears a dress, below demons crawl around a pool. A floating monkish figure reads a book.

De Gier strode onward.

Triptych. Three confrontations with the subconscious threefold?

Panel 1: Whorish moped woman and hellhound. Panel 2: Self-cursing monk. Panel 3: Deadly skeleton dance.

The members of the gang of muggers that attacked de Gier a few minutes later wore dark sweatsuits painted with white dayglow skeletons. The battle resembled a Japanese B movie where the white hero (de Gier wore a cream-colored sports jacket) is assaulted by bad guys in black. White uses special throws that makes Black keel over like ninepins. De Gier obliged, moving nimbly like the athlete he was, kicking and punching, using shoulder throws, even successfully trying out the complicated turn-throw (opponent's left arm grabbed by defendant's right hand), somersaulted sideways, but in the end Truth beat Fancy. The tallest and biggest skeleton retreated ten yards, then rushed, butting de Gier's chest with its hard-plastic death head. De Gier staggered, spread his arms, slumped over backwards.

Torture Field's cobblestones opened into a bottomless hole. The vanquished hero fell, kept falling, fainted.

5

AN OLD MAN ABOUT TO LEAVE

Grijpstra and Inspector Simon
Cardozo observed de Gier eating his hot oatmeal porridge,
carefully spooning the gray paste from the edge of his bowl.
The raisins, banished to the center, he kept for later.

"You in pain?" Grijpstra asked.

"Never," a nurse in spotless whites, by the name of Sayukta,
formerly of the Dutch colony of Surinam, a brown-skinned
woman with roots in India, said sweetly. "Your friend is full of
opium and belladonna. He's doing just fine."

De Gier saw Sayukta double: a gracious golden twin who
caressed him with four hands and smiled at him with two full-
lipped mouths. A comforting hallucination? With the compliments of Bosch?

"Your patient is not my friend," Grijpstra said.

"Yours maybe?" the nurse asked Inspector Cardozo.

"Certainly not, Nurse," the inspector said gruffly, annoyed
by the way she pronounced the word "friend."

"Because he is so handsome," Sayukta said. "Quite rare in straight men, such beauty. No wedding ring either. So I was thinking . . ."

"All yours," Grijpstra said gruffly.

He and the inspector would have made real-guy jokes if de Gier's roommate, behind a screen, hadn't been harrumphing in a frightening manner. De Gier's visitors pointed at the screen and wiggled their eyebrows. De Gier mimicked too, relaxing his jaw and neck muscles so that his head hung sideways, drooling.

"Acchch," Grijpstra said compassionately.

Cardozo, who didn't like death, sighed deeply.

"My ribs are broken," de Gier said peevishly.

"Maybe cracked a little," Grijpstra said.

"Happens all the time," Cardozo said. "You're aging now. Bones get brittle."

"You wouldn't even be here," Grijpstra said, "if Cardozo hadn't flashed his police card at the paramedics."

Inspector Cardozo, youngish looking under a load of wild curls above a corduroy suit in need of dry-cleaning, said that de Gier's ribs might be a trifle damaged but were certainly not broken. Ketchup and Karate, by chance, happened to be driving past Stulp Church and had noticed a mugging/manslaughter in progress. Their timely interference had saved de Gier's life.

"Ketchup and Karate?" de Gier asked, mildly interested in spite of the injected opiate. "They made an arrest?"

"The bad boys had run off," Grijpstra said. "You had lost consciousness. First things first."

"Ketchup reported they had seen you at Singel Canal," Cardozo said, "and then later, near Torture Field they noticed the Skeleton Gang hanging out. Two-thirty in the morning, nobody about but their ex-sergeant and dressed up bad boys. K&K went home but came back again, once they considered what might have happened."

"Back in the car, back to the inner city," Grijpstra said. "They checked out the alleys and sure enough, there you were being clobbered. What did you do to those poor skeleton fellows? Annoy them in some way?"

"Showing off again?" Cardozo asked.

"Good thing you had some back-up." Grijpstra smiled.

De Gier started on his residue of raisins.

Inspector Cardozo listed more reasons as to why K&K had not made an arrest. They weren't on duty. Their private car was not connected to police communications. De Gier seemed to be in need of medical attention. The Skeleton Gang had a reputation for violence. To go after them would have taken energy and time.

Grijpstra also reported that the yacht mentioned by their prospective client, young Ambagt, did appear to exist. Water Police constables saw the *Admiraal Rodney* moored at a quay near Grass Road Complex on the Northern side of Amsterdam harbor. There was even a telephone number that Grijpstra found through Information. Grijpstra called it. He was put through to Carl who promised to pick up Grijpstra and Inspector Cardozo by sloop at Dry Dock Point opposite the Central Railway Station. Grijpstra checked his watch. "Right now. We're late. See you," he told de Gier. "Get better. You may be needed."

De Gier gave his empty porridge bowl to Sayukta. The nurse left the room. "I thought," de Gier said, "that Detection G&G had refused the job, Henk."

Grijpstra shrugged. "Sure. But I thought I'd just take a look at the vessel. Curiosity. We *are* detectives."

"Will we let those bastards force us?" de Gier asked.

Grijpstra stood quietly in the open door.

De Gier touched the bandage covering his chest. "You think this scares me?"

"There is a draft," the dying man wheezed from behind his screen. "Mind closing the door, gents?"

Grijpstra disappeared. The door clicked behind Cardozo's back.

"They're gone, sir," de Gier said.

"Gone is good," the dying man said. "I'll be gone too. The euthanasiasts will be helping out soon. Won't that be something?" He laughed weakly.

"You don't mind?" de Gier asked.

The dying man sighed contentedly.

"Aren't you getting any porridge?"

"No more porridge," the dying man said contentedly, "ever." He giggled.

"Want to watch TV?"

"No more TV," the dying man said contentedly. "TV used to be okay sometimes but now with all the advertising. . . . First they describe Babywipes and then the next spot sells chocolate. And they expect you to keep watching?"

"Your family?"

The dying man grunted happily.

"Is your family coming to see you?"

"No more family ever," the dying man said contentedly.

JANWILLEM VAN DE WETERING

"Would you mind calling the exotic lady?" He giggled. "Nice nurse?"

De Gier pressed his red buzzer.

"Ain't she something?" the dying man asked after Sayukta had come and gone. "I didn't need to spit, you know, I was pretending. I wanted to feel her arm around my neck again."

Constable First Class Karate, impeccably uniformed, carrying a plastic report file, entered the room smartly. "Everything hunkydory, sergeant?"

Rage made de Gier speechless.

Karate, his back perfectly upright, his legs parade-parallel, sat on the straight plastic chair. "Ketchup and I did save your life. You could maybe be grateful?"

De Gier's rage continued.

"Okay," Karate said, "Something else. Remember what you said about Hieronymus Bosch? That wasn't nice you know."

De Gier forced his mouth to form and emit words. "As soon as I get out of here I'll throw you off Easter Dock."

"Comparing us to Hieronymus Bosch imagery," Karate said.

"Ketchup too," de Gier said. "Off Easter Dock, unless I can find filthier water."

Karate opened his file. "Ketchup," Karate said, "is off duty this morning. Instead of sleeping in, he researched Bosch in the public library. This here is a portrait of Hieronymus himself. Photocopied out of the encyclopedia, enlarged and laminated; no skimping on energy or money. This is for you. First we save your life, then we bring you presents."

"This is Bosch?" de Gier asked. He studied the kind old-man's face. "The one who created all those horrors?"

"Authentic," Karate said. "A portrait done by a contemporary artist."

De Gier held the picture at arm's length. "Where did this honeybun find my monkish confrontation? Where, in his sweet pure mind, did Bosch see an old whore on her moped, and her starving hyena hound?"

Karate didn't listen. "You told us we were black-winged minidevil's henchmen, drawn by Bosch."

De Gier studied Bosch's long strong tapered fingers, quietly resting on a drawing board. "Miles Davis had such hands."

Karate spoke with some intensity. "Bosch was a good citizen, paid his taxes, an important man in his town, he organized religious processions, he helped support the poor."

"Nice face," de Gier said, caressing, with his fingertips, the smiling old eyes of the medieval painter.

"A God-serving thinker," Karate said. "Like me and Ketchup. Me and Ketchup celebrate mass Sundays. The Virgin Mother has her niche in our house. We burn candles."

De Gier reached for his water glass and pain pills. His sore ribs moved. He groaned and fell back against his pillows. Karate passed him the glass and pills.

"Thanks to corrupt cops like you," de Gier said tonelessly, "crack gets dealt to kids."

"That makes us black-winged horrors?" Karate asked. "We are having the best time possible, considering the circumstances and our talents. What would you rather have us do? Watch goldfish in the constable's room, in between comparing numbers of open warrants and available cells? Lament politics? Collect guilders for the next birthday party of some worthless colleague? Join the Criticizers Club for coffee and cake at head-quarters each Sunday?"

"Your cooperation with criminals," de Gier said, "kills kids."

"You know," Karate said, "there is a serious kids-surplus in Holland. Kids grow up and buy cars. Ever consider the slow-ing flow of traffic? Will that get better when the population doubles?"

"We won't take the Ambagt job," de Gier said.

Karate looked at his motionless hands, perched on his knees.

"You know," de Gier said, "that Grijpstra and I retired."

Karate got up, marched to the door, came about face, stood to attention. "Do your job," the constable barked. "Your shin-gle at Straight Tree Ditch says nothing about doing nothing. It says 'detection.' "

"Bye," de Gier said.

Karate banged the door. The dying man sat up. He smiled at de Gier. "How silly of me," he said, "all my life I wondered about it and I could have seen it if I hadn't been keeping myself so busy." His voice was both hoarse and deep. "It's both beau-tiful and simple."

"What?" de Gier asked, but the dying man had died.

6

Hurrah And How-De-Do

"Where is the sloop that was supposed to pick us up?" Grijpstra asked Inspector Cardozo at the quay at Dry Dock Point near the Central Railway Station.

Cardozo waited patiently, on the legal side of the harbor's sign, ONLY OWNERS AND CREWS ALLOWED. Grijpstra looked at the moored sailboats. He remembered that de Gier liked to stop off here, in the past, in the midst of duty. The sergeant would admire foreign flags, weathered sails, frayed ropes, exotic types sucking bent tobacco pipes and sporting massive earrings. The sergeant would prattle about the mouth of the Orinoco river, the East Coast of Papua New Guinea, the Russian peninsula of Sakhalin, even the Dutch North Sea islands. Setting up desires, Grijpstra thought now. A process that was now proving to be painful. Cracked ribs and hospital beds? All due to long ago's daydreams. And he, old-buddy Grijpstra, got sucked along with them. But was that bad?

The spring day, observed by present-day Grijpstra, was

pleasant. Crested grebes, their pointed heads crowned with tufted feathers, flirted as they swam around each other. A great blue heron winged by slowly. A finch chanted from within weeds sprouting between the quay's cobblestoned walls. Young women in tight shorts and T-shirts were raising sails on a yacht. Grijpstra enquired about their destination. "We're going to win the Inland Sea race today," a girl said. "Men are losers now. You won't be needed."

"There," Cardozo said.

A sloop rowed by six uniformed sailors approached smartly. A boatswain, wearing a hat with visor, stood in the bow and saluted. "Mister Grijpstra and Inspector Cardozo?" the boatswain asked smartly.

The beautifully crafted wooden sloop slid across the waves of the river IJ. The passengers shared a caned bench between the rowing sailors and the commanding boatswain. The sailors, muscular young men with sparkling teeth, pulled long oars.

"Hur-rah," the boatswain sang. "How-de-do," the sailors responded.

Inspector Cardozo thought how wonderful life could be and how his life was not. How he still lived with his parents and took a bus to work every morning. How he looked forward to Thursdays because his mother didn't cook on Thursdays. Thursday nights he sneaked out for sushi. Simon Cardozo thought about the brand new three-storied super yacht towering above them, with a gleaming streamlined steering tower in front of a shiny helicopter clamped to the aft deck.

Different ways to deal with a lifetime.

What he faced here, Cardozo thought, was a heavenly floating castle for billionaires who were offering his former superiors a million dollars to take care of an exciting Caribbean problem.

Small-timer Simon Cardozo wondered about other people's big time.

"Could this be that houseboat the little fellow was talking about?" Grijpstra asked. "Big, eh, Simon? Must be something to keep that tub clean and going. Nicely turned out though."

"Careful please," the boatswain said, helping them step on the gangway that had been lowered by the ship's automatic hydraulic crane.

Carl Ambagt, dressed in a tailored merchant marine officer's uniform, welcomed his guests. "Now you believe me? You think the Tax Office owns toys like this? Want the ship's tour?

"Agile like a shark," Carl said, "Strong as a whale." He walked ahead on the deck of sandpapered teak, across the main cabin-suite's Tibetan rugs, guiding the way through the living quarters for the owners, past a bar room decked out in white marble, a gallery of modern art, a gadget-equipped kitchen.

"Crew's quarters are below," Ambagt said. "Furnished oriental style—tatami-matted floors, brightly colored lacquered furniture, lots of fans and gongs and pipe racks." He indicated a door. "Cup of Chinese tea for the gents?"

"Your mother is aboard too?"

"Who?" Carl asked.

"Is she alive?"

Carl gestured widely. "Do you know that the *Admiraal Rodney* measures three hundred and fifty tons? Cruises at thirty kilometers an hour, sails seven thousand kilometers without taking on fuel? That, if we leave tonight, we could be in the Caribbean in a mere eight days?" He addressed Grijpstra. "And that de Gier and yourself will meet us there? On St. Maarten? To start up your quest?"

"No," Grijpstra said.

"Oh yes," a gruff voice said. Skipper Peter Ambagt, in a stained admiral's uniform with bedraggled braid, leaning on a gold tipped invalid's steel tripod, greeted his guests. In contrast to his diminutive son the man was a giant. Father and son had the same square faces but the skipper's large nose was bulbous and obscenely purple. His scraggly eyebrows hung down dismally and his long sideburns needed brushing.

"You smartasses are going to recoup our loss on the old tank tub," Ambagt Senior said, slurring his speech in between hiccups. "I am glad to see you're here to clinch the deal, Mister Clever."

"I was just curious," Grijpstra said. "Your son mentioned your houseboat and we wanted to take a look."

"Houseboat? Trying to be funny now?" The old man tried to focus his eyes. His unsteady hand pointed at Cardozo. "And you are the fuzz here?"

"Inspector Simon Cardozo," Grijpstra said.

"And you are in charge here," Cardozo said, looking at the gold ornamentation on Ambagt Senior's hat.

The old man, without turning around, addressed the servant standing behind him. "A cold one, my dear." Ambagt Senior lowered his body into a deck chair. "Carl and I hold Liberian captain's papers." His long yellow teeth showed in a wide smile. "That's in Africa." He pointed at decorations pinned to his tunic—silver monkey heads, trailing multicolored ribbons. "Issued by the Head Honcho there. He personally pinned them on, just in time, a day before His Excellency was executed." He stood to attention for a moment, then noticed his visitors again. "Cardozo?"

"Sir?" Cardozo asked.

"Your name is familiar."

"It is?"

The skipper snapped his fingers. "St. Eustatius cemetery, that's where I saw that name. Your ancestors made good deals on that island. Jewish Amsterdam merchants with Portuguese names because that's where they came from. Inquisition time. Remember?"

"No, Skipper Peter."

"So *now* you know." Ambagt Senior dabbed his swollen nose with the tip of a blood stained handkerchief. "St. Eustatius, The Golden Rock." The skipper looked over Cardozo's head. "The golden past, alas." He looked at Grijpstra. "One million smackaroos for you and your partner, ten percent up front, balance to be collected when you recover the *Sibylle* loss." His cane fell while he bent his cadaverous body toward Grijpstra. "Is that a deal, Lucky Fatso?"

Cardozo picked up the cane and gave it to Skipper Ambagt.

He wasn't thanked.

Grijpstra said "No."

The sloop, wind pushing, sailors pulling strongly, crossed the IJ river on the return trip to Dry Dock Point. Grijpstra enjoyed the sea breeze. Cardozo looked nervous. "You know," Cardozo said, "Ketchup and Karate planned the attack on de Gier."

"Hur-rah," Grijpstra chanted along with the rowing sailors.

"To put some pressure behind Ambagt & Son's proposition," Cardozo said nervously.

"How-de-do," sang Grijpstra along with the rowing sailors.

"Because de Gier refused to accept that job."

"Hur-rah."

"And now you are the one who refuses."

"How-de-do."

"You know you are the endangered party now?"

"Hur-rah."

"And so am I," Cardozo said. "Because I am with you."

"Please," Grijpstra said.

"I think we are about to be pushed overboard and drowned," Cardozo said.

"Please," Grijpstra said. "My dear fellow. We are in a sloop owned and operated by Ambagt & Son. Nothing could be safer."

"Operated by Ambagt & Company employees," Cardozo said. "Not by Ambagts."

Grijpstra had to laugh. "So who could possibly push us over?"

"That police boat," Cardozo said. He pointed. Behind a foaming bow wave a harbor patrol boat approached at full speed. Blue lights sparked above the cabin. A siren wailed. The boatswain in charge of the sloop looked up in fear. He pushed his rudder. The patrol boat, alongside now, didn't have enough space to turn. The sloop's portside oars splintered against the steel side of the patrol boat. Sailors, boatswain and passengers raced to starboard. The sloop capsized. "Didn't I say so?" Cardozo shouted shrilly.

7

Rifle Fire In A Nature Reserve

"I keep telling you," Katrien said to the commissaris during breakfast, while beheading her egg, "and you just sit there smiling like a retard. Is this Alzheimer's now?" She looked worried. "Yoohoo? Jan?"

"Who are you?" the commissaris asked. "Do I know you?"

Katrien got angry. De Gier was spending his second day in the hospital and Grijpstra, according to Nellie, kept kneeling in his bathroom while filling up the toilet bowl with slime imbibed at the bottom of the river IJ. Inspector Cardozo had found out that the water police who had run the sloop down were intimate friends of Ketchup and Karate. Nothing but trouble everywhere and the commissaris was putting too much cream into his coffee. All this was bad.

"Cholesterol," Katrien said. "Think of your waistline."

"What waistline?" the commissaris asked. "And what do I have to do with de Gier and Grijpstra?"

"More than with me," Katrien said, "and K&K knew that."

Grijpstra and de Gier were dear boys, she would admit that, and not inexperienced, not really dumb, quite capable of solving simple problems but the minute a situation became slightly complicated there they were at the commissaris's door, begging for their master's guidance. "Without you there would be no Detection G&G Incorporated."

"I told you a million times," the commissaris said, "don't exaggerate, dear Katrien."

Katrien swore, while sweeping her hands about furiously and raising her voice, that, on the contrary, she had been minimizing the situation. Grijpstra and de Gier had, during their lengthy police training by her husband, changed into the commissaris's efficient projections. A triumphant triad had scoured the Amsterdam underworld. Grijpstra/de Gier, marionetted by their chief. Tweedle Dee/Tweedle Dum, and the Holy Ghost on top. Now that G&G (Katrien smiled disdainfully) were working in their own so-called business, was she to understand that the situation had changed?

"But they are *not* working, dear," the commissaris said. The commissaris cut himself a large slice of honeycake, buttered it thickly, ate the slice quickly. "So-called or otherwise. Grijpstra keeps Nellie happy by shopping with her and watching TV, de Gier has his plantation of weeds and Nietzsche if he isn't reading in Spanish."

The commissaris reached for the Gouda cheese. His wife slapped his hand.

"All that fat," his wife said. "Better go for your walk, dear." She pleaded. "You know what is going on here, don't you? I happened to see Nellie yesterday. The woman is right. Ketchup and Karate recommended *you* to those yachting people. That

Antillean business is well beyond G&G's powers. Those Rotterdam folks definitely need you in charge of their project. Those are bad guys, Jan. They lost their illegal goods and they are poor losers. They'll do anything to even things out."

"Nellie and you?" The commissaris shook his head. "Tarot cards again?"

Katrien ate her diet biscuits with sugar-free imitation fruit spread. "Nothing to do with you."

"Nothing is good," the commissaris said.

"All my effort for nothing," Katrien said. "The cards say you will have a nice time with this case." She bit her lip. "And I have to baby-sit. I am jealous I suppose."

"So what you are saying," the commissaris summarized professionally, "is that our potential client, Ambagt & Son, while wandering about the fun Caribbean island of St. Maarten in between sailing their royal cruiser, happened to run into Ketchup and Karate who like to spend their time off in the Netherlands Antilles. Ambagt & Son are in the crude oil business, K&K are in the corrupt police business, in Amsterdam of all places, hub of the criminal universe these days. Skipper Peter and young Carl knew at once that K&K are bad. There is a discrepancy of lifestyle. The Amsterdam Municipal Police pays real wages but even when two constables first class, both childless, combine their salaries the happy couple cannot afford a summer cottage in well-heeled Philipsburg, St. Maarten. Mortgage free. Like their superb apartment in Amsterdam, overlooking the river. And they fly across the ocean like evil-faced gadflies. On what kind of money? Could I have one of those biscuits, do you think?"

"Never," his wife said.

JANWILLEM VAN DE WETERING

She gave him one anyway.

"Tastes like fax paper," the commissaris said. "No. Tastes like unprinted E-mail." He thought. "Some combination, Katrien. Two policemen serving Lucifer in our magic city here, connecting to St. Maarten, owned by Dutch and Italian gangsters. Can you see that meeting? A tropical bar? Striptease performed by selected beauties from, didn't I read that somewhere, Santo Domingo, home of the western hemisphere's most luscious . . ."

"Yes," Katrien said. "I see it. So do you. Wouldn't you like to do the selecting?"

"Bongos," the commissaris said. "You can hear good bongos in Amsterdam now but real bongos, no. And out there, there'll be Mexicans on trumpets and black drummers out of New York, taught by Tony Williams or even," the commissaris smiled dreamily, "or even by Jack de Johnette, Katrien."

"How nice." His wife began to clear the table.

"I am only sketching in the circumstances," the commissaris said. "While all this goes on in the background it turns out that Ambagt & Son has suffered a severe loss, a tanker-load of crude oil taken by pirates. The amount involved could be their entire working capital for all we know, but they have no recourse as they themselves are illegal. Liberian citizens selling Iranian energy to Cuba right under the nose of Uncle Sam?

"And even if they were still Dutch, and reported the piracy to the Dutch *Rijks* Police in St. Maarten? A lieutenant in charge of a dozen constables trying to safeguard tourists going wild in casinos and stripbars and worse? Besides, the piracy took place in international waters, the high seas. Yo ho."

"What?" Katrien asked.

"Yo ho," the commissaris said enthusiastically. "Not a chance, Katrien. But what happens? Haven't I always said so? Good luck comes to those who are lucky."

Katrien banged a ladylike fist on the table. "You did not, Jan. You used to say that good luck comes to those who keep trying."

"I don't think so now," the commissaris said, "I gave in. I no longer believe in positive thinking. Things don't get better and better, things just are, and you can always fit in with things somehow. Things just happen, I happen along."

"*Shit* just happens," Katrien said. "Like me getting old and ugly. You going off on your own again. Having fun."

The commissaris banged a gentleman's fist on the table. "No, Katrien. I marry you and you are beautiful and then you are a grandmother and baby-sit and you're still beautiful. You were just fine then, you're just fine now."

"I look like shit," Katrien, smacking her hips with her hands. "Look at me. Bah."

"You know," the commissaris said. "I find you more elegant as you grow older."

"I am just fine," Katrien said. "Everything is just fine. Crime is just fine. Crooked Ambagt & Son running into corrupt Ketchup & Karate is just fine?"

"It just *is*. I call it fine because I prefer laughing to crying." The commissaris shrugged. "And it will be gone in the end. Look at our world, Katrien. Think back a little. A meteor hits a planet. Because of that impact dinosaurs will eventually be replaced by us, human monkeys, as the dominant species. Now look ahead a little. A few million years pass like a flash and another meteor will hit the same planet. This time the planet

JANWILLEM VAN DE WETERING

changes into empty space. All is gone. Even the records, for there is nobody left, nobody to recall that anything went on. I can't even say that anything went on *here* for there won't be a here. Just empty space where the planet burned out."

"You know," Katrien said furiously, "I think you're dreaming up your own universe. You got bored. You had to dream up some action, so you dreamed up this giant tanker so that Grijpstra and de Gier would have something to do again, and you could lead them into trouble." She poured coffeeless coffee. "Enjoy."

"This," the commissaris said, tasting, "isn't even unprinted E-mail. This is embryonic. This is not even a concept. This is pure cyberspace sh—"

"Jan!"

"You used that word just now."

"I am a woman," Katrien said. "Women can say anything now. You're an archetype."

"Of what?"

"Of the old wise man."

"I am?" the commissaris asked. He kissed her cheek. "What do wise old men do? Stick to their diet and walk briskly in one of Holland's last enclaves of pure nature?" He put on the hat with the pheasant feather Katrien bought him for his birthday, grabbed his cane and limped out of the house.

The commissaris parked his old model Citroën behind the windmill at the entrance of the nature reserve north of Amsterdam. He grumbled and groaned as he hiked along the shore paths. Insects rose from cattails and ferns and successfully penetrated his armor of bug spray. Summering boating people

sipped lukewarm beer while singing along with radio trans-
mitted advertising jingles. A giant helicopter carrying nature
reserve-watching tourists thundered over the protected wetlands. The commissaris reached a graffiti-covered bench and sat
down to enjoy the remnants of silence. He observed waterfowl.
He reflected that this was his life now. There was the investing
on behalf of Grijpstra and de Gier, of course, but the money
kept increasing. No challenge there. Most days looked alike.
The money business required glancing at the financial paper,
analyzing his computer screen twice a day, attending to the
pains in his legs. Left thigh becoming too sensitive? Sell winners. Right thigh bone feeling hot? Buy recent losers. That
interesting kind of splitting cramp with twisting and soaring
red-hot arrows that reached both his knees? Sell anything that
the analysts were telling him to hold on to. He didn't really care
to do this kind of work now; there was too much money in the
account anyway, the boys would never have any need of it. De
Gier considered the stuff a useless burden and Grijpstra no
longer believed he could please Nellie by buying her more
kitchen gadgets. It would be better if G&G were to engage
themselves seriously again. It no longer interested the commissaris to watch de Gier grow ever more silly-named weeds in his
paradise-loft, while waiting for Eve's apple. Grijpstra might
have his apple now, fed to him thrice a day by the queen of his
dreams, but Grijpstra was gaining weight, hardly played his
drums and kept painting the same dead ducks.

And what about his own quest? A superior garden reptile
to have a monologue with, but Turtle's interest seemed to
be waning lately. Besides, what did he require the turtle-
conscience for now? Did he need advice to make choices? Yes

or no to another holiday with Katrien? Holiday from what? Katrien was minding the grandchildren, she was done with travel. Perhaps Turtle might advise some discreet drinking, even whoring, at expensive locations, some private brothel on Apollo Avenue, or maybe an apartment in Beethovenstreet with a stately goddess specializing in pleasing old gents, catering to senile perversions, but should he even consider such a waste of his decreasing energy?

The commissaris rubbed his aching body against the back of the park bench. He tried to visualize a goddess in the Beethovenstreet apartment. Perhaps a somewhat mature woman in a long simple dress, hardly any makeup, gradually opening up to a more intimate conversation while she stepped out of her gown, yesyesyes, but even so, the woman could be his daughter, or if she happened to be younger, his grand-daughter—once he considered those aspects the end result, if any, was sure to fall short of expectations. Still, he had better continue his enquiry. If not he would be like other old men whom he saw fading away while they roamed the city's parks and nature reserves. Former directors of downsized corporations, once powerful city officials forced into accepting early retirement, now being quacked at by water fowl peering at the human ghosts wandering between willows and cattails.

The commissaris dutifully observed black coots, busily swimming about. There were fat coots with white bills and slender coots with red bills. They kept nodding their heads, not because they wanted to confirm his soul-searching but because their biological programs made them bob their heads forever. Walk-bob-head. Swim-bob-head. The commissaris had gotten up to look at tall water lilies when he heard shots.

The Bosnian Serbs are attacking, the commissaris thought. The Tutsis invade the Hutu camp. Ceylonese Tamils are launching a suicide attack. Arabs on the rampage. A German young intellectual has finally, after watching too much evening news, converted to fundamental Neo-Nazism and now has to prove himself by killing me.

Or was it a flipped-out hunter hiding between the bushes at the other side of the brook? The "silence" area between the Amsterdam satellite towns of Abcoude and Ouderkerk does qualify for pheasant hunting but it wasn't the season now. The shots weren't fired by a shotgun. No loud bangs here but sharp cracks, normally associated with the firing of an automatic assault gun. An American liberation weapon, the M-16 used by the Dutch Army? The Kalshnikov used by Eastern European forces?

Now bullets whined close to the commissaris' head.

He knelt between waving grass plumes. The tall pheasant feather on his hat was hit and snapped in two.

Katrien had been wrong once again, the commissaris thought when, back at the windmill parking lot, he got back into the old Citroën. The situation wasn't dangerous at all. All the shots had missed him. De Gier's cracked ribs were healing nicely. Grijpstra wouldn't be sick to his stomach forever. These harmless assaults could be explained as invitations to return to the good life. As encouragements, loving touches from the guiding hand of a benevolent spirit.

Yessir, as far as he was concerned, and he *was* concerned now, the invitation could be accepted.

The commissaris whistled a popular football jingle, "Kick Ass

Hahahah, Kick Ass Hahahah," following an arrangement for mini-trumpet, drums, percussion keyboards and voice, composed by de Gier. He stopped at a carwash on the way home. He noted with pleasure that the weather happened to be superb. He was still whistling when he pushed his front door open.

"Oh no," Katrien said when she saw his face.

He kissed her cheek. "What's wrong, my darling?"

"And I can't go along to take care of you," Katrien said. "You knew that. You're slipping out of reach again. And I have to play grandmother here. Stay away from those tropical beauties, Jan. Don't overeat now. Don't forget your pain pills. Stay close to G&G, they like to protect you. Beware, dear."

"Let the enemy beware," said the commissaris, hissing the tune of "Kick Ass, Hahahah."

The commissaris, stumbling about the loft, found a pith helmet and a tropical suit, with a tunic that buttoned all the way up to the chin. He shouted. "A *tutup* coat, vintage Dutch Indies, from the good old days!" He held the coat up. "Dad used to wear this, on the plantation, Katrien, during the twenties. Real shantung, still as good as new. I bet you this sort of thing is in fashion again, I'll be the king of the Caribbean." Back in the living room, duly uniformed complete with cork-and-linen helmet, the commissaris marched stiffly around Katrien, stopped, clicked his heels, saluted.

"What do you think," he asked shyly. "Does this look okay on me, Katrien?"

Katrien laughed, then cried.

8

DOUBLE PRICE

The nice thing about life, the commissaris thought, during the meeting in the Run Street billiard café, is that nothing ever works out as advertised. Grijpstra's and de Gier's show-off talk apparently was based on very little. The strip-lady might exist but if she did she had that day off. The balcony was empty. The pianist wasn't there. The billiard table was hidden below its dust cover.

Grijpstra talked about nurse Sayukta's visit to de Gier's loft to see if he really grew weeds there. "A mutually useful relationship, sir. Sex traded for insights. The nurse is an adept of the Hindu sadhana. De Gier needs practice after all that reading."

"That so?" the commissaris asked de Gier.

"Never," de Gier said.

The commissaris rummaged in his briefcase. "I have a map of the Antilles here."

Although Ambagt & Son's proposal, on the commissaris's advice, had been accepted by Detection G&G, including the commissaris himself as on-the-spot counselor, de Gier had not been convinced the job was a good thing. Grijpstra tried to persuade his laggard partner. "The Caribbean is good for you, Rinus. Sayuktas galore, and not the tame version you see in Holland. Out there they water-ski, nude."

De Gier thought that the wild Sayuktas, roaming their own habitat without any measure of control, could make him ill. He wanted to stay in his loft with his meadow parsnips and green-headed coneflowers. "While using a nature-cured healthy body the spirit develops."

"Please," Grijpstra said. "You should get rid of your mangy rat buds and dogshit poppies. Why do you think those noxious weeds survive in the city?"

The commissaris spread his map between bottles of fake beer. "Look here, Rinus, these are the islands where *Sibylle* lost her cargo. St. Eustatius, here. Saba. And here is St. Maarten where the *Admiraal Rodney* is going."

Grijpstra was in daily telephone contact with their clients. Young Ambagt reported that the yacht was now in Bermuda. Some minor engine trouble, nothing bad, but not something that could be repaired on a resort island either. It might be better if the *Rodney* headed for Florida. "The Ambagts want us to fly to Key West and board their boat there."

"And from there to the Antilles." The commissaris looked pleased. "That's where this adventure started."

Grijpstra thumped the map. "YesyesYES."

"You're going to be seasick, Henk," de Gier warned.

Grijpstra slapped his partner's shoulder. "Key West! I read about it. At the dentist's office. Supposed to be beautiful. KLM charter flights connect Amsterdam directly to the Florida Keys but it will be more fun if we go to Miami and drive a car from there." Grijpstra's blunt forefinger traced the route. A hundred and forty miles of speedway and bridges connecting islands. "This bridge here is over seven miles long. Gulf of Mexico on the right side, Caribbean on the left side. We rent a Cadillac, that would be all right, wouldn't it, sir? And play CDs while we drive. I'll bring my new Wallace Roney."

"Sir," de Gier said. "This is ridiculous. Are we going to give in to bad guys? Because they slapped me about and dunked Grijpstra?"

"Nah." The commissaris estimated distances on his map. Key West, the most southern point of the USA, was at some distance from Bermuda—about a week's steady going for the disabled *Admiraal Rodney*. He suggested that they leave the next morning, make Grijpstra's car trip, spend a few days in Key West and while waiting for father and son Ambagt, look around. "Yes. That's it. We'll do that."

Katrien, like de Gier, had also accused him of putting himself into criminal hands. And there was the matter of rank. Ketchup and Karate were mere constables, trying, Katrien said, to pull a staff officer down. Peons taking on executives. "But so what, Katrien?" he had replied. "Can we afford to underestimate talent within the lower echelons?" The strength, energy, even intelligence of Ketchup and Karate were not to be sneezed at. Certainly, he had misgivings about their motivations. He did not assume that the two rascals longed for the good old days of pre-drug trade peace and quiet. K&K always tended toward evil. "They're in this for the money, Katrien. But they can be of help."

"Shouldn't you devise a plan that would punish those two

little weasels?" Katrien asked. "Poor Grijpstra and de Gier . . . K&K are *bad*, Jan. They could have gone after you too. No, don't look stupid now. Everybody knows you go hiking in the nature reserve every day, they could have pushed you off a dike, run you over with a tractor"—Katrien laughed, she knew she was exaggerating—"they could even have shot you."

"Haha," laughed the commissaris.

He wasn't into punishing people. Punished people, like beaten dogs, tend to get nasty. It is better to wait for people to do something right for a change and then flatter them to high heaven. Besides, K&K, together with Inspector Cardozo, linked him to the might of the Dutch state. Piracy, the commissaris thought, wasn't this something? Michiel the sailor's corpse pecked by seagulls, a fact documented—according to Grijpstra—by a color photograph. Captain Souza, found in his cabin in a helpless condition. They were obviously confronting a cruel and daredevil enemy. Any help would be nice.

"I say," the commissaris said, "Grijpstra, I forgot to ask you. What happened to the *Sibylle*'s captain, Souza, that poor chap."

"Taken home to Aruba, sir."

"Young Ambagt said so?"

"Yes sir, the *Sibylle* captain was helicoptered to St. Maarten and ambulanced to the airport. Something wrong with his legs. Poor circulation. Gangrene in both feet."

"And the captain knew nothing about the assault on his vessel?"

"Too intoxicated, sir."

"Aruba," de Gier looked at the map. "And the yacht, the *Rodney* is now in Bermuda's harbor? Didn't you say that

Ambagt & Son once had their office in Bermuda? Before they became sailors?"

The commissaris quoted a police file shown him by Inspector Cardozo. Peter and Carl Ambagt, some twenty years ago, started their career as Rotterdam-based car thieves. The garage they kept on the Schiedam Dike was a "chop shop" where stolen cars are quickly taken apart. Parts were then sold all over the country. Carl did the stealing, mostly of expensive Ford models, and Peter was in charge of chopping and dealing.

Peter Ambagt was arrested and spent a year in the jail at North Canal, Rotterdam. Carl was released on probation.

Prosecutors underestimated the size of their case. Shortly after Peter was released the Ambagts started their crude oil business in Bermuda, well-capitalized.

"Capital earned by the sale of car parts?" Grijpstra asked. De Gier thought this quite likely. The total value of a car's parts is about three times the value of the new car. The Ambagts would have sold them at wholesale so their prices would have been lower. Suppose you do a car a day. Say three hundred cars a year (allowing for off-days) at twenty thousand each. That would be six million a year, gross.

"Costs?" Grijpstra asked.

De Gier was still calculating. Help. Rent. Having dinner in the "The Meuse" Yacht Club. Peter Ambagt had a male Chinese prostitute habit to keep up in the Cat's Creek quarter his file had said. Then there were Carl's linen blazers and Swiss gold watches. Say they made a profit of three million a year, say they kept it up for five years, that would give them savings of fifteen million as starting capital for the oil business. Yes?

The commissaris didn't see how the calculation could be too

far out. According to Cardozo's police file the Ambagts's subsequent oil business was conducted from far-away Bermuda, well out of reach of the Dutch police. The Ambagts started off by buying Russian oil and shipping it to South Africa. South Africa at the time was unpopular with all western countries. The embargo included crude oil. South Africa has no energy sources of its own. Red Russia couldn't deal directly with the white Protestant Boers but would sell to anybody via third parties. "And then . . ." the commissaris hit the table top with his small fist, ". . . haha!"

"Haha what, sir?" asked Grijpstra.

An absolute wonderful construction, the commissaris said. How did the rascals ever think of it! Real smart Alecs those two. The Russians had to be sure they would get their money so payment was arranged with a letter of credit, a transfer of dollars guaranteed by a Bermuda bank. The cash was released as soon as the Russians could prove delivery of the oil. The South Africans paid Ambagt & Son, Ambagt & Son paid the Russians, and in between was *paperwork*.

"Bureaucracy," the commissaris said. "You know what Professor Mindera of Erasmus University says about bureaucracy. *The only thing that saves us from the bureaucracy is its inefficiency.*" The commissaris raised an all-knowing finger. "Bureaucracy is based on lack of trust. Its paranoid fear requires tedious paperwork. Eventually even the best of us get irritated by dotted lines and multiple choices. Frustration with red tape tempts us to beat the system. Become crooks."

"Professor Mindera said all that?" de Gier asked.

"The latter part I said," said the commissaris.

The Russian paperwork was unbelievably complicated but

Peter Ambagt learned how to fill in the forms. After a year of regular business the old man placed an enormous order. A fleet of chartered tankers filled up in Leningrad. He didn't apply for a letter of credit and blamed the paperwork delay on his banks. The loaded tankers were taking up valuable Leningrad harbor space. Peter Ambagt telephoned his Russian suppliers: hadn't he always paid, wasn't he trustworthy, the papers were in the mail. "Please send off your tankers. Please? Pretty please?"

"Da," the Russians said. "Yes."

Russian tugs pulled the tankers to sea. Off went the oil fleet.

"Ah," de Gier said, thinking ahead. "So Ambagt & Son were paid by the South Africans as soon as the tankers hit Capetown but Ambagt and Son never paid the Russians. A fortune was made for their cost was zero. But didn't they run a risk here? Didn't Russia send Ivans?"

"Ivans?" Grijpstra asked.

"Ivan Bondsky," the commissaris said. "Ivan shoot-the-pheasant-feather-of-my-hatsky."

"What?" Grijpstra asked.

"But there was a change of regime in Moscow," the commissaris answered his own question. "No more Ivans." He laughed. "And that's how Ambagt & Son could purchase a thirty million dollar FEADship."

Grijpstra pointed an accusing finger at the commissaris. "Shot a feather off your head? Didn't you just say that? Where did that happen? While you were walking behind the windmills at Abcoude? In the nature reserve?" Grijpstra's heavy jowls trembled with fury. "So K&K got you too! Used that idiotic Kalshnikov that hangs above the fireplace at their Amstel apartment."

De Gier's face also flushed with anger. "An untrustworthy weapon. Shoots large caliber bullets too." De Gier's finger pointed accusingly. "You never told us. That's not good, sir."

"We'll get the little fuckers," Grijpstra said.

"Now, now, gentlemen," the commissaris soothed. "Personal weaknesses cannot be taken care of on their own levels. We know that. Yes?" He peered over his little round glasses. "You, de Gier, as a student of Buddhism, and lately Hinduism, is it? Yes. Well, as a student of eastern philosophies you should know by now that Ketchup and Karate will not raise their level of being by anything we can do to them. Only their own effort, which is part of their own quest for insight, may, as a side effect, make them decent. Knowing that we will set our attitudes aside and use K&K purely for their talents."

"For their egotistic ruthlessness," de Gier said.

The commissaris smiled. "Absolutely."

"I understand," de Gier said.

"He understands nothing, sir," Grijpstra said.

"Ambagt & Son don't understand anything either," the commissaris said, "and ignorance makes their practices worse. Figure for yourself. In Bermuda they had a nice villa with a pool and a few expensive hobbies maybe, nothing that couldn't be financed with an easily produced cash flow. Was that enough?"

"Enough is too much," Grijpstra said. "Nellie keeps saying that. She doesn't even want me to buy her flowers."

"Less is better," de Gier said.

"You know that now, do you?" the commissaris asked. He peered over his glasses again. "That's nice. But did the Ambagts? I don't think so. Bermuda was near-heaven but they were still paying some taxes. A FEADship that happened to dock in Bermuda harbor gave them the idea they could improve their independence."

Grijpstra looked unhappy. "Nellie gave the car I bought her to her sister. She got a used bicycle, rides it to keep her weight down."

"Used bikes are mostly stolen," de Gier said.

Grijpstra nodded. "Maybe she stole it herself. She used to do that. Stole them from the market where thieves sold stolen bikes."

"Now," the commissaris said. "As soon as Ambagt & Son had invested a sizable part of their income in the *Admiraal Rodney* the necessity to augment their cash flow increased." The commissaris nodded triumphantly. "See? My cousin who's in shipping says that a vessel's upkeep is about fifteen percent of its purchase price a year. That's a lot more than what their Bermuda villa was costing. Another five million a year to make somehow, and their position in the oil market deteriorating."

"Cuba won't pay too well," de Gier said, "and Iran won't supply too well."

"With Carl and Peter in the middle," Grijpstra said.

"And now," the commissaris said, "the Ambagts want us to recoup the losses caused by the piracy of the uninsured cargo of their chartered supertanker *Sibylle*."

"And offer us one miserable million," Grijpstra said sadly.

"I vote that, considering the way we have been treated so far, we double our fee," de Gier said.

"Enough is too little?" the commissaris asked. "De Gier, I want you to order tickets right now, Amsterdam to Miami, open returns, first class, and make sure Grijpstra's Cadillac is

waiting in Miami. CD player included. We leave tomorrow."
The commissaris looked unhappy. "Double fee? Really, Rinus.
Greed. You of all people."

"Vengeance," de Gier said loudly. "Not greed."

Vengeance was unacceptable too, Grijpstra said. How could
de Gier feel a need for revenge, surely not after all his meditations in the loft, his spiritual reading, the communication with
magical herbs. Was Grijpstra to conclude that the method de
Gier was using, the *sadhana* as he called it, did not work? Could
Grijpstra assume that his own way of behaving normally,
staying within parameters dictated by common sense. . . .

"You don't want to get even?" de Gier asked.

"With Ketchup and Karate?" Sure enough Grijpstra wanted
to get even. "We'll get them, Rinus." Grijpstra didn't mind
the ordinary beating de Gier had gotten, and the feather off the
commissaris's hat, well now, that wasn't too bad was it? But he
himself had almost drowned in unspeakably filthy IJ river
water.

"There are moments," the commissaris said, "that I expect
just a little more of you two."

Grijpstra leaned toward the commissaris. "Don't you feel
intimidated, sir?" De Gier touched the commissaris's arm.
"They did use a Russian assault rifle on you, sir."

"Come to think of it," the commissaris said while he cleaned
his spectacles, "they did make me nervous there, just for a
moment."

9

Vultures Circle Mount Trashmore

Black-winged yellow-billed vultures followed the blue jeep below with interest. Colombians living in Key West, Florida, call the vultures *chulos*, the same word they use for bandits.

"Stewy" Stewart-Wynne looked up. His jeep had been rented only minutes ago from an office in the golden hill's shadow. Florida is flat but Key West is proud of her homemade mountain. It is a bother to transport garbage produced by some fifty thousand Key Westers to Miami, so the refuse is used to manufacture a landmark, Mount Trashmore, tirelessly pushed up by growling tractors that cover the garbage with sun-reflecting sand. Some is exposed and contains rotten food. The vultures peck and tear around the ever-busy tractors. Their stomachs filled, they spread wide wings, hop away from the steep slopes and use thermals to leisurely soar for hours. Vultures are lazy. They hardly move their wings.

"Hello, foul-faced gobblers of carrion," the Englishman

joked from his open jeep. "Is my perfumed presence offensive to you?" He was in a good mood. He had just finished his last business project. A couple of more months of gazing out of the window back at the London office and Stewy would retire. After that there would be nothing but contentment. Walk the dog three times a day in spacious Hyde Park, without forgetting bucket and spade—Jasper was a volume crapper—water the flowers in his little solarium once a day, take care of the stuck-to-the-fridge shopping list once a week, that would be it for the duration. Anne would continue to suck oxygen from a steel bottle, and smoke cigarettes of course. Fortunately she wasn't much bother. Waiting for eternity, Anne would keep smoking while Jasper the dog jerked and dreamed and Stewy, well, he would be just fine he expected. Read *The Times*, watch some movies, listen to comedians on the BBC, have a half pint of bitter at the pub around the corner.

Fine by me, Stewy thought. Fine by me.

"Stewy, old boy," the boss had said. "I hear the Caribbean is one of your former stomping grounds. It seems we have a little trouble there. You might go out there and take a look. What say, Stewy?"

"Yes *sir*," Stewy said.

"Agent" (his official work title) Stewart-Wynne was in luck that day. Originally employed by the British financial giant Quadrant Pty. Ltd. as an investigator of dubious insurance claims he had, due to age and an unwillingness to become "computer literate," been told to "take things lightly." And now he was back in the field. Facing adventure. He hadn't told his boss that he knew almost nothing about the Antilles, except for what he had noticed during a visit to Anguilla. Anne could still walk then, it had been a few years ago. A brief holiday spent in a bed & breakfast. The owner of the ramshackle former colonial "villa," Jonathan, had made an impression. The tall distinguished looking black man was supposed to be a "seer" but behaved normally enough, except for conducting cere-monies with believers. Chickens were killed, there was a bon-fire, the congregation dressed up and Jonathan showed the whites of his eyes, mumbled, sang, shook a rattle, banged a drum, a choir of young girls singing rhythmic refrains behind him. The music, and the general performance, reminded Stewy of rap with a touch of Sting. He had, in spite of British arro-gance, become fascinated by his host, however.

On his return to Anguilla, he found the bed & breakfast still there. Stewy, at company's expense, took the best room. He told Jonathan about his investigation. Jonathan helped out. The enquiry pointed at the nearby island of St. Maarten. Another lead took Stewart-Wynne to its twin island of St. Eustatius. All lines of enquiry met in Key West. Stewy checked Key West out. It wasn't necessary because enough proof had been obtained and even recorded. He could have returned to London and wrapped things up but his expenses were well within budget, so why not celebrate to top this thing off? Closing his career, Agent Stewart-Wynne sneaked in a nice secret week of vacation. His conscience was clear. This was the final occasion for realizing some of his fantasies. "I am a cowboy," Agent Stewart-Wynne shouted, at the wheel of his brand new bright blue rented all-American jeep. "I am John Wayne and I do things with boys."

The real John Wayne would do nothing of the kind, Stewy knew that, but *his* John Wayne did what master Stewart-

Wynne dictated. And if *his* John Wayne had to live in Key West's four star Eggemoggin Hotel, well, there the splendid fellow stayed.

Stewart-Wynne's personality had many aspects. At St. Maarten and St. Eustatius he had enjoyed being a hiker, observing nature. On the small island of Anguilla he was the British odd man out, riding a donkey. Perhaps his personality had split because Anne wasn't with him this time. His wife was his anchor. Anguilla's seer, Jonathan, had raised that possibility during a long night's dialogue where much marijuana was burned. Jonathan had suggested Stewart-Wynne should use all his personas. Jonathan compared the so-far dull British middle-class gent to an airplane found on Anguilla. The Cessna had crashed and broken a wing. The pilot disappeared, probably after stealing a sailboat. Pleased Anguilla constables had confiscated a consignment of cannabis products found in the airplane. The useless plane stood at the side of the road. Jonathan owned a melon field and his cart had broken down which was a nuisance for the field was at the other side of a three-mile-long road.

Jonathan unscrewed the Cessna's wings, hitched his donkey to the plane, loaded it with melons and saved himself some trouble by hauling his products to the farmer's market. Then the donkey hurt a leg. A friendly mechanic got the plane's engine going so the next load of melons was motored to market. "I could also," Jonathan told Stewart-Wynne, "*fly* the melons to market. I still have the Cessna's wings and there is enough technology on Anguilla to get them reattached. All the airplane's capacity was there, just as you, as a human being, have all human capacities in you too."

"*Is that so?*" asked Stewart-Wynne politely.

That was so. The human being, Jonathan proposed, has infinite possibilities.

"Is that so?"

That was so, too. The Cessna did not have to fly melons a short distance away however and Stewart-Wynne, for the moment, did not have to use his supernatural gifts. There were times, however, said Jonathan, where we need all our talents, "Like you will, Mistah Stewy, in Key West, in the very near future."

"How do you know, Mistah Jonathan?"

Jonathan had been busy with a chicken again, and pieces of cloth, and his drums and rattles, had danced around a fire in a white robe at full moon while the female choir sang musical backdrop.

"Wonderful nonsense," Stewy thought, driving under circling vultures in his rental jeep on his way to the center of Key West where he was to airmail a postcard to Anne and have a leisurely and superb dinner afterward, in Key West's fine restaurant, Lobster Lateta. Certain to be quite expensive, and so what, one might ask?

Stewy wasn't pressed to inform Quadrant Ltd. in London. The report was in his head and the cassette was in his hat.

The vultures, meanwhile, observed the doomed cowboy. Vultures recognize potential dead flesh. Stewy had packaged his in tall snakeskin boots, with silver toes and high rubber heels, tight jeans, a plaid linen dress shirt and a two-gallon hat. Stewy intended to leave those clothes in the hotel; Anne would be too amused if she were to see them in his suitcase. She might tell his boss at Quadrant. The boss would be too amused too.

He saw, in his rear mirror, a dented Chevrolet, an early

seventies model, a semi-wreck, the type used by beach bums. Stewy remembered he had seen the vehicle before, driven by the same long-haired guy. A junkie, Stewart-Wynne thought. A drunk. People like the Chevy driver were deliberately avoiding chances of work. Most Key West hotels and restaurants displayed HELP WANTED signs. A shame really that the driver of the car behind him had fouled up his life almost as if on purpose. Now *there* was someone the vultures above should be interested in.

Always something, Stewart-Wynne thought angrily. Now why was he being followed by a bad guy? Finally, at the end of his career, about to realize a little harmless dream, a man finds himself faced by possible new trouble. Stewy recalled another clever saying produced by Jonathan. Life is not one damned thing after another, no, it's the same damned thing over and over again, the same desire to fearfully hold on to pleasurable moments.

He decided to disregard the circling birds of carrion, the pervasive sweetly foul stench wafted down from Mount Trashmore, the rust bucket-driving bad guy. Besides, his rear mirror had emptied. The bum had probably taken a side road. Stewart-Wynne was John Wayne again.

"Use all your aspects," Jonathan of Anguilla had said, "in Key West you will need them."

John Wayne needed nothing, except a gourmet meal and, after that, drinks, in a trendy bar.

Stewy parked the jeep in front of the Key West post office on Whitehead Street. He had bought a picture postcard for Anne. The picture showed the last Floridian Native American chief, Billy Bowlegs, about to shoot, through the chest, an officer of the ever-victorious American cavalry. Anne, anti-American since Vietnam, enjoyed contemporary Indians versus Whites movies. She would giggle, in between smoking and coughing, whenever a representative of the dominant white race bit the dust while the noble Indians smiled wisely. Billy Bowlegs had bitten the dust himself at the time but on the picture postcard he was allowed to win. The American officer who was about to be killed looked just like John Wayne.

While he nimbly jumped out of the jeep Stewy saw a dead sparrow, resting on its beak. It happened that the parking lot was empty. In the absence of vehicles the eye automatically focused on the little animal corpse. The sparrow, leaning forward, appeared to be both humorous and pathetic. The dead bird was spotlighted by sun rays breaking through the foliage of palms. It was late in the afternoon, and the low incoming sunlight, fragmented and contorted by the exhaust fumes of passing traffic, seemed shot through with blood.

John Wayne sucked in his belly behind his snakeskin belt, tipped his huge hat over his eyes and, postcard in hand, swaggered lankily past the dramatically illuminated dead sparrow.

Ominous omens everywhere. "Use all your aspects," seer Jonathan had warned.

Behind victim Stewart-Wynne the Chevy's long-haired driver eased his muscular body quickly beneath Stewart-Wynne's parked jeep. In his hand glistened a set of spanners and a pair of pliers. Stewy noticed nothing.

10

AMERICAN SCENES

The commissaris, Grijpstra, and de Gier, were waved goodbye to at Amsterdam's Schiphol Airport by Katrien, Nellie and Sayukta. They had a pleasant flight with good weather during take-off and landing, and thunderstorms in-between that they could look down on.

Their reserved Cadillac waited at Miami Airport. The Avis girl explained how to get out of Miami and onto Route 1 to the Florida Keys and ultimately to Key West. Her Haitian-French accent was so attractive that the nodding listeners never took in a word. They made a number of wrong turns and reached Miami's back side where de Gier had to drive artfully to avoid unhappy kids and the beer cans they were throwing. The commissaris, in the rear, ignoring de Gier's cursing and Grijpstra's wails, tried to read the Avis road map. The Cadillac was followed by a van filled with young adults with felted hair, robbers according to Grijpstra, tourist-killers, armed to the teeth. The tension of the chase took the detectives into their past.

Grijpstra took command. "Get us out of here, sergeant."

"That is understood, adjutant. At your orders."

De Gier clicked his rear lights on and off so the driver of the chasing van would believe that the Cadillac was suddenly braking. He did indeed think so. In order to avoid a collision the felt-haired driver stamped on his own brake and the sudden loss of speed caused him and his companions to lunge forward and strike their heads against the van's windshield. The Cadillac, meanwhile, increased speed. De Gier twisted his wheel a little in order to give the impression that he was about to make a sharp turn to the left, then made his car turn all the way to the right. Another feint? Yes, the car made a left U-turn. The complicated maneuver unsettled the pursuing van. It slipped off the tarmac, plowed through a row of trash cans, skidded into a field, destroyed thorn bushes, veered off a palm tree, collided with car wrecks and turned over slowly.

The commissaris finally understood the road map and guided de Gier to a highway where the Cadillac joined steady traffic on a Miami bypass. Cars in parallel lines were driven by neat old men wearing straw hats.

"If you keep following Route 1 signs," the commissaris told de Gier, "we'll reach the Everglades soon." He read the reverse side of his map. "Ibis and giant white heron, eagle and bear, panthers even, and then we'll cross those bridges you mentioned, Grijpstra, between two bodies of water, connecting a long stretch of islands, terminating in Key West."

Grijpstra had inserted a CD into the opening in the car's dashboard. Four stereo loudspeakers emitted the sound of the trumpet of Wallace Roney. "So What?" The outskirts of Miami flashed by. Skyscraping hotels mirrored each other in a thousand windows. The Cadillac moved smoothly. Peace had returned. "Yes, indeed," the commissaris said, closing his eyes for a moment to be able to concentrate on Herbie Hancock's piano. The notes were impeccably clear, Roney's trumpet entered again and guided the commissaris to gain insights. Just for a split second he almost knew what everything was about.

The commissaris, hands folded on a slightly protruding stomach, head resting on velvet covered foam rubber upholstery, snored softly. Grijpstra thought dreamily about two supertankers moored to each other, one spouting, one sucking. Could such an event have happened? Robber tankers sidling up to victim tankers. Pirates jumping from one deck to another. A machine gun rattles. Pumps and tubes being dragged across gunwales. Sailor Michiel bleeds to death. Captain Souza raves and rants in his cabin. Nobody pushes the emergency button? No SOS signals flash through cyberspace? No Coast Guard cutter approaches at full speed? Nothing but empty sea and sea gulls hacking into the squirming flesh of a foully murdered young hero? De Gier switched the Cadillac into cruise control, fifty miles per hour, the speed limit announced on signs along the two lane road. Swamps stretched to the horizon on both sides, an expanse of flat greens and yellows with an occasional cluster of bushes and pines. White and gray herons and egrets waded thoughtfully, cormorants and crows sat on telephone and electrical lines, an osprey peered down from a large untidy nest built on a giant billboard showing a leggy and breasty woman sipping whiskey, the same glossy color as her hair.

De Gier listened to the jazz trumpet, trying to play each note in his mind along with the performing genius. Grijpstra listened along, drumming on his knees, softly, because the CD's percussion was soft too, especially while swishing the cymbals although there were quick rattles on the tom-drums because a drummer remains a drummer.

"Heh," sighed Grijpstra ecstatically.

How pleasant it all can be, de Gier thought contentedly.

The Everglades receded into forgotten background. Speedboats left futuristic white stripes upon the azure water. Pelicans accompanied the car, like policemen riding Harley-Davidsons around a limo transporting a governor on tour. Beach houses hid under palm trees. Key West was approaching. The figures indicating distance became lower and lower. Key West would be Mile Zero.

De Gier wanted to eat but Grijpstra and the commissaris were dozing happily. The CD player performed Duke Ellington's "Caravan." He moved cruise control up to 60 mph. Grijpstra mumbled and the commissaris sighed. "Caravan," de Gier knew, was inspired by a camel caravan trotting. Little bells sounded while the animals, in the joy of motion, rhythmically moved their long legs in unison. The ideal journey, de Gier thought, keeps going. The ideal traveller forgets departure, ignores destination. None of the moving images matter—he does not wish to stay, he is not afraid to leave them. He enjoys the passing show.

De Gier vaguely thought of food again. Key West, according to the leaflets, was Lazy Gourmet Heaven. There would be the stone crab that offers its tasty fighting claw and grows a new one when thrown back after amputation. There would be the differently tasty lobster tail. There would be giant shrimps, there would be fish of all colors, sizes, tastes, denominations.

And Florida's mainland would provide tossed salads, fruits covered with whipped cream, vegetables for the thus inclined.

A special dish would be ragout of conch, a humongous shellfish, an endangered species not caught in U.S. waters but Key West's supply is ample for the nearby Bahamas and the Antilles don't mind robbing their part of the ocean in exchange for dollars. Then, eventually, there would be key lime pie, the ultimate association of lemons, eggs, crust and cream.

"Hunger," groaned the gradually waking Grijpstra. "Maybe a little taste of something?" the commissaris whispered from the rear seat. He studied a new map. "Key West already? Cross the bridge, de Gier, turn left onto Roosevelt Drive, turn right onto Duval Street, second block on the left. There is a restaurant called Lobster Lateta."

"Hotel?" Grijpstra asked.

"Eggemoggin Hotel," the commissaris said. "Lots of stars. Eat first. Shall we do that?"

Food was served on the restaurant's sidewalk terrace with a view of Duval Street. Shopping tourists, in slobby-snob attire, wandered along on the sidewalks; restored antique cars moved slowly along well-kept tarmac. Female bikers thundered along at five miles an hour. The riders, dressed in identical orange bib-overalls over brown T-shirts, wore First World War steel helmets. Some were hardly able to reach their machines's handlebars. A heavily made-up desiccated old woman rode a rickshaw pulled by a body builder with a gold painted chest and a bamboo penis holder, aggressively pointing forward. A single-file jazz band goose-stepped slowly along, one foot on the sidewalk, one foot in the gutter. The leader was a Native American wearing a feathered hat and playing the trombone. The band consisted of white and black musicians. It played a passable version of Monk's "Rhythm-A-Ning."

The commissaris saw Stewart-Wynne's jeep as it came roaring along, before his companions did. Time slowed down, as it had done before when he faced a life-threatening situation, but then there had been evil on the other side: a criminal holding a gun, a fight on a railway platform—he had almost been pushed under a train. He had faced death in illness too, to the point where he had detached from his body and floated up from a hospital bed and looked down on Katrien's head and noticed her first gray hairs. He had despaired then, thinking she might need him, and gone back to fight those lethal microbes, greedy, out to tear the flesh off his bones. Now the threatening image seemed friendly. The commissaris liked jeeps. He remembered American troops driving down an Amsterdam street in a jeep, the first Allied soldiers he had seen during the liberation. He wanted to welcome the square engine hood, the chromium plated headlights.

The deadly machine hurled closer. The bright blue vehicle hit the Cadillac, parked correctly on the other side of the street, sideways. The jeep bounced off. The Englishman hung onto the steering wheel for dear life. His mouth was wide open. He was probably shouting. The jeep hit other parked cars, grinding their fenders with its own, causing clouds of sparks. The jazz band tried to scatter but merged again and poured itself into an ethnic art gallery, bumping into African tribal sculptures and sliding about on Oriental rugs. The rickshaw shot into an alley, where it broke its carrying poles and jettisoned the old woman. The body builder climbed a palm.

The commissaris, using the uncommonly long length of

what had to be only a split second, chose to forget his lame leg for the moment. He jumped across the table and shoved Grijpstra, chair and all, to the side. Grijpstra's foot was in the jeep's way, he shrieked while pulling it back. De Gier, aware of the danger before Grijpstra was pushed over, shoved guests out of the way of the roaring jeep—then, to save himself, ran into a decorative garden at the rear of the restaurant and fell into a shallow goldfish pond that was partly covered with water lilies in flower. The jeep, having climbed the wooden steps leading to the terrace, followed de Gier, splintering furniture in its path. "Out of the way!" yelled John Wayne, with a British accent. (The commissaris mentioned that later: because of the slowing down of time, he had been able to notice how "put on" the all-American cowboy's voice seemed.) "Wayay-ayayay . . ." Stewart-Wynne screamed with his last breath. The jeep entered the goldfish pond too, as it was vacated by de Gier, and was suspended from its rock wall, all wheels spinning. De Gier turned the car's ignition key. A fearful silence became filled with groans and curses. Guests picked each other up. A woman, raised by the commissaris, wailed about irreparable damage done to her hand-painted silk dress. She pointed a shaking finger at Stewart-Wynne's limp body. "I hope that drunk hurt himself." She narrowed her eyes and asked, "Or do you think he is stoned?" She mimed inserting a pill into her mouth. "Some mind-altering substance? Maybe he was out of it?"

"He won't get back to it," the commissaris said, studying the unnatural angle between the driver's head and torso.

A police-cyclist arrived. The athletic looking young man wore khaki shorts and a blue shirt above a polished gunbelt hung with law-enforcement paraphernalia, polished boots and high socks. The cop knelt next to the corpse and sniffed at its lips. "I did that already," de Gier said. "No liquor, but look at this." He showed the policeman the inside of the jeep, where the accelerator was detached from its hinge. "And here, this isn't right either." The brake pedal was pushed in. "The poor fellow had no controls; it's amazing the steering wheel hasn't been fussed with also."

The policeman stared at de Gier.

"How come, huh?" de Gier asked.

"How come," the policeman asked slowly, "you know so much, huh?" He touched de Gier's shoulder with a powerful hand. "You stay close, buddy." He spoke into his radio transmitter. "Sergeant Symonds? Harry here. Situation at Duval and Louisa, Northside. Dead tourist in cowboy outfit at the wheel of a Mount Trashmore rented blue jeep. Lobster Lateta Restaurant, sixty percent destroyed. Quarter of a million collision damage to Duval-parked cars, Darn-Dikes's bikes, Aunt Tata's rickshaw, Golden Boy's genital wear and the Stompers's instruments. The chihuahua in the ethnic gallery is in a defensive coma. Apart from the driver, nobody seems to be hurt. Amazing, huh? Probable criminal intent and a wise-ass witness. Sergeant? Mind sending the van and some technical backup? And an ambulance for the corpse."

"Ten-four," a musical (veiled, and jazzy, de Gier thought) female voice said. "Thanks, Harry, and out."

11

PORTRAIT OF A COMPANION BIRD

The commissaris and Grijpstra had a meeting in their suite at the Eggemoggin Hotel. Grijpstra had exchanged the damaged Cadillac at Avis Key West. The commissaris telephoned Carl Ambagt. The FEADship had, Carl reported, just sighted the Bahaman island of Eleuthera. The *Rodney* was still going slowly. There had been, Carl complained, a blockage of air in the cylinders. The air had been bled out meanwhile. The air had gotten in because of clogged fuel pipes. The clogging was caused because fuel taken on at Bermuda had gummed up. The gumming up was caused by "poop."

"Poop, Mr. Ambagt?"

"Little-animal-poop," Carl said. Microbes that live in fuel oil only partially consume their daily intake. A residue is excreted by the parasitic organisms as gummy poop. Not, Carl said, an entirely unknown phenomenon; poop in fuel lines has slowed down naval battles. "You never heard of microbe poop? No? It was a first for me too, but here we are, slowed down to five knots." Carl had gotten his information from his ship's engineer—twenty years of service with the Royal Dutch Navy. Carl said he believed the entire story was baloney. Some crew member probably forgot to open a fuel line somewhere, so the engine sucked air instead. Diesel engines choke on air. So what to do? Admit guilt? Never. Invent microbe poop.

"I see," the commissaris said, puzzled.

Whatever happened, Carl said, the *Rodney* would dock in Key West for repairs. Any day now. The *Rodney* was a perfect vessel but oversights will occur and the ocean does not forgive weakness. Everything would be taken care of in due course. Sometime soon they would all be on their way to the Antilles, to see some action.

"Not all of us," the commissaris said and filled his client in about a jeep hitting Lobster Lateta and the Key West Police holding on to de Gier for further questioning.

"I hope he brought his gloves," laughed Carl.

"Beg pardon?"

It was okay, Carl said, he had to hang up now. The boatswain was reporting seaweed in his vessel's exhaust.

Carl sounded nervous. "He has to lower a diver."

"Good luck," the commissaris said.

"You think de Gier will be arrested?"

"Could be." The commissaris's aching legs were bothered by an onshore breeze. He lay down and covered himself up with a cotton blanket. Grijpstra rested on the next enormous bed. Together they analyzed the confrontation at Lobster Lateta. Grijpstra's theory, an arranged simultaneous failure of brake and accelerator, seemed acceptable. The gentleman/cowboy was not drunk. He didn't look like a substance abuser either. De Gier, before he was escorted to the police van, had reported on its mechanical malfunctions, but the jeep was new with not two thousand miles on the odometer.

"Not logical as a mishap," the commissaris concluded.

Grijpstra's theory included a "hellish machine," a Dutch legal term, indicating a device intentionally installed to cause physical harm.

De Gier entered the room after midnight.

"Gallivanting?" the commissaris asked.

The enquiry had taken up some time. De Gier had been told not to leave town and to be prepared to be picked up at any given moment.

"Trying to be clever," Grijpstra said. "To the police of all people. To the *American* police. Don't you watch movies? They kill you here for being clever."

"Sergeant Symonds," de Gier said, "takes us for big players. Our profiles are wrong. We can't be tourists. We're a godfather with two lieutenants. We're here to be *bad*."

The commissaris sat up. He smiled gleefully. "Is that so?" He rubbed his hands. "So what's the Key West Police sergeant like?"

De Gier reported. "Black female, mid-thirties, tall, attractive, lot of strong white teeth, efficient, intelligent, can think for herself."

"Did you charm her?" Grijpstra asked.

"Not the type."

De Gier had, after spending over an hour in a badly ventilated cell, spoken the truth to Sergeant Ramona Symonds. He and his two friends were eating lobster tail and stone crab claw at their cozy little table in the classy restaurant when a jeep careened off Duval Street and aimed straight for them. Subsequently, as a former Amsterdam Murder Brigade detective, now self-employed as a private eye, de Gier had alerted Harry, the bicycle-cop, to technical points of interest. Harry, however, seemed to have a personality disorder. An extreme case of paranoia? Or someone who likes to annoy his betters?

"Harry is a dear," Ramona said. "So what brings you here, my former colleague?"

De Gier and his associates, an ex-police non-com and a retired chief-detective, had been invited by the shipping firm of Ambagt & Son to join the directors on their yacht for a journey to the Netherlands Antilles.

Yes, the invitation was connected to a professional project.

No, de Gier could not divulge further information.

No, nothing illegal. "Really, Miss. No? You prefer to be addressed as Sergeant? Really, Sergeant."

What was Ambagt & Son's business?

Crude oil in tankers.

No, no drugs.

So far the to-and-fro had been easy, rhythmic, a round of table tennis, ping-pong, ping-pong.

After that some tension occurred. "No kidding," the sergeant said, straightening her shirt, adorned on the sleeve with three small gold chevrons. "Crude oil? That's not a big product here in Key West, you know that? And I know the FEADship you mentioned. The *Admiraal Rodney*, right? She destroyed one of our quays, behind the Hotel Singh, not six blocks from here. That was last year. A FEADship is just about the most expensive type of private yacht that plies our seas. Made in Holland. Just like you.

"And you live in . . ." she checked de Gier's passport, ". . . in Amsterdam. Isn't that where heroin is supplied, free of charge, by the city?" Sergeant Symonds rummaged through a stack of papers. "It so happens that I just read something on that. Here. A newspaper clipping, an article on Amsterdam drug use. *Heroin Heaven*." She nodded angrily. "Something my kid brother from Detroit would like to try out. It would make him happy."

De Gier said that drug *trafficking* in Amsterdam was illegal.

"But isn't the city a hub for the international trade?" Sergeant Symonds asked. De Gier denied it. She didn't hear his answer as her phone was ringing. She picked up the receiver, listened, thanked the speaker, replaced the receiver. The large brown eyes under artfully curved eyebrows searched de Gier's face. Her soft voice vibrated. De Gier's spine vibrated too. He assumed she sang, in a choir in a church perhaps. "The jeep driver was murdered," the soft vibrating voice said. "You knew that."

De Gier knew nothing.

"Didn't you tell me just now that you're a private eye?" the sergeant asked. She curved her thumb and index finger around her eye.

De Gier said he was.

"And before that you were a Murder Brigade detective?"

He was.

"Many years?"

Many years.

Amsterdam, Sergeant Symonds said, was a lovely city, she had spent a week there, as a Police Academy student, during an exchange program. She had stayed in the youth hostel near

Vondel Park. Low priced. Nice people. Free beer at the Heineken brewery and a harpsichord and two flutes concert at the cathedral, the Wester Church it was called, she believed. Beautiful music. Raw herring at a street stall, with onions, hold the capers.

De Gier said he was glad she had liked his city.

"But there was quite a bit of trash floating in your canals."

The trash problem had been handled since then, de Gier said. Dogs had been trained to use the streets's gutters. Car theft was down somewhat and street crooks playing the shell game were now being detained and lectured on human values. The problem of stolen bicycles would be next. Mugging was an exclusive now, done only by foreigners who could not obtain free heroin at city clinics. When caught these unfortunates were promptly deported.

"You retired early?" Sergeant Symonds asked. "How come? Col-league?"

De Gier thought that the sergeant pronounced the syllables in an irritating manner.

"No pension?"

De Gier admitted to not having waited for his pension.

She poured from a green metal thermos. De Gier tasted. "Delicious." She said that she had bought the coffee at the Fleming Street supermarket. She wheeled her chair back, half-opened the lower drawers of her desk and used them as foot rests. She looked innocent, friendly, across the rim of her coffee mug. She asked if de Gier, an experienced criminal investigator, would care to think along with her. Now wasn't this an interesting case? Where to start though? At the presence of three foreign ranking for-mer po-lice-men? Okay?

"Okay," de Gier said, disturbed somewhat by the way she cut up the words "former" and "policemen."

Okay, Symonds said. She was pleased he was thinking along with her so nicely. And these three pension-ignoring former policeman, sorry, the commissaris was collecting his pension, yes? Good. But the other two disdained a monthly income for the rest of their possibly long lives? How come? Did the new born private eyes enjoy private resources? And another thing, the trio arrived in Key West, drug-town of the Florida Keys, straight from Amsterdam, drug-capital of Western Europe, and these three in-di-vi-du-als . . .

De Gier didn't like the way she said that.

. . . were driving a new rented Cadillac in the sergeant's jurisdiction, aiming the expensive vehicle at the most elegant restaurant in sight, Lobster Lateta—jeez, just a little ball of dark chocolate with a bit of whipped cream on the side would be around nineteen dollars at LL—and there said trio met, in the most violent way imaginable, even for Key West (where a Cuban shot his friend last week for refusing to share his bacon, lettuce and tomato sandwich), a British gentleman dressed up in a thousand dollars' worth of Lone Ranger clothing—now, wasn't all this somewhat extraordinary, yes?

"Maybe goddam crazy?" The sergeant looked neither innocent or friendly now. "Right? Colleague?"

"Not crazier than anything else." De Gier declared that, after having reflected and studied the miracle of existence, anything—and he meant more than a gentleman/cowboy dying, a rental jeep racing between a trombone-playing Navajo and a rickshaw-riding mummy, more than the Milky Way galaxy, more than the occurrence of a universe, or even the phenomenon of space—de Gier declared that anything at all came about by happenstance, was just there, for no reason.

The sergeant stared at him.

"Chance occurrences," de Gier said, "explain you and me too." He smiled reassuringly. "And there is no guilt."

Sergeant Symonds smiled widely. She liked that. A perfect construction. Philosophically correct. And didn't de Gier speak nice English. Weren't Dutchmen true internationalists? She herself had taken Spanish as second language. In Key West one simply had to.

De Gier appreciated the compliment. He returned it too. Spanish was indeed a beautiful, but difficult language. He himself could barely read it.

"Is that so?" asked the sergeant politely.

De Gier saw her in a straw hat (he was wearing one himself) and he and she were walking on a clean raked beach, as their hands touched and they stopped for a moment to kiss, while she pressed her bosom against his chest, and violins behind the mangroves—never mind the violins, just a double bass and a guitar and maybe some piano, a young Ella Fitzgerald singing a ballad in scat—while de Gier imagined these pleasantries the actual scene was changing.

Ramona jumped up, leaned on her desk, spoke raucously as if coffee beans were being ground in her throat. She said they weren't here together to sweet-talk each other. Nothing accidental had occurred. The offed Brit was no tourist in a cowboy hat but a fucking bank inspector out of London. He was here on duty. His fucking inspection had been broken off by violent unnatural fucking MURDER. By deliberate fucking with his fucking rented car. Okay?

"You're sure?" de Gier asked, no longer just erotically but also criminally interested. "How so?"

Symonds stared again. She sighed. She had sat down. Her voice became veiled and jazzy again. "Now, col-league. I am only supposing. I construct a hypothesis based on observed facts. I personally visited Stewart-Wynne's hotel room which is in the same hotel where you happen to be staying."

"Eggemoggin Hotel?"

"Couldn't you find anything more expensive?"

De Gier smiled expectantly. He noted the coffee grinder was starting up again. "So?" the sergeant asked hoarsely, "is that why you left the police? You prefer the luxury of corruption?"

De Gier kept smiling while spreading his hands in innocent defense.

She showed him a visiting card retrieved from the Englishman's hotel room. THOMAS STEWART-WYNNE, ASSISTANT DIRECTOR, QUADRANT BANK, MAYFAIR, LONDON.

"You think the victim was on the trail of some financial trickery?" de Gier asked.

Symonds nodded.

"A big loan gone bad? So the other party wanted to get rid of the inspector? Hence the death ride on Duval Street?"

Ramona used her phone. "Harry? Mind coming up here a moment? You and Bert?"

A white-coated technician and Harry the bicycle policeman brought in three Polaroids. De Gier was allowed to look too. The technician used a pencil as pointer. "Here is the hinge of the accelerator, cut through, but not quite. See that spring here and the hook? Shouldn't be there. Kick the accelerator and this breaks and that hooks on, and your vehicle is out of control at full speed. Now for the brake, same thing other way round, ram the pedal but nothing works. So here we go, subject drives along Duval revving his engine a bit to make an impression, the thingamajig catches and he is going at full speed, so now he hits the brake but he just keeps going. The technician laughed sadly. "On Duval, when the cruiseships are in, at the height of the season!"

"Couldn't he have switched into neutral?" de Gier asked.

Policeman Harry didn't think Stewart-Wynne had time to consider that option, "not in a car with everything just a bit different, plus he is a Brit used to driving on the left side. Not a young man either. Slow reactions."

Sergeant Symonds looked at de Gier kindly. "Some nightmare, huh? So did *you* mess with that jeep, Rai-nus?" She said his name carefully, after glancing at her notebook where she had written it down in large square letters.

Good work. The sergeant had kept her voice flat. Friendly information, shared with a pal, changed imperceptibly into accusation. De Gier knew the trick. He had performed it himself often enough. The relaxed suspect confesses. As soon as he does, handcuffs click. The suspect is a prisoner and the detectives have a beer around the corner.

Stupid suspect.

"No," de Gier said flatly.

Bert the technician and Harry the policeman left the room.

Symonds sighed. "You know what is interesting, Rai-nus?"

De Gier found the whole thing interesting, that he was interrogated here at an air-conditioned American police station for instance, by a beautiful uniformed woman. Politely. Correctly.

That the lady had caught him, could lock him up if she felt like it. He didn't know any black women, not intimately. He would like to. Perhaps he could get her to help him spend his treasure, here in out-of-the-way Key West, in the lawless Bahamas, even in sinister Mexico. Swimming deep under the surface, between colorful coral reefs, his legs between hers.

"Hello?" the interrogating officer asked.

"I have no idea what is interesting, Ramona."

Sergeant Ramona Symonds turned a framed photograph on her desk. De Gier was faced by a starling-like bird with a black face, a reddish brown crest and glittering orange eyes. "My companion bird," Symonds said. "Mynah and I live together. My human companion took off, she accused Mynah of being too noisy and me of being too quiet." The sergeant looked across the golden frame. "You live alone?"

"With plants," de Gier said.

"Gay?"

"The plants?"

"You."

"No," de Gier said.

"But you live alone."

"Plants are company," de Gier said, "I don't quite harmonize yet but the barrier is dented."

"You can't get it up with women?"

It wasn't that so much.

"Should I mind my own business?"

De Gier explained, adjusting the ends of his mustache, holding on to his chin, trying to ignore the accusation in the bird's eyes in the frame, that he couldn't offer women commitment. Besides, he didn't want kids. There were enough kids around already, crack smokers and destroyers of streetcars.

"Do you have a girlfriend?"

A brown lady from Surinam, de Gier said, a Hindu woman. Hindus believe in not expecting anything, in uncomplicating life, in finding fulfillment in nothingness.

The sergeant frowned. "A Surinam seaplane crashed here last week. It was overloaded. The pilot had bags stacked on his dashboard."

De Gier shrugged. "Not that Surinam."

The sergeant pointed at a filing cabinet. "A robbers's nest. I have piles of documentation in there. The Colombians use the location as a warehouse."

De Gier waved the filing cabinet away. "My friend is a nurse."

"How do you know her?"

"I met her in the hospital."

"You were ill?"

"I was mugged," de Gier said.

"In Amsterdam?" Symonds asked. "In Heroin Heaven? Or was the violence connected to your present project?"

De Gier shrugged wearily.

"You understand," the sergeant said, barely audible above the humming of the air-conditioning, "that I am going to investigate this case fully. If there is the slightest reason to suspect that your pals on the *Admiraal Rodney* are engaged in the drug trade I will grab you too." She bent toward him. "I am personally interested. My brother in Detroit used to be a dear little fellow. Clever too. Got A's in math and science. He fed my goldfish. You should see him now."

"Ambagt & Son tell me they deal in crude oil," de Gier said.

"Hashish oil?" Symonds asked.

"Stuff you make gasoline out of," de Gier said.

Symonds turned the photo toward her. "Hi, Mynah."

De Gier predicted a retreat into niceties.

"So your Hindu princess expects nothing from you," Symonds asked nicely.

"Hindus belive in Nirvana," de Gier said. "Nirvana is empty. There is nothing there. How can you expect something from nothing?"

"Her ancestors came from India?"

"They must have," de Gier said.

"India is a dungheap," Ramona said. "Believers in nothing create nothing but misery. Any religious faith is a silly assumption that there are gods and that the gods are interested in our welfare."

"Sayukta came to see me on Earth," de Gier said.

"To do what?"

"To guide me."

Sergeant Symonds looked at de Gier's fly.

De Gier followed up on his symbolism. "She is a tunnel, the Hindu goddess Kali is sometimes represented as a hole in a stone."

"Sayukta is a tunnel?" Symonds asked. "A hole you can enter?"

"A hole to let me through."

"And she'll come along?"

"She is there already."

"Vagina-priestess Sayukta-Kali," Symonds said. "Interesting how we keep mixing up sex with mysticism. My hole in a stone was called Mary-Margaret. Biblical names. I found them attractive. I saw all sorts of far-reaching potential in our connection."

"Didn't work out?"

"The more you expect," said the sergeant, "the less comes of your expectations."

De Gier got up and looked out of the window. The window faced a yard where a large black man in a cream colored gown danced around parked police cars, motorcycles and bicycles. The man had braided hair, each braid ended in a decoration. The decorations looked like small animal skulls. The dancer's necklace was made from large orange glass beads. He wore open sandals cut from car tires and was shaking a rattle made from two coconuts, adorned with pink seashells.

"Rat skulls." Symonds was standing next to de Gier. "Priest Ratty of the First Voodoo Church of Key West blesses our transport." She waved. Priest Ratty waved too. "He is returning a favor. We're patrolling the black district more regularly now."

"Apartheid?" de Gier asked.

"In America?" Sergeant Symonds gaped at him. "Apartheid in free America? Tell me you are kidding."

"So why is there a black neighborhood that wasn't patrolled regularly before?"

"Little kids are being bothered there."

"Why are you bothering me?" de Gier asked. "I have nothing whatever to do with your dead banker."

"You do," the sergeant said. She raised a long tapered finger. "You were the only observer in the restaurant who saw something was seriously amiss with that jeep." She raised another finger. "You tell me you are about to cruise on the *Admiraal Rodney* which is expected here within a few days." She raised a third finger. "You and the fat guy and the old gentleman who directs you *and* the murdered man, Stewart-Wynne, stay in the same super-expensive hotel." She raised her little finger. "I checked around today. The hotel has its own yacht harbor. The harbor master tells me that Stewart-Wynne asked him where boats of the FEADship type would go for repairs here."

"Ach," de Gier said.

"The *Admiraal Rodney*," Symonds said. "The vessel you are about to board was mentioned by name by a bank inspector who was about to be murdered. Doesn't the yacht belong to Ambagt & Son? Your very own client?"

De Gier shook his head. "Why would I mess up a jeep belonging to an unknown person in such a way that the victim will direct the deadly vehicle at me while I'm having dinner?"

Symonds gazed at the portrait of her bird. "Does the Dutchman really think we believe him, Mynah?'

"Can I go now?" de Gier asked.

Symonds walked him out of the building. Priest Ratty hadn't finished his ceremony yet. Sergeant and detective waited for the dancer to finish his song.

De Gier was taken to the hotel in a voodoo-blessed motorcycle and sidecar.

"Please tell me why you are here," Symonds said while they waited at a crossing.

"Piracy," de Gier said. "Well outside your territory, Sergeant. Near the Eastern Antilles. The cargo of a supertanker. The *Sibylle*."

She saluted. De Gier watched the Harley drive off, gurgling powerfully down the hotel's driveway between palm trees waving huge leaves. Ibises, white and pink, on stilt-like legs, marched across a lawn, looking conceited behind their long curved bills. Palm rats moved about noisily in the crotches of their trees. A waiter, smoking secretly on a balcony, coughed, his cigarette glowing brightly. An acoustic guitar sounded the theme of a Miles Davis composition from behind the screened windows of the dimly lit bar. An electric organ pecked fiercely under the long flowing guitar notes. A drummer caressed a cymbal. A large-breasted slim thirty-year-old in a bikini, striding along slowly holding hands with an old man, smiled at de Gier. He nodded a friendly greeting at the couple while crickets spread a silver sheet of sound reaching out to moonlit sea waves.

"Nice place," de Gier thought.

12

Airborne Seals

Breakfast was served by young waiters. Carefully braided ponytails, adorned by orange ribbons, hung down red tunics above short white pants. The waiters wore rope sandals. They cooked little steaks, large mushrooms, sliced potatoes and tomatoes in cast-iron black pots above charcoal fires. They flip-flopped pancakes and folded omelets with a flick of the wrist in long stemmed pans. They served choice foods circled by arrangements of herbs and edible nasturtium flowers on large white plates. They peeled mangos, kiwis and other tropical fruits that were new to the Dutchmen, or, if requested, squeezed them in hand-held electronic devices. A baking machine, displayed prominently on the terrace, produced fluffy rolls, another machine spat out sliced honeycakes. A baker in striped trousers caught rolls and cakes in little baskets that the waiters plucked from his hands and distributed freely.

Grijpstra, dressed in a green beach suit that he had bought

earlier that morning, looked, from under the long visor of his purple sun hat, at his fellow guests.

Breakfasting men flirted with the waiters, female escorts buttered toast for their older companions. Jewels glittered on the fingers of the women, gold watches gleamed on the hairy wrists of the men.

"The commissaris would like all this," Grijpstra said.

"Don't you?" de Gier asked.

"Sure," bragged Grijpstra although he secretly thought the performance pitiable for some of the women were mere girls and some of the men were decrepit graybeards and what the hell did they think they were doing together?

"Aruba will be much like this." De Gier had just returned from the airport where the commissaris had chartered a small jet for the day. He smiled at the woman who had greeted him the night before. "You think this is heaven, Henk?" He touched Grijpstra's arm. "Look at that boat. A classic."

Grijpstra looked at the three master sailing slowly by. "Yes." He waved at a waiter and ordered a double helping of peach pie. "Don't spare the whipped cream."

De Gier produced a pocket set of binoculars. "That's beautiful. I'd love to go along."

"No problem, sir," the waiter delivering peach pie said. He fetched a leaflet and read the itinerary. The schooner would leave the harbor in another hour and sail by some of the smaller islands nearby. There would be dolphins, rare birds, military maneuvers and sponge fishing to watch. Snacks and drinks on the half hour. A nice clean bathroom. The waiter said he sometimes went on the cruise himself. "Romantic," the waiter said. "For you and your friend here. Sea air also speeds up digestion."

De Gier read the folder. Dutch and Scandinavian fishermen sailing schooners had visited American shores for centuries via the Iceland and Greenland route, even before Columbus cried victory on the more southerly route.

The waiter recommended the sunset trip. "You'll both love it. Even more romantic."

"We'll take the early round trip," de Gier said.

Grijpstra said that the romantic part didn't turn him on so much and that, unfortunately, he would be busy all day.

"Part of the job," de Gier said. "This is a piracy case. Piracy has to do with the sea. The commissaris left instructions that we should be thinking *water*."

Back in the suite de Gier turned on the radio. A red headed young man with a long ponytail was making the beds. The forecast came on. The announcer predicted rain, drizzle and fog, with winds gusting to twenty-five miles and more. De Gier turned the volume down. Grijpstra peered through the crack of the bathroom door. "What did he say?"

"Who?" de Gier asked.

"The weather fellow?"

"Nice," de Gier said. "Sunny mostly. Bit of a breeze maybe."

"It's going to be bad, sir," the young man making the bed said. De Gier snarled at him and held a finger upon his lips. The young man cursed, started crying and ran from the room.

Grijpstra, alarmed by the banging door, exited the bathroom. "Were you bothering that poor fellow?"

"Me?" de Gier asked.

"Why did he call you 'Asshole'?"

De Gier held up the coffee mug brought in from breakfast. "I inadvertently spilled some coffee on him. Must have hurt."

"You know this is homo country?" Grijpstra asked. "Did you see all those German male sex tourists on their rented blue bicycles on Duval this morning?" He raised his eyebrows. "Never fails to surprise me. An entire area of human life I can't even imagine." He pointed at the radio with his shaving brush. "You sure the weather is good?"

"Top of the morning," de Gier said. "Why do you think these super rich tourists hang out here? The weather is guaranteed. Even hurricanes wouldn't dare come near."

The schooner captain, a gangly hairy giant, looked as if he belonged to a different human species. *Homo habilus maritimus*, de Gier thought. The captain preferred, in view of the predicted bad weather, that the passengers come back the next day. Grijpstra couldn't hear him because de Gier was blowing a conch shell, that he had bought minutes ago, near his ear. De Gier pushed Grijpstra up the gangway and called the captain's attention to a sign on the quay. *Daily* roundtrips. "We'll pay extra if you like."

"Cash?"

De Gier peeled off banknotes, slowing down until the captain, who had introduced himself as Noah, commander of the sail and motor vessel *Berrydore*, relented.

Sailors hoisted brown sails. The captain started up his engine. The sixty-foot schooner maneuvered gracefully between the docks and other vessels. Incoming boats, escaping the coming storm, blew their horns. Motor launches and dinghies raced between the city's quays and the yachts anchored outside the harbor. A shrimp boat, resembling a gigantic butterfly with its nets raised to port and starboard, sounded a powerful blast, commanding more space. Military sloops were hoisted up the sides of a destroyer armed with missiles. Red and green floating markers indicated narrow channels of passage. A wreck, exposed by the falling tide, was covered by resting cormorants, drying their outspread wings. The shrimp boat was surrounded by pelicans catching fish offal tossed to them by sailors. Frigate birds planed effortlessly hundreds of feet above the turmoil, resting their small white heads on puffed up, blood-red feathered chests. The *Berrymore* used both her sails and her engine, speeding up to reach open sea. Captain Noah, sporting a fluffy beard that seemed glued to his boyish face, turned the wheel. He shouted commands. The sailors reefed all sails. The captain told de Gier that the *Berrymore* hailed from Maine, a forgotten state up north where she had been born more than a century ago. Warm winters in Florida, cool summers in Maine, the ideal existence. Each year the ship left the Maine coast late in the autumn and covered over two thousand miles of open ocean; in late spring she returned. "There and back, there and back, I can do it blindfolded."

"Dangerous?" de Gier asked.

"This side maybe." The captain pointed at hardly noticeable differences in color in the bluish-green sea. Subtly changing shades indicated reefs and sand banks. A thin line of foam warned of a strong counter current. Gull-like birds, "skimmers," stood on an invisible boat, a smuggler sunk by a Coast Guard cutter, that went down in shallow water.

"You get some illegal traffic?" de Gier asked.

Lately yes, the captain said. It had been quiet for a while but the government was tightening budgets and the various agencies, Coast Guard, Customs, Marine Patrol, DEA, and what have you, couldn't do as much as they liked. "Punishment is up though," Captain Noah said. "Does hold us down a tad, you know."

De Gier looked up. "Us?"

"Who else?" the captain asked. "Cocaine and pot are profitable products." He scratched his unkempt beard. "If an opportunity happens to flit by and one happens to feel courageous . . ."

"That happens?" de Gier asked.

It happens, Noah said. Supply routes were mostly in the Colombians's hands now, but Colombians couldn't do everything He himself had driven a five-ton truck from Key West to Dallas. The truck's loading door was locked and he wasn't given a key. The Colombian client was a vague acquaintance, a xylophone player in a Key West combo. The man had since been murdered but was then in charge of a motor launch and a warehouse between Duval and Simonton Streets. This was some years ago. Captain Noah had just gotten his truck driver's license. The xylophone player offered him three thousand dollars for the trip. A few days's work, and what could possibly happen? Just outside Miami the truck was stopped by a State Police cruiser, checking license and registration. The cruiser escorted the truck to a weighing station. Weight was fine, no overloading. "Have a nice day," the cop in the Boy Scout uniform said. "Bye bye, sir."

"So?" Grijpstra, who wasn't feeling well but couldn't help being interested, asked.

Noah, back in the truck's cabin after his confrontation with the law, suffered a sudden bowel movement. "Total," the captain said. "I had shit filling up my boots. I had to clean up in the sea for no motel would have let me in." He pulled his beard desperately, reliving bad moments. "Fear. Pure and simple. I felt nothing else. Nothing untoward was going on but there was shit between my toes."

De Gier tried to visualize the situation. "What kind of punishment would you have been in for if the state cop had checked your cargo?"

The captain shivered. Much pain, for he had no big bills to pass to the lawyer to share with the judge. He would have been in for endless abuse by sadistic guards and gangs of perverted prisoners. "I would have been marked for life. No personality can stand that."

"Did you deliver your cargo?"

"Not complete a Colombian job?" The captain pointed at his crotch. "Risk a load of buckshot hitting my boys here?"

It's all relative, de Gier thought. Get your testicles mashed for a mere three thousand dollars between Key West and Texas, find a few million while rummaging in a deserted basement in Blood Alley in Amsterdam.

"There's really too much risk involved now," Captain Noah said. "Prices are kept high by Washington but if we try to beat Those In Charge there isn't much in it." He spat, missing his passengers' feet neatly. "Get it? What I delivered in Dallas was just a bit of pot, the puny effort of a few small-fry Colombians and I got to hold up my hand too but the real bucks . . ."

The wind was increasing.

De Gier enjoyed the fresh sea-air, the grinding of ropes through wooden blocks, the cracking of taut sails. He thought about past glory, when the Dutch were still tough sailors, yohoho and a jar of jenever. Playing pirate with a wooden leg and a blunderbuss loaded with broken and bent nails. A cursing parrot on one's shoulder. Commander Rinus Rowdy Roughneck. "Yes, Milady, take off your blouse, you about-to-be-ravished Duchess de Portobello y Veracruz, never mind the ransom money, we'll worry about that later."

"What do you fellows do when you're not, eh—what we shall we call it—enjoying your holidays here?" Captain Noah asked.

De Gier said he was on perpetual holiday.

"For some time?"

"For some time."

"And before that?"

De Gier used to be employed by the city of Amsterdam, Holland.

"Yes," the captain said. "Big business goes to the big guys. City officials for instance. You got out rich, did you?" De Gier remembered the banknotes he had been peeling off his roll just now. "Bit of good luck, I used to be a policeman."

"Bad cops," Captain Noah said excusingly, "bad customs officers, bad drug enforcement agents, and whatever else is chasing us free men. Meanwhile the real business flies it in." The captain pointed at a large cargo airplane, losing height, aiming to land at Boca Chica naval airport.

De Gier looked at the gray plane, marked with the American white star. "The military, right?"

"Ferry to Mexico," Captain Noah said. "Maybe not that particular plane, the military do have other jobs of course.

"Those in charge," the captain said.

De Gier watched the transport plane disappear behind palm trees and shaggy pine trees. A flying whale stuffed with Mexican heroin?

"But the sea stays beautiful." The captain laughed. "I used to lose my cool, in the old days, before I learned that things don't get better, before I quit complaining." He swung a victorious arm. "Ride the currents, don't fight the natural course of events."

The *Berrydore* reached open sea. White breakers crashed against its hull. Captain Noah ordered the sails to be reefed further. Grijpstra and de Gier were attached to the railing with ropes ending in hooks. The ship kept changing direction to avoid shallow areas and onshore currents. Every time the *Berrydore* changed tack the passengers had to free themselves from the railing, struggle to the other side and attach themselves again. De Gier was good at it, Grijpstra needed help.

Grijpstra looked pale. De Gier indicated points of interest: Key West hotels fading away in fog, the chimneys of the island's huge generator, green lines that were small islands showing up on all sides. There were dorsal fins cutting through the schooner's wake. Dolphins. Later there were other dorsal fins, triangular, sharp. "Sharks, Henk. Remember the movie *Jaws*? That was filmed around here. The shark that ate small boats? That was a white one. Very aggressive. There must be lots of them here. Look. See that?"

There were brightly colored floats, marking crab and lobster traps. "It's not good when their lines entangle our propellers or rudders," Captain Noah said. "It could pull us down, or rip planks out of her bottom. Old boat. Wood gets weak."

The fog got thicker.

Grijpstra used his handkerchief to cover his mouth.

"Or we could break up on those sandbanks," de Gier said. "Right, Captain? Waves would wreck her in no time at all. The power of water."

The fog got even thicker. "We only see this once or twice a year," the captain said. "Good thing we have electronics." An apprentice-sailor, who studied science at the University of Miami and was making good use of vacation time, explained the instruments on the console. A black plastic box was attached to a battery outlet. Its minute screen came to life.

"It may take some time before we have a position reading," the student said. Captain Noah didn't think there was all that much time because the fog had swallowed all the red nuns and green cans marking danger to shipping, and what now? The student abandoned his box and measured longitude and latitude using compasses and a set of parallel rulers. The chart kept slipping because of the schooner's movement. The compasses were bent somewhat and the plastic rulers had been in the sun, causing to them to lose their straightness. No matter, the trick was to persevere. Not easy though for the compasses fell off the chart board and pricked the student when he picked them up. Ah, the little computer was working now. Very nice. So, if this was the schooner's position and the next red buoy was there, just a moment now, type in the buoy's position via the little computer's tiny keyboard, there we go, see, this figure here was the compass course, oh dear, the computer was losing power— oops, touched the wrong button, reprogram the computer real quick, according to the code, anyone know the code? It was indicated in the little handbook. Anyone see the little handbook? There we are, start over, input the code, there, she lights up again, input the two positions, the ship's and the channel-nun's, there you go, that's our compass course. "Steer 310 degrees, Captain Noah. Hard ahead. One eighth of a mile and the red nun will be in sight. This computer is accurate up to thirty feet. Can't be wrong. Connects to six satellites. Satellites aren't bothered by fog. Let's go, Captain Noah."

The course had to be wrong, Captain Noah said. 310 degrees would take them to the Northwest and the red nun they were looking for would be south of the schooner, he remembered that. Was the little computer malfunctioning perhaps? See, it was losing its screen lighting again. Maybe its batteries were weak and would have to be replaced. Triple A batteries. Were there any around?

A quarter of an hour later the schooner ran aground on a sandbank, after having been advised by the Global Position System Finder to follow varying and conflicting courses. The GPS, a device that is also used on aircraft, indicated that the schooner was flying at a forty-five thousand feet elevation. Clearly something was wrong with someone. Grijpstra, who had been vomiting and sliding about, and falling even, rather painfully so, was leaning against the side railing to which he was still locked. De Gier freed him. Grijpstra, using gravity, made his way down the steep cabin ladder. He dropped down on a bunk. He told de Gier that further effort was useless. It was over now. He would stay there.

The wind stopped gusting and the fog was burned off by a cheerful sun. The schooner was facing small islands topped by palm trees surrounded by mangroves that were new to the captain. He checked, using his binoculars, for possibly known points. A cargo ship, a mile away, closer to the islands, might be able to pull the *Berrydore* free of the sand bank. Or was the cargo ship in trouble too? She definitely listed. He dropped the binoculars, frightened by the roar and whistle of jet fighters coming in low over the schooner's masts. Crew and passengers—Grijpstra, pacified by the lack of movement, had come up—cowered, covering their ears. Helicopters hovered close to the helpless *Berrydore*, keeping the sun behind their threatening shapes—a bevy of insect-faced dark shadows that turned this way and that, observing a target through bulbous glass eyes and via waving antennas, carrying warriors clustered behind open sliding doors. The soldiers pointed machine guns and assault rifles until Captain Noah, gesturing widely, dancing on his long legs, bowing deeply, pointing at the *Berrydore*'s American flag behind him, drooping sadly across the schooner's railing. The helicopters seemed to accept the captain's surrender, temporarily anyway. The lead chopper, after dropping a few feet, then gaining altitude again, while staring through its gigantic bug eyes, banked sharply. It was followed smartly by the other machines: a flock of man-eating birds of prey, now headed for a more interesting target.

Ahead in the lagoon the cargo ship, stuck on a coral reef, was being strafed and bombed by the fighters. Once the sleek airplanes roared off the helicopters made low slow passes, peppering the dying hulk with small-arms fire. The student sailor whimpered while tenderly embracing a mast. Other crew members were still kneeling, hands on ears. Grijpstra, in between final retching, looked miserably placid as if the overwhelming attack was only to be expected. De Gier was on the schooner's foredeck, leaning out above the bowsprit, trying to miss nothing of the impressive spectacle of wanton destruction.

The downside of adventure (what harm had the cargo ship's crew done to be torn up by mechanized pitiless demons?) seemed irrelevant in the rush of elation. Why pity losing parties? Victorious violent thoughts flashed through de Gier's mind. He reminded himself to choose a martial planet for his next incarnation. Constant warfare. Be part of devastating forces during a brief but splendid existence. Blow up his next home altogether. What would a temporary habitat's loss matter in an endless universe that provides endless bodies for the same soul? De Gier shouted encouragement at the helicopters swooping down at a sandbank that had just been strafed by screaming jets.

Captain Noah was about to give up grovelling to appease superior powers when an enormous airplane thundered low over the *Berrydore*, close enough, it seemed, to shear off the boat's dainty topsails. The machine, dwarfing large passenger planes, had opened the flaps in its smoothly curved olive green belly. Dark objects of miscellaneous sizes fell out. De Gier, expecting the falling things to be bombs, dived headlong off the schooner, hoping to be able to use the water as a shield. The larger objects turned out to be rubber rafts, the smaller, weapon-containers and soldiers. De Gier, swimming between the rafts, dived when he saw masked heads popping up from the ocean. The heads bobbed while the men treaded water, searching for their rafts's locations. The soldiers, swimming now, wore black wetsuits and protective goggles. Their feet were extended by flippers. They held on to assorted types of guns, ready to spread more devastation. They climbed into their rubber boats which were equipped with powerful outboard engines. The boats reared up and rushed at the remains of the cargo vessel. Guns fired again. Steel cables flashed from mortar-like tubes, hooks attached themselves to the cargo ship's railings and gunwales. The warriors pulled their bodies, hand over hand, along the steel cables and leaped aboard.

As soon as the sea around the *Berrydore* was free of boats and warriors, Captain Noah dropped a line to the lonely swimmer and pulled de Gier aboard. Far away the Stars and Stripes were raised on the cargo vessel. The jet fighters returned again, streaking ahead of their own sound that thundered over the schooner as the planes dove and strafed an island beyond the cargo ship. The schooner's crew ducked despairingly when another giant bomber dropped more rafts, containers and men. The lagoon, once again, was speckled with the heads of attacking soldiers. "Frogmen," Captain Noah, crouching next de Gier on the safe side of the schooner's cabin, shouted over the clamor of rapid gun fire. "An Amphibious Special Forces exercise. These must be what they call the 'Dead Men Keys.' We're well off course."

De Gier, glad he had left his personal papers back in the hotel, tried to squeeze water out of his jeans and jacket. Grijpstra, moving on elbows and knees, approached slowly. "You okay?" de Gier asked. Grijpstra didn't hear him; the nearby explosions of missiles and grenades had deafened him. He sighed and collapsed.

After more American flags appeared, one to each conquered island or sandbank, a rubber boat captain hailed the *Berrymore*. The officer seemed genuinely outraged. "What do you think you are doing here? This is restricted territory. Nobody comes here. We could have shot you, you idiots. You are under arrest."

Captain Noah cited fog and his own stupidity. He promised he would never get his schooner stuck on a military sandbank again. He told the officer how much he and his crew had enjoyed watching the show. He mentioned the warriors's efficiency, courage and patriotism. He told the officer how much he would have liked to have been a military man himself.

The rubber boat captain relented. He spoke into his handheld radio. More rubber boats appeared and pushed and pulled the schooner free. Grijpstra was sick as soon as the *Berrydore* began to move on the billowing swell. The vomit hit his shoes, not the frogmen's heads below, because de Gier pulled him away in time.

"Wasn't that something?" Captain Noah asked de Gier after saying goodbye to his liberators. Grijpstra was ashore already, leaning against a palm tree. "Anything else I can help you folks with?"

"Tell me about the oil trade," de Gier said.

"Hashish oil?" Captain Noah asked. "A friend of mine brought it in, in dud gas tanks in antique Jaguar cars that he sold to collectors. One of his girlfriends told on him. He has been in jail for a while now."

"Crude oil," de Gier said. "The raw material for fuel. Comes in on supertankers. Gets lost sometimes."

The captain was interested. "Here? Near Key West?"

"Near St. Maarten," de Gier said. "Antilles. This side of Puerto Rico."

"I know the area," Captain Noah said. "I sometimes visit St. Kitts and Nevis, in the British West Indies. You want some leads? It would cost you a commission."

"I need a lead," de Gier said.

"Good grass on some of those islands," the captain said. "There are airstrips too. Someone picked up fifty tons of the shit once, flew it straight to Paris. It was a jumbo load. I could get you an introduction. Will cost you a few thousand, okay?"

De Gier was confused. "In a tanker *plane*?"

"You want fifty tons of hash oil?"

"*Crude* oil," de Gier said. "A supertanker, a ship, the *Sibylle*, got herself pirated near St. Maarten. The cargo was property of Ambagt & Son, operating out of the FEADship *Admiraal Rodney*."

Captain Noah had seen the *Rodney*. "You want to know who the pirates are?"

"I need to find the cargo." De Gier smiled apologetically, "It wasn't insured."

The captain whistled. "We're talking millions."

"I'll pay you five hundred dollars," de Gier said.

Captain Noah kept whistling.

De Gier whistled along.

"Two hundred now," the captain said, "three hundred when I give you some relevant information. Can I reach you anywhere?"

"I'll find you," de Gier said.

Captain Noah wrote down the number of his cellular telephone.

De Gier peeled off two bills.

13

SAINTLY MUSICAL CRIES

The pilot of the commissaris's chartered Learjet had called Aruba airport to make sure that a cab would be waiting. The cab's driver was a big black man in colorful clothes. His vehicle was a large model Mercedes, some fifteen years old, nicely kept up.

"Hotel, sir? You are Dutch, are you? I thought so. I am from Curaçao so I speak Dutch but on this dumb island only English is spoken."

The commissaris said he was looking for an oil tanker captain by the name of Souza. The driver knew no tanker captains although there should be some around, cruising their ships between Aruba's Lago refinery and the U.S. The driver did know Colombian and Venezuelan schooner captains who brought in produce from the South American mainland. He turned toward his passenger, sitting forlornly in the middle of the huge rear seat, comical under his outmoded pith helmet but otherwise quite correctly attired, in his shantung tropical outfit, with a golden watch chain across the modest bulge of his small stomach. "Vegetables and other organics."

"Oil," the commissaris said.

"Organic pick-me-ups, I would be referring to, sir," said the driver, "or push-me-downs, as the case may be."

"Crude oil," the commissaris said. "Would there be a meeting place for merchant marine officers on Aruba?"

"Sniffing organics, injectable organics, edible organics, smokable organics, up-the-rectum organics, even smear-on-the-genitals organics." The driver hadn't started his car yet. "But you don't have to visit a bar for that, sir. I can bring samples to your hotel. Less risky for you. You are in luck, I am the exact contact you have been wishing to meet, sir."

"Captain Souza," the commissaris said. "Master of the *Sybille*, a supertanker. An alcoholic and a pornographer, if I have been informed correctly. A black man. A citizen of Aruba."

"We have hookers here too," the driver said. "Not quite the quality you might find on Curaçao but not bad either. Discount hookers. Specialized. Whatever you like, sir. Please specify ages, measurements, colors. I will bring them to your hotel. Rubberized of course, no risk of picking up the nasties, sir."

"Captain Souza," the commissaris said, "was flown in, ill. Possibly both feet were amputated. I am sure you can direct me to someone who could help me find the captain."

"An oil skipper," the driver said. "The Sabaneta Hotel bar does attract seamen. Suppose you give me a hundred up front and a hundred if I can find your man. I'll drive you anywhere. Two hundred in all plus whatever the meter says."

The commissaris leaned forward. "You have no meter."

"If I had a meter," the driver said, "it would say about a hundred when I take you to the final destination of today, sir."

The seamen's bar in the village of Sabaneta, ten kilometers from the airport and five from the Lago tanker-harbor on Aruba's St. Nicholas Bay, was furnished with rough-sawn wooden tables and bright plastic yellow chairs. The music was live, performed by two black trumpet players, a guitar playing Indian (from India) and a tall round-faced white man as leader. The leader's long hair was silver-gray and hung down smoothly. The long mustache, peeking out under the large luminous eyes and high cheekbones, made him look catlike. The leader doubled as a percussion player, using a set of calabashes and metal bells hanging down from the ceiling. He also sang scat, with occasional long brittle cries that, whenever they escaped his wide chest, instantly halted all background playing although the trumpets sometimes supplied dialogue, either musically commenting on the leader's cat calls or asking their own questions. The commissaris, looking about the large room to see if he could pick out possible tanker captains, paid no conscious attention to the music but became aware, after a while, of vibrations in his spine and skull whenever the shrill cries sounded.

The establishment was an "everything place" the driver said. One could eat, drink, gamble, use substances, dance and consent to be taken by hostesses to rooms in the rear. The hostesses wore neat cotton dresses and simple white high heeled shoes, as if they were visiting each other for tea and cookies. They spoke Spanish. The driver said the young ladies were coastal Colombian, and had come to Aruba to earn their dowries in two weeks, the maximum duration of visas issued by the Dutch Maréchaussee, military police sent all the way from the former colonizing nation of The Netherlands.

"Come here," the driver said to one of the girls. *"Que venga aqui, amor."*

The hostess smiled at the commissaris. *"Lo que quieres, viejito."* She sat down on his knee.

"Whatever you wish, little old man," the driver translated, adding that "old man" was a term of endearment. "Margarita is to be married in Barranquilla next month. The house is rented but hasn't been furnished yet. Your contribution will be appreciated." The driver closed his eyes in ecstasy. "Oh, to donate one's sperm to the purchase of a bedside lamp." He winked at the commissaris. "Margarita has been tried and approved." He raised an appreciative finger. "A-1 Fancy."

"Tried by you?" the commissaris asked.

"By who else?"

"Gracias," the commissaris said, and added that he didn't have the time. *"Que no tengo tiempo, desgraciadamente.* I am here for *trabajo,* work, my dear. I am looking for *el capitan Souza del buque Sibylle,* pirated *cerca la isla holandesa Sint Maarten."*

"I don't know your friend captain Souza. *No lo conozco."* The girl smiled and got up. She touched his hand. *"Hasta luego."*

The commissaris lifted his pith helmet. *"Muy amable."*

"Really," the driver said. "You speak the language."

"My wife Katrien is taking Spanish lessons," the commissaris said. "She wants us to retire to Spain. We make up conversations together. We never agree on any subject we bring up." He looked at the hostess drinking a cola drink at the bar. "Amazing, don't you think?"

"Your wife Katrien?"

"She, too," the commissaris said. "But I was referring to Santa Margarita over there. To think that the dear little thing would actually go to bed with me."

"For money." The driver looked at the girl. "With me, too." He shook his head. "I couldn't do it. Not with me. Not for all the money in the Caribbean. Maybe it's different for women."

The commissaris thought so too. "Perhaps they can switch off their imagination."

"Unbelievable," the driver said.

The commissaris couldn't believe it either.

"I am glad I don't have to believe," the driver said.

The commissaris said that there might come a moment when there would be no need to believe anymore, a moment of revelation where everything would become clear. Maybe a release from having to believe would occur during death.

The driver crossed himself in fear, although, he told the commissaris in a low voice, he wouldn't mind death because death would liberate him.

"From what?"

"From me," the driver said.

Fried rice was served, with side dishes of smoked and fried fish, and pickled peppers, the biting taste of which, the commissaris thought, complemented the shrill cries of the cat-faced scat singer.

The waiter knew one Emilio Souza who had a brother who commanded a tanker. Emilio was a famous figure in Aruba. Emilio would, after drinking his fill, be taken home by his donkey. The donkey drank too but not as much as Emilio. Emilio Souza no longer visited the Sabaneta bar. His, and the donkey's, liquor bill had long ago reached its limit. Perhaps the pair visited the Divi Divi Bar now. The Divi Divi Bar was situated in Ponton. At the driver's request the waiter called the Divi Divi. He came back to say that Emilio was banned there too and was now living on credit in Venezuela. The waiter didn't know where in Venezuela. Emilio's wife Solange lived in Aruba, in Boca Mahos. Solange was Mexican, the waiter had met her. Some years ago that was. He said she seemed a nice woman. Maybe too smart though. Pregnant and barefoot but her eyes were too twinkly. "Can't have that," the waiter said. "Can't let them see through us."

The commissaris gave the waiter twenty dollars.

"Is Boca Mahos far from here?" the commissaris asked. The waiter and the driver laughed uproariously. In Aruba nothing was far. The commissaris, a citizen of the immeasurable plains of Holland, could not imagine the smallness of the island of Aruba. The waiter brought a cordless telephone. The commissaris, after having been given a number that the waiter looked up for him, managed to raise Solange. Solange said she had nothing to do with Emilio and even less with her brother-in-law, the tanker captain Guzberto Souza. *"Todos chingados!"* She broke off the connection.

"Chingados?" the commissaris asked.

"Mexican for 'the fucked'," the driver said. "Not fuckers, she would have said *chingadores* if she had meant fuckers."

"Pity," the commissaris said. "I do have to meet with Guzberto Souza. Won't you try? Tell her I wouldn't mind paying her."

The driver touched in the number. "Solange, you will

receive *monedas, ducados, dinero sancto, plata chingada, patatas de oro.*"

He looked at the commissaris. "How many monies, ducats, holy coins, fucked-up silver, golden potatoes?"

"Fifty?"

The driver said that Solange said she would see them. "Fifteen minutes through vales and hills. Nice trip, sir."

"After dessert." The commissaris wanted to hear more calabash and bell music. The dessert was stewed pears under a breast-shaped cone of stiffly whipped cream with a cherry as nipple. Margarita served the final course. She wanted to know whether the commissaris really didn't want to make use of her body. She specialized in older clients. It wouldn't take long.

"Gracias, pero que me pardona por favor," the commissaris said.

"What was your wife's name again?" the driver asked.

"Katrien," the commissaris said. "My name is Jan."

The driver thought that was great. "Jan is scared of Katrien," he told Margarita. "Katrien beats Jan. Don't you know, the puppet couple of olden times? Jan Klaassen and Katrien? Punch and Judy? She always beats him. On his wooden head."

Margarita didn't know the couple. Were they literature? She didn't think Gabriel García Márquez had ever mentioned the puppet couple.

"Gabriel who?" the driver asked.

"The Colombian Nobel prize winner," the commissaris whispered.

The driver slapped himself on the forehead. "Of course."

The combo's two trumpets and guitar played what the commissaris recognized as a Bach cantata he had once heard in Vienna. The trumpets wove the melody through the guitar's

THE PERFIDIOUS PARROT

rhythm, then dropped back so that the leader could repeat the theme with his weirdly elongated cries. The silence returned, and was framed by the percussionist with pedantic little dry knocks on his gourds. The clicking made the Colombian hostesses turn and shake their hips and bosoms, the clients stood next to their partners, ramrod straight, hands on backs, chins extended. The trumpets played a duet, Vienna mezzo-sopranos with Mexican innuendos. The catlike white leader played a snare drum, using both rim and skin, alternating clicking with reverberating staccato rattles.

The driver was happy. "This is *it*, sir." The commissaris agreed. Perhaps he should stay here on Aruba. He could send for Turtle. Katrien could stay behind with the grandchildren. They could E-mail each other.

In order to defuse music-generated tensions the hostesses took their pleasurably excited clients to the café's back rooms. Margarita escorted a red-headed first mate in his splendid whites. Bartenders busily pumped draft beer, creating immaculate white-cuffed glasses of golden fluid. Waiters rushed about carrying trays of broiled snapper and grouper.

"The band leader is a guru," the driver said. "He realized his true nature in Amsterdam. Because they still know shit there he came to us."

"Ach," the commissaris said. He had been cleaning his eyeglasses, blaming possible dirt or steam for the appearance of a halo above the catlike man's head. "And what does he do when he isn't making mystic music here?"

"He gambles in the Hilton."

"He wins?"

"He loses," the driver said.

"Thank you," the commissaris said before leaving the Sabaneta bar. He passed a hundred dollar note to the band leader. "You play wonderful music."

"Specially composed and performed for your benefit, Commissaris."

The commissaris failed to recognize the guru.

"I used to call myself 'Puss in Boots,' "* the singer said, pointing at his high leather shoewear. "Amsterdam North, twenty years ago. I kept busy keeping unemployed assholes busy, on the dike. Steal and share. Remember that time, sir? You did not agree with my idealism. Made me do some jail time. To take care of karma I worked for National Assistance for quite some years but what I do now seems more suited to my mission."

"I came to see a captain Guzberto Souza of a pirated super-tanker, the *Sibylle*," the commissaris said.

The percussionist touched his gourds. The trumpets blared, the guitar trembled. The commissaris's spine began to vibrate again. The sensation became almost unbearable when the singer started his thin brittle singing.

The commissaris bowed.

The guru nodded.

"Bad behavior," the driver said, starting the Mercedes. "But he is out of it. Good musicians usually are. I would be if I could make good music." Unfortunately the driver was no musician. He did have the Judds on CD. He had done that much.

---

* see *The Corpse On The Dike*

14

THE LETHAL DELIRIUM OF THE AMPUTATED

"Divi-divi trees," the driver said while the Mercedes drove slowly along a dusty Aruban country road to avoid straying goats. "The monsoon pushed them over, it always blows from the same side, but they never quite go low enough to touch the ground."

"Beautiful," the commissaris said. The trees were more like bushes in a dried-out landscape, sandy with some rocks and clusters of thorny low-growing plants. The commissaris admired some giant blossoming cacti. Small thrushes looked from black nest-holes in ten-foot-tall pale green stems. Other small birds drank nectar from the white cactus flowers. Ramshackle cabins showed up along the road, behind fences put together from odd sized twigs. Dogs scratched themselves lazily in the shadow of parched fir trees. Children stared from sagging porches. The driver said that the island was once covered with forest, that water welled from between the rocks and was drunk by deer and rabbits. How did he know that? Because those animals had been drawn on cave walls. By whom? By Arawak natives. The Arawaks fled Venezuela, pursued by their enemies, the Caribs. The cannibalistic Caribs came after the Arawaks, killed them off, and ate them. Columbus came after the Caribs and massacred them. Eating the Caribs wasn't necessary, there was plenty of pork and fish and the Bible did not prescribe eating Caribs.

The driver knew what the Bible prescribed, he had been to Bible school in Curaçao. He knew the book by heart. The Bible prescribed manslaughter only.

"And after Columbus, you came," the driver said. "White Dutchmen massacred the Spanish. I would have liked to have seen that. My granddaddies did, you brought my granddaddies from Africa. They must have been sickly, you couldn't sell them stateside. So we got to live here and sell you drugs and Margaritas.

The commissaris sighed.

The driver sighed too.

Solange, wife of Emilio Souza (but she had applied for divorce she told the commissaris), was small and graceful, with long braids. She wore jeans and a plain white T-shirt. She spoke English with a Mexican accent. Her small house was plastered and whitewashed under a roof of baked red tiles. It was surrounded by a large vegetable garden, fenced with barbed wire to keep out goats and long-legged chickens. "The house is in my name," Solange said. "The chingado bailiff didn't want to believe me so I had to hire a chingado lawyer."

She breathed deeply. "Emilio Souza, *el chingado*."

Solange served lemonade, made with the fruit of her own lemon tree. "You guys looking for Guzberto? Fifty bucks is not enough, señores." She laughed sadly. "A woman alone." Two little girls had been dropped off by a small schoolbus. They came trotting down the path, swinging their cloth bags. "Three women alone. You know what the chingado lawyer charged me to write this?" She showed them a letter. She rubbed her hips. "You know what my income is? No? Minimal unemployed single caregiver allowance. We could starve without the veggies and the chickies. You know what the chingado bailiff and the chingado lawyer asked me? 'Amor, amor, how do you do it?' You know what I said? I said nothing because they were on top of me."

She crossed her arms defensively. "So now what do you want me to say?"

The commissaris had floated away on Solange's stream of words. The question shocked him back. "Hello. Yes." What was it he wanted her to say? Right. "Do you," he asked solemnly, "know where we can find your brother-in-law, Captain Guzberto Souza, master of the supertanker *Sibylle*? If so, would you tell us please?"

"Not for fifty bucks." The woman looked at her small bare feet. "I could have told you earlier but then you wouldn't have come here." She addressed the driver. "You with your dumb talk, man. Holy silver money. Golden potatoes. Where do you get that dumb talk, man?"

"I am a poet," the driver said. "I didn't want to insult you. I talk that way. I think you are a goddess."

She made a fist.

"I think you are a goddess too," the commissaris said. He asked for an envelope and if he could use her bathroom. She brought him the envelope from the lawyer's letter and showed him the way to the outhouse behind the garden. The panels of the structure had been filled in with the ribs of palm fronds held by neatly made frames of narrow boards, individually sawn out of driftwood. The outhouse roof was fitted together with odd pieces of corrugated iron, of different rusty colors, a metal quilt of sepias and tender rose and red shades. A cracked but gleaming toilet bowl stood on a fundament of orange cement blocks. "A work of art, ma'am," the commissaris said, feeling guilty, for his own garden was a weed field and its toolshed, since the last windstorm, had been leaning against a fence that was ready to topple over too. "Emilio thought it up," Solange said. "He can start things but he can't finish them."

"You made it?"

"I make everything here."

Solange pointed at her gardens. "I have a septic system, it makes the vegetables grow, and it does rain sometimes. I save the water. See, the gutter? The drums? There is a cistern too. Someday I'll get the pump fixed maybe."

The commissaris used the outhouse and came back with the envelope. "Here you are."

"Can I look?"

"After we leave please," the commissaris said. "It's more than fifty dollars, ma'am."

"Guzberto was taken to the clinic of the nun, Sister Meshti," Solange said. "His legs had to be cut off and he kept shivering and crying. Guz smoked bad cigars that made his veins shrink but he said it didn't matter because he was drinking too and the alcohol made them swell up again. Not true either." Solange's head shook until her braids swung above her small head. "More macho shit."

The commissaris thanked her. He got into the car. "To Sister Meshti's clinic if you please." The Mercedes was turning out of the driveway when the driver looked in his rear mirror. "Solange is running after us. You want me to stop?" The commissaris opened his window. Solange was crying. "I never told you, Guzberto is dead." She pushed the envelope into the car. "Here. I don't want it."

The commissaris got out. He returned the envelope and hugged her softly. "There, there, dear."

She whispered in his ear. "Too much *chingado* money." She kissed his cheek. "You are an angel hiding under a piss pot."

He took off the pith helmet and offered it to her. Maybe her daughters would like to play with the thing. But she said that he needed to keep his head covered, the sun might give him cancer, his hair was so thin.

"What was going on?" the driver asked.

"Happens to me all the time," the commissaris said. "Women come on to me. My wife thinks it is charisma."

"Really," the driver said.

The clinic where Captain Guzberto Souza lost first his legs and later his life was a wooden barn set precariously on the slope of a hill. A covered passage led to a cave. The Mother Superior was a thin German standing on large bare feet. She wore a gray cotton dress under a stiff white hood. An unvarnished insect-eaten cross hung against her flat chest. Her unfocused eyes were protected by thick eyeglasses. Her wrinkled face was burned a deep tan. "Yes, dear?" Her mouth held few teeth.

"The Capitan Guzberto Souza," the commissaris said. "I

JANWILLEM VAN DE WETERING

would like to know if he told you something about his ship being attacked by pirates."

"Zey still exist?" the nun asked, "Ze piraten?"

"They stole the oil," the commissaris explained, "that the Capitan was transporting in his tanker."

"Zat is why ze Kapitan had no money?" Sister Meshti asked. "I did not understand. Kapitane earn good money."

The commissaris and the driver were taken to the nuns's living quarters within the cool cave. They sat on straight-backed cane chairs around a heavy square table. A young nun brought glasses and a plastic jar filled with iced tea.

"Sister Johanna," Sister Meshti said.

Sister Johanna spoke the soft Dutch of southern Holland. "Guzberto was a nice man. I got to wash him every day. Never gave me any trouble."

"He had no legs zen," Sister Meshti said. "We zought we could save ze Kapitan but ze poor fellow got fevers and ze antibiotics did nuzzing and his condition was very bad." She looked sad. "All ze Kapitan wanted was gin but we don't give zat."

"Strange," the commissaris said. "Piracy of his ship, must have been a traumatic event, yet he never told you about it."

"Poor man was sick," Sister Meshti said. "Bad wizdrawal."

Sister Johanna spoke up. "Guz was bothered by big black frogs." She indicated how big the frogs had been. As big as Sister Meshti. "And afterward Guz's toes would itch and I had to scratch them. He had no toes. I scratched anyway, under the sheets at the foot of the bed. *Zkrrtzch, Zkrrtzhch.* He always felt better afterward."

Sister Johanna blew her nose in a red bandanna. "Guz was

frightened of the big black frogs. They were all wet and they attacked him."

"You were paid for taking care of the poor Kapitan?" the commissaris asked Sister Meshti.

She shook her head. "Guz had no insurance. Ze shipping people did not pay eizer." She found a folder and looked through its papers. "Ambagt & Son."

"Nobody paid for the work you did here?"

"Nobody," said Sister Meshti.

"God did not pay either?"

"Who?" Sister Meshti asked.

Sister Meshti said that she and Johanna sometimes went begging, in their donkey cart. They called on the accountants of the hotels and casinos. She usually got some money out of the accountants, she had been an accountant herself, long ago, in Cologne, where she was in charge of the administration of a chemical concern. She liked numbers. She did not have too many numbers to take care of now. "But zat's okay."

"Surely *you* know who God is," the commissaris told sister Johanna.

"Who?" asked Sister Johanna, smiling sweetly.

"Do you have an envelope?" the commissaris asked Sister Meshti. "And could I use your bathroom please?"

"You don't work for the firm that employed that no good Captain Souza do you?" the driver asked after they had left the clinic, where they were waved out by the happy nuns.

The commissaris said that he had been hired by detectives to do some research.

"Why were those nuns all over you?" the driver asked.

"Nuns are women," the commissaris said. "It's because of my charismatic presence. Even that Margarita liked me."

"Really," the driver said, stepping on the gas, for the commissaris was in a hurry to get back to his chartered Learjet. "Pity we couldn't locate that drunk for you, but I did have a nice day. Just pay me a hundred. The gasoline is free."

"You have an envelope?" the commissaris said. "You can open it after the plane takes off."

"And it will be empty," the driver said suspiciously. "Listen here, sir. I'm no woman in need of appreciation. You know what I am? I am a pimp and a drug dealer. Guys like you give me nothing."

The commissaris passed him a hundred dollar bill.

The driver passed it back.

"You prefer the envelope?" the commissaris asked.

The driver found one on the airport. The commissaris took it to the airport's bathroom. "Don't open the envelope before my plane leaves," the commissaris said as he gave it to the driver. "Thank you for putting up with me all day. What is your name please?"

The driver was called Maurice Mazlof.

"Goodbye Mr. Mazlof."

The driver stood to attention while the Learjet pierced low clouds. Back in the Mercedes he opened the envelope. It was filled with folded toilet paper.

15

THE LOWER LEVEL

"The lower level?" the commis-
saris asked at breakfast on the Eggemoggin Hotel's terrace.
"Isn't American an expressive language? What do they mean? A
hellish cellar? What do the police want with you on the *lower
level*, de Gier?"

De Gier wiped his mustache with a napkin handed to him by
Grijpstra, swallowed the rest of his coffee, put half a bagel with
salmon, cream cheese, onions, and capers into his mouth,
spread his hands in a gesture of innocence and followed the
waiter who had delivered the message.

The commissaris's cellular telephone in his pocket rang.
"Hello-ooh," said Carl Ambagt. "Rain, drizzle and fog, did you
hear the weatherman say that this morning? He likes saying that,
but it is clearing up nicely. You bothered by bugs there? I've
been slapping mosquitos all morning. We have arrived. We're in
dry dock. Close to you. Within walking distance. Repairs to the
Rodney won't take up much time. Throw out bad parts, put in

good parts. Costs an arm and a leg though. But who cares, eh? With a bit of luck we can leave before sunset. Are you ready?"

"Yes, Mr. Ambagt, sir," the commissaris said, watching a mosquito sucking blood from his right hand. His left hand held the phone. He turned the bitten hand and tried to squash the mosquito on the tablecloth but the mosquito saw that coming.

"Beds are made," Carl Ambagt said, "drinks are iced. Sailors have changed into crisp uniforms. We are eating crêpes with powdered sugar tonight, and Dad isn't all that drunk today."

"Crêpes," the commissaris said, snapping his telephone shut. He missed the blood-digesting mosquito. "What did we get ourselves into? Culinary kindergarten?"

Grijpstra accepted more plum compôte, served by a smiling waiter. Spooning cream into his bowl he reminded the commissaris of what had been done to them. "Feather removed from your hat. De Gier still can't breathe deeply. And I . . ." Grijpstra coughed.

"Vengeance," the commissaris said, swiping at the mosquito. The animal landed slowly, nursing a broken wing. The commissaris smashed it. "We should not give in to our lower emotions, Grijpstra. This project is no more than a character exercise. Our adventurism is pure, like that of the knights of old." He watched the bloodstained tablecloth with satisfaction. "What did the waiter call the location where Sergeant Symonds is lurking, waiting for fearless de Gier?"

"The lower level," Grijpstra said.

The commissaris nodded. "We are not of the lower level, Grijpstra, we have vanquished egocentricity, small-mindedness, the need to revenge insults and pain inflicted on our illusionary egos."

"Sir," Grijpstra said.

The lower level was a parking lot contained by concrete corner pillars holding up the hotel's main building. The lot had a wide view of the sea. Sergeant Symonds had assumed the lotus position on the saddle of her Harley Davidson. She wore shorts. She was watching pelicans planing elegantly above the blue-green surface, ready to drop like rocks as soon as they spotted shoals of small fish. The sergeant laughed. "Bunch of flying comedians. I am glad they are back. Fishermen were shooting them but the new laws give them a chance now."

"Protected?" de Gier asked.

Ramona waved at the sidecar connected to her motorcycle.

De Gier got in.

"You have the right to remain silent," the sergeant said. "Anything you say can be used against you. You can make one telephone call. If you can't afford an attorney the city of Key West will hire a lawyer for you." She bent down to him. He could smell her perfume. "Yes, the pelicans are protected because they attract tourism to the area, Rai-nus. Murderers do not attract tourism, Rai-nus. We do not protect murderers."

She reached for handcuffs, gleaming on her gunbelt, but changed her mind. The Harley roared. The tip of her boot put the motorcycle into gear.

Police-psychology, de Gier thought. Bag of tricks. Pelican-talk, then show handcuffs. Intimidation by evoking fear of shackles and the desire to enjoy nature.

The motorcycle and sidecar passed small wooden houses. Hedges blossomed, flowers grew from pots dangling from veranda ceilings, palm trees grew everywhere, tall palm trees with clusters of red fruit, little fat palm trees with huge leaves, palm trees in the shape of giant fans. Oranges, grapefruit and lemons gleamed between moist green foliage. White lattice work contrasted with pale blue or rose window shutters. Ramona shouted above the thunder of the engine that the houses had been built by ships's carpenters of the previous century. Sailors brought tropical seeds from Tahiti and New Zealand. Key West, as found by early conquistadores, knew only the grays and greens of swamp mangroves but the imported fauna thrived on local soil.

Waiting at a traffic light Sergeant Symonds told her prisoner that the police Harley was a Dyna Glide model, capable of going one hundred sixty miles an hour, without the sidecar of course. "Only in America, Rai-nus. What do you guys ride in Europe? Japanese rice cookers?" She shook her head. "That stuff isn't real."

De Gier looked at the real handcuffs on her gun belt.

"Did you ride a motorcycle when you were an Amsterdam cop?"

De Gier mentioned a twin cylinder BMW.

"Were Harleys too expensive out there?"

"They were, Ramona."

Here I am, de Gier thought, stuck in a baby carriage, being pulled along by Nanny Chauvinista making goddamn conversation.

Ramona served gourmet coffee in her office. "I really appreciate being able to arrest you, Rai-nus. I was lucky. You want to know what I have?"

"A new incriminating fact?"

The sergeant looked pleased. "Yes sirree."

"May I know what new incriminating fact?" de Gier asked.

"You know," Symonds asked, "what the old incriminating facts were?"

American police methodology, de Gier thought, wouldn't be essentially different from what he was used to. Sergeant Symonds would have had to convince a high ranking authority, a police chief or a judge, that an arrest was justified. De Gier set forth a possible theory formulated by the arresting officer, based on facts:

"*Fact 1:* Victim T. Stewart-Wynne drives his jeep into a restaurant where Suspect de Gier is having dinner with two associates.

"Hypothesis: Victim was to meet Suspect in that very restaurant. Victim was attempting to park close by when he lost control of the vehicle.

"Defense: There is no proof that Victim and Suspect knew each other. The jeep's malfunction just happened to occur in that particular location.

"*Fact 2:* A bicycle-policeman investigates the jeep after it has stalled inside the restaurant. Of all people present only Suspect is interested in Victim's corpse.

"Hypothesis: Suspect is the killer, he is checking whether his attempt succeeded.

"Defense: Suspect is a former police officer, he is interested in the deadly accident out of habit.

"*Fact 3:* Both Victim, an employee of the British financial company Quadrant, and Suspect, a former policeman, are connected to Ambagt & Son, a shipping company working out of the Liberian-registered FEADship *Admiraal Rodney*. Ambagt & Son claims it deals in crude oil. Victim stayed in the luxury hotel Eggemoggin. So does Suspect. Key West is a strategic location for the drug trade.

"Hypothesis: Quadrant financed Ambagt & Son's dealings but wasn't paid back. Victim looks for possible wrongdoing and obtains proof of drug dealing. Victim threatens to call the cops. Ambagt & Son hires Suspect to get rid of Victim.

"Defense: Suspect says he doesn't know Victim and denies being a hit man.

"*Fact 4:* The rented jeep's brake and acceleration systems have been tampered with, changing a means of transportation into a deadly weapon.

"Hypothesis: Suspect did the tampering with the object of murdering Victim.

"Defense: Suspect says he did not.

"Yes?" de Gier asked.

"Perfect," Ramona said. "You've hit all the nails on the head. All you have to do is keep denying everything. But now . . ." she bent across her desk, smilingly aggressive, as if she was going to grab his crotch—a uniformed guard and her helpless slave—". . . what new fact showed up which allows me to arrest you?"

"Somebody saw something?" de Gier asked. "But there was nothing to see. I am innocent. You are misinterpreting something."

"*Two* somethings?" Sergeant Ramona Symonds of the KWPD asked triumphantly. She reported, staring over de Gier's head as if she was addressing a godhead throned behind him. "Victim," Ramona said, using a professionally modulated voice, "stayed for five days in the Eggemoggin Hotel. He was very busy during the first four days. He dressed in regular clothes and drove a regular rental." Symonds looked at her notes. "A two-door beige Geo compact. He didn't bother the chamber boy, wasn't interested in Cocaine Annie's services—Annie, an expensive prostitute, works the Eggemoggin, officially, as a masseuse.

A very classy lady. . . . But on the fifth day Victim suddenly changed his persona." She glanced at de Gier briefly. "Do you follow me?"

"I am with you, Sergeant," de Gier said brightly.

Symonds smiled triumphantly. "On the fifth day, Victim dresses up as an expensive cowboy, pinches the chamber boy in the buttocks, orders Cocaine Annie into his room and demands special sexual acts, changes the Geo for a rental jeep, complains about the food—beefsteak too well done, wants it rare—laughs loudly while drinking champagne by himself."

"Manic?" de Gier asked. "Abnormal excited behavior after a period of colorless depression? Can Victim be diagnosed as bi-polar?"

Ramona ignored the interjection. "Hypothesis: Victim successfully closed his investigation. Victim parties and Suspect . . . ," (Ramona was staring de Gier in the eyes) "which is you, Rai-nus . . . gets him." Sergeant Symonds leaned back in her chair. "Defense: Suspect denies having gotten Victim at this crucial point of proceedings?"

De Gier laughed. "He does, Sergeant. And what you have there is old. I mentioned it already. No proof, you know. Nothing doing."

Symonds was smiling too. "I have enough here to make a jury listen to what the prosecutor has to say, but there is more." Her smile widened. "So much more. You want to hear?"

De Gier was shaking his head. It all sounded ominous. Perhaps he should have stayed in the police force, on the power side of the table. "Tell me," he said quietly.

"The Key West Post Office," the sergeant told him, "is on the edge of our black district. Someone has been bothering kids there. We patrol the area more frequently now. A woman cop out of uniform was watching the parking lot on the day Stewart-Wynne died. She saw a long haired white male subject sliding under a blue jeep, holding tools. She thought he was making repairs. The man looked disheveled, the jeep looked new. The contrast was of note, of course. You know the police are always looking for contrast?"

"Yes," de Gier said. "What else did your lady constable see, Sergeant?"

"A white gentleman in a cowboy outfit drove the jeep away, after the disheveled pseudo-mechanic had done what he did."

"It wasn't me," de Gier said. "I don't have long hair and I don't look disheveled."

"Wig? Different clothes?" Sergeant Symonds read from her notes: "Tall white male subject, military posture, huge mustache, six feet tall, wide shoulders.

"Hypothesis: Suspect had somewhat changed his appearance while changing the jeep into a lethal weapon."

De Gier grinned. "It still wasn't me."

Sergeant Symonds looked serious. "Policewoman Susan G. Wilson begs to differ. I took her to Hotel Eggemoggin last night. She saw you in the bar, listening to jazz. I didn't point you out to her. It wasn't necessary. She recognized you at once. She'll swear to it too. That's why you're under arrest now."

De Gier dropped his hands to his knees.

"Defense?" Symonds asked.

De Gier shrugged. "My name is Janneman Jackrabbit and I know nothing."

"Who Jackrabbit?"

"A Dutch children's song," de Gier explained. "Little kids

chant it when they're accused of getting into the cookie jar."
He sang the line for her, beating time with his hands.

"This is no joking matter." The sergeant got up and looked
out of the window.

"You don't really wish to hold me on these trumped up
charges," de Gier said.

"Policewoman Susan G. Wilson has a good reputation,"
Ramona said icily without turning around. "I can hold you
until you rot."

"Please," de Gier said. "Did I mess with a jeep in a post
office parking lot while I was eating key lime pie in Lobster
Lateta in the company of two witnesses?"

"Your accomplices?" Sergeant Symonds turned sharply.
"Hired by Ambagt & Son, alleged macro-drug dealers operating from a tax-free floating palace that keeps visiting Mexican
ports for no obvious reasons. Are you aware that Mexico sup-
plies half of all cocaine, heroin and cannabis products consumed
in this country? How do you think you can wiggle out of that,
tell me!"

"Release me on bail," de Gier said. "I will find you the real
killer, who I now know to be a former military man who looks
just like me."

"Former? How so?"

"Men in the U.S. military service do not look disheveled nor
do they have long hair. I will be looking for a renegade, dis-
honorably discharged." De Gier jumped up. "It shouldn't take
me long. Let me do this for you."

Ramona Symonds approached the prisoner. Her pouting lips
touched his cheek. She whispered. "I thought you would never
ask, my dearest."

16

HELL ON THE HIGH SEAS

The FEADship *Admiraal Rodney* left Key West for St. Maarten the next late afternoon. De Gier was not on board. Grijpstra had tried to take over the pursuit of Stewart-Wynne's killer, citing his exchangeability with de Gier. Hadn't he been in Lobster Lateta when the British Quadrant bank inspector died there? Wasn't he de Gier's partner and fellow private eye? Wasn't he also working for the owners of the suspect *Rodney*? Wasn't he, like Stewart-Wynne, associated with the Ambagt people?

Why not let go of poor de Gier and take the much superior Grijpstra, who, besides, did not like to sail on small boats.

Sergeant Symonds said she would just love to but she couldn't, really. De Gier had already been arrested and to change paperwork via Monroe County's bureaucracy was just too much work. "I truly like you better," Sergeant Symonds said. She liked the commissaris even better but the commissaris wasn't interested in taking over de Gier's precarious position. Besides, the commissaris did like to sail on small boats.

The commissaris accompanied Grijpstra to pay de Gier's bail: fifty thousand dollars in five hundred bills of one hundred dollars each. Quite a sizable package. The commissaris got the cash after G&G's Luxembourg bank guaranteed payment by fax through an American correspondent. While Ramona counted the cash the commissaris studied the portrait of Mynah. "I keep a portrait of Turtle on my desk."

Ramona looked at his wedding ring. "Not your wife's?"

"Katrien," the commissaris said, "keeps changing. Turtle is more eternal."

Ramona looked serious. "You're looking for eternity, sir?"

"Who isn't?" the commissaris asked. The unchangeable, symbolized somewhat by Turtle's timeless face, fascinated him. "The wisdom of an ancient reptile, beyond fear and desire."

"You're neither?" Ramona asked.

"I am free in essence," the commissaris said, "I think. But then, who isn't?"

"Mynah is noisy," Sergeant Symonds said, "especially when he imitates the sound of my cappuccino machine."

Grijpstra would not believe that a bird could do that.

Ramona imitated the bird's imitation of her cappuccino machine. Grijpstra applauded.

"But you do love your wife," Ramona said to the commissaris, "even if she does keep changing."

"Certainly, certainly," the commissaris said, "and you love your . . ." he checked the rest of her desktop. "Of who you do not keep a photo here?"

Ramona said that it was all over with Mary-Margaret and that she couldn't believe that it had ever not been all over for what, after all the arguments and disappointments, does a human relationship amount to? Isn't it just a battle between opposite egos? Domestic violence. Cause for most calls for police assistance. "Is it the same in Europe?" Sergeant Symonds asked. Grijpstra said domestic violence had always upset him. It was nice to be away from that now. Also at home. Although his second wife did sometimes resemble his first, she didn't throw things.

The commissaris studied the bird's photo. "Except for Mynah you have no close relationships?"

"What is it to you?"

The commissaris smiled. He said in an avuncular tone, "Ramona, my dear . . ."

Ramona, mollified by the commissaris's act, said that an older man was her friend now. She sometimes felt bad about that, she had drawn some satisfaction from being gay, but some older men were okay, perhaps. She smiled at the commissaris. "You could be okay, but my old man looks more athletic." Prompted by the commissaris she said that her friend lived in a lane behind Petrona Street, in one of the ships-carpenter-designed little rectangular houses, overshadowed by flame trees. During spring and early summer the trees seemed to be on fire due to their exuberantly orange and red flowers. Ramona's friend was a retired psychiatrist who had come to the conclusion that all human personalities are irreparably unpleasant. Unmarried and childless, he led a scholarly life among inherited antiques, brought in long ago by Key West wreckers. Behind his oleander hedge her friend mildly disliked people, although he sometimes tolerated Ramona's company and was fond of her bird who liked to come with her.

"Gabriel likes to cook for us."

"Do you and Gabriel do it?" Grijpstra asked.

"I beg your pardon?"

Grijpstra scratched his chins. "I sometimes wonder if happy couples do it."

"Do you and your wife do it?" Ramona asked.

Grijpstra admitted to gradually preferring to think about it.

"With your wife?"

"Sure," Grijpstra said.

"Does Gabriel make you feel safe?" the commissaris asked, using his grandfatherly mode again.

"I comfort him," Ramona said. "Gabriel, even if he dislikes it maybe, still lives in the universe. The universe is essentially female. The female sometimes comforts."

"Mutual safety?" the commissaris asked hopefully.

Yes, perhaps. Ramona said that she liked spending time behind Gabriel's protective hedge and the sign that hung from a flame tree's branch, nicely written in the old man's precise hand, carmine on white. THE LION IS OKAY, it said. If one touched the gate the lion, well inside the house, growled; if one opened the gate the lion would roar just behind the front door. The growling and roaring were randomly programmed by a Sony-made device, or was it Philips Electronics?

"De Gier did not murder our Englishman," the commissaris said as he left the sergeant's office.

"Of course he didn't," Sergeant Symonds said.

"Do return him some time," Grijpstra said. "We need him for routine jobs."

"So do I," said Sergeant Symonds.

17

The Devout Art Of Wrecking

"You're looking all disgruntled," the boatswain on the *Rodney*'s gangway said, "but the weather forecast is good. Good weather all the way to Puerto Rico." Grijpstra wasn't reassured. He had studied the commissaris's maps again. Puerto Rico to St. Maarten still seemed some distance. "And after that?" Grijpstra asked, worried.

"Winds higher than thirty-four knots not expected." The boatswain did expect a bit of a breeze around the Virgin Islands.

Grijpstra, a few minutes later, replaced the snacks he had taken from the refrigerator in the luxurious cabin he and the commissaris were sharing. The ship was moving. "De Gier was right," Grijpstra said. "This is going to be bad."

The gold telephone on a night table between the beds played a little song which the commissaris remembered from his student days, a ribald chorus sung by a strident male voice accompanied by tuba honking and drum thumping. The commissaris picked up the phone.

Carl Ambagt informed his passengers that the *Admiraal Rodney* was about to leave port. He invited his guests to the bridge, to enjoy their farewell to Key West. Carl mentioned sun-kissed beaches, Victorian houses with bizarre towers, pagoda-shaped pine trees, a crumbling brick fortress, rare tropical birds riding the thermals.

"Our client is being a poet," the commissaris said in the ship's corridor. "He is actually quite funny sometimes. That's annoying, Grijpstra. I don't like it when the enemy tries to twist himself out of my characterization. Carl is a despicable bounder. Bluffing scoundrels should have no eye for beauty. Atypical and therefore unacceptable misbehavior, Grijpstra. Hitler pets his loving dog. My half-witted brother-in-law reads Cormac McCarthy. You are a sensitive and creative percussionist. None of that fits."

"De Gier?" asked Grijpstra.

The commissaris scowled. "My star pupil? He who makes no progress? He who is getting worse maybe?"

"Your wife?"

The commissaris sighed. "Only Turtle."

The ship, hitting a wave, shuddered.

Grijpstra belched defensively.

The Ambagts waited for their guests on the *Rodney*'s bridge where the first mate studied his monitors and auxiliary screens and a sailor moved the wheel with a single finger. A servant brought deck chairs to the teak aft deck and placed them in the shadow of the helicopter parked there. A coffee table, a marble black woman, nude, lying on her back, holding up a plate-glass sheet with her hands and feet, bore an artful array of nuts and cheeses, and colored alcoholic beverages in decanters.

"Welcome," Skipper Peter said, "to our priceless yacht, Mister Detectives."

Key West's south coast slid past the slowly moving vessel.

Skipper Peter pointed at the Martello Tower rising above a tourist beach. "That's where Key West's wreckers used to keep watch."

Grijpstra wanted the shore to stop sliding.

The commissaris was mystified by the term "wreckers."

De Ambagts explained while the servant poured bourbon for Peter, a cola drink for Carl, iced tea for the commissaris and "please, nothing" for Grijpstra.

Key West's first wreckers, said Peter and Carl, were Calusa Indians. After their extermination Europeans took over. "Key West" is an English adaptation of the Spanish "Cayo Hueso." Cayo = boil. Hueso = bone. Key West started out as a skeleton covered sea-blemish. The bones were of murdered shipwrecked sailors.

The island might look peaceful, Carl said, pointing at trees, beaches and buildings and calling attention to flowering vines, orange trees, the cloud-shaped gum trees, the green velvet lawns, a cute couple of old gay gents on their tandem bicycle riding down a gravel path, and equally cute heterosexual combinations, walking along slowly, wearing identical straw hats and holding hands, the terraces of restaurants with yellow and blue parasols and—Peter interrupted his son gruffly—stores selling stuff nobody needs, T-shirts with funny texts, pre-torn jeans, fishnet underwear, plastic turds glued to the visors of pink hats, day-glow hats stuck through with tin foil fish. "But in the old days, hey?" shouted Skipper Peter, "when there were still some *real* folks around?"

"Real folks?" the commissaris asked.

Carl said that his father was referring to pirates and wreckers. The real-motivated.

The explanation continued. The Calusas, the Florida Indians, used to be peaceful, Carl said. They caught broilable fish and deer. They grew tossable salads. They were happy and healthy and lived in palm-leaf beach houses, pleasant even at the height of summer, because movable screens could direct cooling breezes. Calusas paddled hollowed-out canoes, visiting families on other islands.

One of the world's paradises, soon to be under the Spanish cross on which hung the Spanish Jesus.

Spanish forces would annihilate the natives but a project of that magnitude, Skipper Peter said, seemingly sober, speaking articulately, takes time and effort. Father Ambagt, peering around his swollen, blood-red nose, compared the changed situation with Rome, not built in a day, not torn down in a day either. The Calusas did not agree with being killed off. They shot poison arrows from the mangroves. Camouflaged canoes floated quietly through narrow swamp channels, before their crews jumped the invaders. Nude Calusa women offered fruit juices to lure steel-helmeted Spanish sailors.

Young Ambagt took his guests to the *Rodney*'s bridge. A ship-shaped icon showed on the computer's large screen. The moving icon was the *Rodney* herself, stationary dots were reefs, stationary lines were sandbanks. Flashing arrows were dangerous currents. Seventeenth-century sailors only saw the sea's surface but the Calusas knew where hidden coral reefs waited to rip vessels apart. The Calusas, dressed up in captured Spanish clothes, entrapped ships, by waving flags, or with lanterns at night.

But the Calusas were still primitives, Skipper Peter said, excitedly waving his tumbler. They weren't good at handling firearms. They didn't adapt to new values.

"Lack of values," the commissaris said.

"Exactly." Carl said. He raised his hand didactically. "Primitives cannot look beyond their own morals. Faced with change they stay stuck with obsolete codes." Calusas still believed in pacts. Pacts, agreements, honor, that sort of thing works when there is plenty of space and resources, but time was running out for that. "Drop all that garbage when a million Spanish are trying to get in. If not . . ."

". . . you will be tortured, raped, and killed," grinned Skipper Peter.

"Fifteen thousand Calusas," Carl said, "that's all we are talking about here, just a little tribe with painted faces, doing a bit of hey-ho around the bonfire, so what you do is invite the dimwits for Big Macs with Mayo and you fill them up with mass-produced chemical hootch and then you beat them all to death."

"Leaving some of the shapelier ones," grinned Skipper Peter.

"If you must," frowned Carl.

"After use, they go too," Skipper Peter said, winking, toasting, smacking, spilling liquor and snacks.

Carl addressed the commissaris. "The Calusas came to an end but ships kept coming and we kept the wrecking habit. Why do away with a good thing?" He smiled. "Right?"

"All that useless stupidity." The commissaris looked at the fading island. "And we could all have had such a good time.

Pool shamanic and western medical knowledge of birth control and euthanasia. Keep the population level. Fifteen thousand Calusas, fifteen thousand visitors. Oysters Rockefeller around the campfire. Blossoming shrubs. Cuban coffee and cigars. Nuzzling under the palm trees. Music. Singing the Reds."

"The Reds?" Carl asked.

"The Blues," the commissaris said, "might not have happened."

Grijpstra forgot his nausea for the moment. He said he liked the Blues, even if only for contrast. Who needs being happy all the time? Who wants to keep singing the Reds around campfires, even while nuzzling firm-fleshed primitives?

The commissaris was about to mention the possibility of going beyond the duality of being massacred by mutual egotism and being bored by bourgeois's get-togetherism when the sea became rougher and Grijpstra started retching again.

"Really, Henk," the commissaris said.

Carl Ambagt hadn't noticed the interlude. "We, of course, improved on the art of wrecking." He tapped the commissaris on the knee. "Listen here. Indians are the thing now, crystals and drumbeat journeys and power animals and bouncing around the tepee, and peyote, but what is it worth, right?" Carl smiled all-knowingly. "Throw in five dollars plus tax and all that Native American bullshit may buy two cappuccinos. Just imagine, the Calusas had been living here for thousands of years and they never thought of inventing a sailship. They had everything here, this is America for fuck's sake, and Native Americans never thought of mixing up a bit of explosive."

"And no wheels," Skipper Peter shouted angrily. "Shit, man, even in Rotterdam we had wheels."

Carl, comically, slapped his forehead. "It's the fifteenth century and nobody thinks of *wheels*?"

"Or oil tankers," Peter wanted to slap his forehead too but missed. His tumbler crashed to the floor. The servant swept up the remains, brought him a fresh glass and held up the Wild Turkey bottle.

Peter sipped. "Where was I?"

"Oil in tankers, Skipper Peter."

"Good boy." Ambagt Senior shook his head in admiration. "The oil business is best. Especially when I do it. Wheels weren't bad, but oil?" He squinted at the commissaris. "Oil is *big*."

"How about drugs?" the commissaris asked. "I am sure the Calusas thought of drugs."

"What was that?" Peter asked vaguely.

"Drugs," the commissaris raised his voice "Mexican ports. The Yucatán peninsula with its cannabis plantations." The commissaris, to show his good will, toasted his host with his glass of iced tea. "The coca jungles and opium farms of South America. Now *there* we make some money."

Skipper Peter looked morose. "Drugs never interested me." He raised his glass. "Bootlegging, sure, but booze is okay now."

Carl accused Native Americans of discovering drugs. "What else was there? No sitcoms or nintendo. The tropical night lasts twelve hours, take out eight hours for sleep and you have four black hours to illuminate with narcotics. If you're that dumb that you can't even invent proper lighting . . ."

". . . oil lamps!" cheered Skipper Peter.

The *Admiraal Rodney*, prodded by the young sailor's finger, turned eastward, taking on the formidable Florida Strait Current. Grijpstra saw deep whirlpools changing into abysmal maelstroms, sharp cliffs circled by white sharks.

"Shipwrecks," Skipper Peter said after adjusting his dentures that kept slipping about.

Key West became white, Carl went on. English Protestant, with some space for adjusted behavioral codes. The congregation looked up toward the preacher who, high on his pulpit, kept an eye on the horizon where sails moved close to the treacherous coast. "Wreck coming!" the preacher bellowed and headed his flock toward the beach. To help out, Key Westers tied lamps to the backs of donkeys and had the animals amble about on the beach. Slowly swaying lights, seen from the sea, indicated vessels leisurely moving about in a safe harbor. As soon as a ship hit a reef the islanders stormed their helpless prey. "Like ants attack a caterpillar," Carl said contentedly. Good pickings were guaranteed. Eastbound ships were loaded with gold, silver and jewels, pillaged in South and Central America. Westbound ships carried luxuries to governors, military officers plantation owners and merchants. Captured passengers produced ample ransoms. Crews causing any trouble had their heads bashed in.

"All that karma," the commissaris said ruefully. "What a waste of opportunities, eh, Grijpstra?"

Grijpstra groaned.

"The wrecking keeps going on, doesn't it?" the commissaris asked Carl. "Used to be ships, now it is jeeps. Mr. Stewart-Wynne's jeep."

"What?" Carl asked.

"Quadrant Bank, London," the commissaris said. "You do business with Quadrant do you not?"

"What?" Skipper Peter asked.

Carl shrugged. "Bank. Banker. Dead banker. Nothing to do with us, Dad. We don't even know the fellow."

"I do know Quadrant," Peter said. "That's a bank in London."

"Do you use Quadrant Bank for your financing?" the commissaris asked.

Skipper Peter had trouble concentrating.

"We used to maybe," Carl said. "Quadrant works the Caribbean. Big bank, I believe."

"Interesting, don't you think?" the commissaris asked Grijpstra. "No drug dealing but Quadrant doesn't seem unknown to our clients." He peered at Grijpstra's face. "Oh dear, are you all right, Henk?"

A young man wearing a cook's hat announced that dinner was on the table. Grijpstra leaned across a railing. Skipper Peter had fallen asleep and was carried to his cabin by the boatswain and a servant.

Carl Ambagt and the commissaris sat opposite each other at the narrow ends of a long dining table. The tablecloth was damask, the plates gold.

The commissaris ate his halibut au gratin. The sound of powerful engines made him look up.

"The American Air Force," Carl said. "Coming out of Boca Chica airfield." He pointed a forkful of noodles at the ceiling. "Always exercising."

The commissaris spooned egg and mustard sauce on his asparagus. "Exercises?"

"Serious training," Carl said. "Ever ready. The Cuban

threat—six vintage MIGs that might possibly cross the straits. Well, it could happen. And those Mexican drugs of yours. They're always watching."

"Of mine?" the commissaris asked.

"Not mi-i-i-i-ne," Carl said, using his Rotterdam sing-song accent.

18

A JEWISH GRANDMOTHER

De Gier had exchanged the Cadillac for a bicycle. The Cadillac was too large for Key West's alleys. De Gier kept thinking another car was following too closely but it was the Cadillac itself, its backside filling its own mirror. De Gier bicycled between blossoming magnolia trees at the edge of the cemetery that covers Key West's center. Stone angels suffocated by weeds leaned toward him from cracked gravestones. Vultures circled above a freshly dug grave. De Gier's bicycle tires crunched over broken oyster shells thrown out by a small fish restaurant. A man dressed in stained jeans and a torn shirt stretched a leg from the curb where he sat between trash cans. The man had a shapely body: narrow in the waist under a wide muscular chest. His long dirty hair hung around unshaven sunken cheeks. The deep set eyes seemed unnaturally large. In spite of his present condition the man looked military. A degenerate soldier?

De Gier veered to avoid the inviting leg. He knew, because

Sergeant Ramona had told him, that Key West is a magnet for homeless men. They are fed by various Christian charities, spend their days on beaches or in parking lots, sleep in junked cars or between mangroves around the golf links. Their daily needs for alcohol and narcotics are financed by scamming tourists. Earlier that day de Gier had tripped over a guitar box, pushed into his path. The mishap caused an uproar. The guitar inside might have been damaged by de Gier kicking the box! The valuable instrument's owner, a big-bellied tramp dressed in a torn raincoat, estimated that the guitar could be more or less restored for fifty dollars.

De Gier shook his head. "You're kidding, buddy."

"Ah?" shouted complainant. "So it's going to be like that is it?" Two other bums appeared. Three men shook hairy fists above their beerguts. "Fuckface Tourist, hand over your wallet."

De Gier remembered good advice given by an instructor at the Amsterdam Police School. De Gier spoke kindly, facing the complainant squarely. "Why are you so nervous, Friend?"

Complainant, suddenly unnerved, giggled shyly. "Me? Nervous? How do you mean? *Nervous?*"

"He has a mental imbalance," the second tramp said when de Gier appeared genuinely curious. "Could be hormones." The third tramp lifted his scarecrow hat. "I used to work in a pharmacy, sir. It's the chemicals that get us. Because of artificial euphorics imbibed by the likes of us the body's natural ability to calm, even cheer itself, decreases." He replaced his hat. He took it off again. "A deficiency which makes us nervous."

"It's the devil's work," the first tramp wailed. "Now we've got to take chemicals to feel normal."

Minutes later, walking from Car Rental to Bicycle Rental, de Gier was waylaid again. This time the bum said that he, that very morning, not less than an hour ago, had been turned around, born again so to speak. The bum, fighting back his tears, stuttering with emotion, said that just now he had met with—well, he didn't know how to describe the entity—a "Higher Power" maybe? Right there, behind that little church, in the shadow of the enormous fig tree, Key West's biggest banyan tree, that's where it happened. Banyans are holy. During the conversation with, well, okay, with God, a gleaming figure made from, well, luminous compressed air?—the bum claimed that describing the Supreme Creator of All isn't easy—it had become clear to this sinner that a new chance was being offered him. What he had to do was return to New York City where, on West Fifty-Eighth Street, he had left his family without sustenance or money. A bus ticket home would cost one hundred dollars. The bum, doing his utmost not to cry, extended a clawlike hand. God had said so. God said He would send a messenger, someone who would pay for the bus ticket for He, well, okay, God, wasn't carrying a wallet.

De Gier wished the born again bum a good journey.

"No dough?"

"No dough."

"Asshole," the bum shouted.

"Why are you so nervous?" de Gier asked kindly, looking his assailant in the eyes. The bum started crying.

And now another homeless person was bothering de Gier. De Gier kept on riding as the tramp behind him shouted that almost hurting his leg was as good as hurting his leg and that he would now sue the negligent cyclist. "What's your name, asshole?"

De Gier wondered why bums kept calling him "asshole". In Dutch the word is not used except in its proper context. Dutch drunks would call him "scrotum." Why the anal angle? He got off his bike, put it against a tree and walked back slowly. The bum got up and said he hadn't meant it that way. De Gier kept coming. The bum's mood reverted a little. He admitted to not having a good day but that didn't mean that he was prepared to have faggot tourists beat on his body. He was a military man, a specialist, "some kind of hero." He postured: feet facing outward, knees bent, arms loose, fingers spread. He used an affected bass voice. "Come and get it."

"A beer?" de Gier asked, sitting down on the curb.

"Now we are talking," said the drunk. "Fish & Chips over there has some cold ones but you do the fetching. They won't let *me* in no more."

De Gier fetched two cold beers for his guest and an iced tea for himself. The beer cans were inserted into brown paper bags. Bare beer cans are not tolerated, the shopgirl said, not even in Key West, "capital of the Conch Republic." Just kidding of course, she said. There never was a Conch Republic but Key Westers like to feel separate. She laughed. How could they be? "Not with all them fool bridges."

"We're not going to play sneaky, are we?" the drunk asked, snatching the beer in bags from de Gier's hands.

De Gier asked what was meant.

"No performance of unnatural deeds," the bum said. He raised a beer bag. "No blowing of tourists in return for fluid ounces. Okay?"

"Okay." De Gier smiled all sneakiness aside. "You were with the military?"

The bum begged time out for ritual. There had to be the snappy opening of the can, the adoring bending back of the neck, the wide opening of eyes to see the source of the divine libation, the actual pouring that connects higher and lower regions, the satisfied swallow, the post-orgiastic "hehhhhhhh," the withdrawal of lips to express inner centering accentuated by the sharp intake of air. "Yes," the bum saluted. "I was a specialist I'll have you know."

"Shock troops," de Gier said.

"Temporary-helicopter-base-builders-protector," the drunk titled his former position, that had involved parachuting into the jungle, armed with knife and carbine, in a camouflage uniform, under a wide-brimmed floppy hat, face blackened, backpack stuffed with quick-energy foods and liquids. It meant making immediate radio contact with two colleagues who had jumped close by. Meeting these colleagues. Cooperating in finding a good location for a future landing site for helicopters. Radioing coordinates to Command. Waiting for giant cargo helicopters that, ten minutes in and out, discharged personnel and provisions. Protecting the site while it is being prepared. Small fighting choppers would fly out of some faraway base to attack enemy locations and use the site to recharge their weapons and take on fuel. They'd attack the now nearby enemy again, several times maybe, at short intervals, until their mission was completed. The entire action might only take a few hours. The big helicopters would return and pick up the site's ground staff. By now the enemy might know where you were but by the time they came in there would be nothing but burnt earth and skeleton trees. And you and your two mates, having blown up the leftover stores of food, fuel and ammo by remote control, would be sneaking through the jungle, hiding there for a few days, running until a safe zone was reached where a chopper could land to pick you up.

"Nice work," de Gier said. "You don't do that anymore?"

The bum held up his second beer can. There had been problems. A bar fight followed by a First Warning. Discussing classified subjects in the presence of hookers was followed by a Second Warning. Drunk in barracks. Three strikes and you're out. Discharge with dishonor, oh dear oh dear oh dear. "Up yours," the bum snarled.

"Up yours," de Gier said kindly.

"With my kind of luck," the bum said sadly, "things usually turn out bad." He accepted being Down and Out for the time being, but there were all kinds of official bodies willing to help down-and-outers. A spiritual reevaluation was just around the corner. It would be necessary to open up for that. Right now he happened to be closed.

"I might require your services," de Gier said.

"Nothing too nasty?"

"Definitely nasty," de Gier said. "Definitely complete. A deadly accident. Technical preparations."

The bum said that this was the Age of Specialization. He himself had only been trained to spot, protect and destroy temporary helicopter bases. After that came the safety of the jungle. There was no jungle in Key West, however. If the police blocked route A1A, the only road out, the law enforcement forces would be sure to get him. Everybody knows what comes next. The pulling out of toenails and electrocuting of genitals in a bamboo cage while being stabbed by infected spears handled by fat women.

"So?" de Gier asked.

"No," the bum said.

Would, de Gier asked, his new-found friend know a colleague, another former specialist, who could bring about mechanical accidents that would kill a third party? De Gier was thinking of interference with a vehicle, cutting of fuel and brake lines. Someone with long hair. Someone who looked like de Gier. With a mustache. If the bum happened to know such a person there was this hundred dollar bill.

The drunk's grasping hand trembled. He leaned against de Gier. De Gier pushed him back. The bum fell over. He groaned. His legs shook uncontrollably. He blew spittle bubbles. The whites of his eyes showed.

De Gier walked to a nearby phone booth and dialed 9-1-1.

"Location?"

De Gier looked outside. "At a crossing." He read signs. "Corner of Walk and Don't Walk Streets. No such streets? Beg your pardon. Just a moment." He left the cell and returned. "Corner Olivia and Frances Streets." No, the incident had nothing to do with him but with a local person who seemed to be having an epileptic fit. He himself was a tourist. Name? "Janneman Jackrabbit. No, I can't spell that in English. Bye, Miss."

Pity, de Gier thought, when he was back on his bicycle again. The idea seemed good enough. If the killer of the British bank inspector had been a military type gone bad, then a brother in arms, given the smallness of Key West, would know said killer. This was America, land of action. He had seen *Sol-*

dier of Fortune in the hotel's lobby. The magazine contained combat stories, essays on the art of killing and foreign areas where desperados could earn good money. There were ads offering "services." De Gier imagined alcoholic former Commandos, Green Berets shooting up, Marines with mental problems. He recalled *The Dirty Dozen*, a movie featuring criminals released to perform misdeeds. This was the country's most southerly extremity, the "Conk" Republic, a dead-end street collecting odd men out. Wouldn't the killer stay put in Key West, while spending his fat fee?

Perhaps a homeless drunk was not a good source of information. Who, thought de Gier, bicycling past ornamental bushes and palm trees, looking into busy bars and bustling marinas, who would know where to find big-spending hit men?

The Eggemoggin Hotel staff? Dear boys, helpful, charming, but would they know where hard core-criminals spend their loot? Sergeant Ramona Symonds of the Key West Police Department would know. De Gier did have his professional pride, however. Would an Amsterdam Murder Brigade detective with twenty years experience seek help from a colleague who insults, humiliates and arrests him? There were other considerations. Man versus woman. White versus black. The competitive element seemed suddenly important. Hetero versus homo. Or was Sergeant Symonds bisexual? Was going either way more likely with women? What did *he* know? Was he into dualism now? This versus that? What about his oriental esoteric studies? Shouldn't he aim beyond dichotomies?

De Gier, troubled, alone and lost, sat on the low wall of the Fleming Street Public Library, framed by decorative travellers palms, so called because they resemble fans, and women wave fans when their lovers leave. De Gier waved his upper body. He directed himself to the only being who had ever loved him.

"Grandma Sarah," de Gier thought. "Are you there? I have been arrested in America. I am free on bail. I am looking for a hit man. If I don't find him I will be food for small rodents. In a badly ventilated cell, Grandma Sarah. I'm sorry I'm bothering you, you hear? I know you are up there in heaven with Canary Pete who sang for me when you asked him, and the doll's house you let me play with Sunday mornings. Remember? Would you mind helping out here?"

Grandma Sarah would have better things to do, de Gier thought, bicycling along unhappily. He shouldn't be bothering the dear woman. What hadn't she expected from him and look how it had all turned out in the end. He could see his grandmother now. She was graceful, tall, with full, sexily curved lips, even though she was ancient. He could feel her caressing hands. He recalled the voice that told funny tales. About an ark filled with animals. Giraffes and cockroaches. Noah's ark.

Noah.

Captain Noah.

Captain Noah of the schooner *Berrydore*.

De Gier passed a red light. Horns sounded. "Ass-hooooooole," the multitude shouted. De Gier hardly noticed. "Did you say 'Noah,' Grandma Sarah?"

De Gier still had Captain Noah's number, on a piece of paper in the breast pocket of his cotton jacket. He found a telephone booth and dialed.

19

Grijpstra's Fearful Freedom

Grijpstra put down the plastic bucket and fell back on his bed. The commissaris took a face towel from a dish filled with crushed ice and placed it on Grijpstra's forehead. "You know what is nice about our situation, Henk?"

Grijpstra's stomach rumbled. "No, sir."

"That we have no back-up," the commissaris said. "Do call me 'Jan.' You can't do it, can you? De Gier can't do it either. I think that you two need a master to look up to. Someone who makes decisions for you." The commissaris shook his head. "You know that's childish, Henk. To live within someone else's set of morals. As if leaders can be trusted. You really revere rule-makers?" He put a calming hand on Grijpstra's noisy belly. "You know what Mark Twain said. *Any fool can make a rule.*"

Grijpstra gestured helplessly. The commissaris passed the bucket. Grijpstra barfed.

"Why do you ignore," the commissaris asked, "the pleasant aspect of our present predicament? We have freedom. You want to shy away from freedom?" He waved fists. "Like in the good old days, Henk, when Dutch freemen sailed about here and behaved any which way they pleased." He patted Grijpstra's rumbling belly affectionately. "So what would please us right now, you think?"

Grijpstra was on his back again. The commissaris dipped his little towel in melting ice. He had learned the therapy from Katrien, in a past almost forgotten, when he was still a drinking man and behaved inappropriately at parties, waylaid women in the corridor of a host's house, drove drunk, saw concentric colored circles whirling in toilet bowls. A bad habit getting worse then. Finally Katrien had confronted him forcing a decision. No more. Very well. Grijpstra never knew the commissaris as a drunk. So now the commissaris could annoy the poor fellow. "Are you and de Gier really pleased wallowing about on illegal found money?" the commissaris asked sternly. "Do you like hiding your treasure behind a million dollar fee offered by little Mr. Slick and his drunken old Daddy-o?"

"But, sir . . ."

"Just kidding, Henk," the commissaris said. "And I did have a good time investing your treasure. Did you check the last bank statement?"

"Doubled," Grijpstra whispered fearfully.

"I was going all the way," the commissaris said. He became more and more cheerful. "If you *knew* what capers I played with your money." He shook his head. "Going on margin, playing puts, going short, wagering the wad, time and again,

Henk. I took every chance no investor should ever take." He laughed. "But what did I care, eh? It wasn't *my* money."

Grijpstra groaned.

"You're right, Henk, I managed to double your loot."

Grijpstra stared at the cabin's ceiling.

"But that's it for now," the commissaris said. "I am bored with juggling figures. It's all in bonds now. One hundred percent safety and an average seven percent yield. Do you have any idea how much seven percent of nine point four million comes to, Henky? You think you and Rinus can subsist on that? Tax free? All you have to do is drive to Luxembourg once a year and fill up your limo's trunk with crisp banknotes. Living off the fat of Luxembourg?"

Grijpstra smiled anxiously.

"Stewed eel in pea soup for breakfast," the commissaris said. "Cream pudding and butter cookies for lunch, pork chops floating in their juice for dinner. A bottle of syrupy liqueur, a good fat black cigar, an extra large hooker for ye old hup-ho. . . ."

Grijpstra gestured pleadingly. The commissaris passed the plastic bucket.

Grijpstra, exhausted, tried to doze off. The commissaris lay down too. The *Rodney* was still swaying a little but found her balance as soon as she faced the Florida current squarely. "The side-wobble seems gone," the commissaris said cheerfully. It was the turning wiggle-waggle that upset the stomach, he explained to Grijpstra, especially when that kind of shimmy was accentuated by the short but not really regular wobbly shaking of rip-tidal waves. The main thing was that they were out of the circular currents, or did Grijpstra think there might still be surprises? The commissaris had heard tornados do occur close to Cuba. "They suck small ships *down*."

Grijpstra sat up.

The commissaris apologized. Everything was okay now. He guaranteed it. "You'll be just fine, Henk. What were we talking about? Our freedom. The chance to finally do whatever we like." He eyed Grijpstra. "Like what?"

"Go home to Nellie," Grijpstra pleaded.

The commissaris didn't think Grijpstra really wanted to cop out now. Nellie was a comfortable woman, Grijpstra had enjoyed that, but he should be about ready for a break now. Tension and action again, that was the ticket. "Adventures, Henk." The commissaris sketched their actual situation: Grijpstra and he, unarmed, in the power of two pathological entrepreneurs . . .

"From Rotterdam," Grijpstra whispered hoarsely.

Indeed. The commissaris had been avoiding that city most of his life but he did know a little bit about Rotterdam. Europe's Number One Port was known for cold winds forever wafting in from surrounding wetlands. No canals, no gable houses, not too much poetry, a lack of art. Dull, straight, a working man's heaven. Rotterdam merchants believed in continuity, in doing business in the long run. Honesty today, profits in the future. Ambagt & Son were clearly exceptions and their very contrariness would be dangerous. The commissaris theorized, combine Carl and Peter's immorality with customary Rotterdam energy and foresight, add irritability caused by having grown up in rain, drizzle and fog, and obtain a multiple danger factor.

Now that the *Rodney* skimmed waves quietly instead of hopping about like a toddler during play-break, Grijpstra could talk again. "We'll never get paid for this, sir." Grijpstra was sorry he had involved the commissaris. This misery was a direct consequence of his mishap in Amsterdam, of finding that silly money. He saw it all now. His and de Gier's greed had opened them up to Ketchup and Karate's tricks. The commissaris was right when he suggested that they still needed guidance. Look where their mistake had taken them. Recommended by corrupt colleagues they were assisting despicable scoundrels, and why? Just to show Mr. Tax Man that they had legal income? Where would this lead to? "To being tossed to the sharks by hired henchmen?"

The commissaris intertwined his fingers behind his head that rested comfortably on fluffed pillows. "Say, Henk, did you ever get that hundred thousand dollars the Ambagts offered up front?"

"Never," Grijpstra said. "We've been losing from day one. You and I will be fish food while that Key West sergeant has de Gier chained up. You call that freedom?" Grijpstra waved limp hands. "We overestimated ourselves. Sarter was right. Freedom is fearful."

The commissaris took a shower. He ordered hot chocolate with Graham crackers. He returned, humming, trying to skip (but his leg still bothered him) to his bed where he slipped under the eiderdown, rubbing his bare feet contentedly. "Haho, Grijpstra."

"Haho, sir?" Grijpstra asked weakly.

"If anyone," the commissaris said, "was ever wrong it was that Sarter of yours. Jean-Paul Sartre?" The commissaris sniffed disdainfully. "Imagine pushing an entire generation of disciples into disgust and loathing instead of urging the young ones to enjoy liberation. Ouch."

"Are you in pain, sir?"

"Hip bones," the commissaris said. "Every evening, at about this time, my hips attract red hot mice. They tunnel through the bone. Aww . . ." He turned, trying to find a better position. "Codeine stumps them." He used his hot chocolate to wash the pills down. "Think of it, Henk. Take away the entire nonsense of judgment, of compulsively defining things as good or bad, where would that get you?"

Grijpstra squeaked with fear.

"That would get you to float free," the commissaris said. "Afloat in the void. Initial dizziness will soon leave you. Watch de Gier. He managed a few times, briefly, and it made him the endearing fellow he is sometimes. I saw you getting close, playing drums. You forget now because you're sick to your stomach. Remember to remember those moments. Find the way back to nowhere."

"Get back to safety with Nellie?" Grijpstra asked stubbornly. "Maybe eat veal croquettes again? Watch funny TV?" He sat up. "You said you had a plan?"

The commissaris's plan wasn't complete yet. He checked his watch. "I have to phone London but they're six hours ahead of us there."

"Something to do with the dead Englishman?" Grijpstra asked.

The commissaris had nodded off. Grijpstra dozed too. Both dreamed. Grijpstra woke up screaming, the commissaris laughing. It was 4 A.M., 10 A.M. in London. The commissaris didn't have Quadrant's number. He was about to enter Telephone Hell, filled with computer voices that offer obscure choices and too little time to choose, repeated dialing of long numbers, sudden cut-off humming, more computer voices, more long numbers, occasionally tired voices wanting to know what the caller wanted to know, crackling pauses filled by bad music.

"You know what?" the commissaris asked Grijpstra. "Why don't *you* phone London, there's a good fellow. I'll go back to sleep to see what happens. Which doesn't mean that I'm not right behind you. Okay? As soon as you connect with Quadrant you wake me. Yes? Yes."

Grijpstra thought otherwise. "But sir, suppose that the Ambagts defrauded Quadrant and that an inspector was sent who figured out how that happened. Who cares? All we have to do is somehow obtain the return of or a payment for the *Sibylle's* lost cargo."

The commissaris raised a hand. The index finger played an invisible phone's keyboard. "Please?"

"No, seriously, sir. Even if the Ambagts arranged for that bank inspector to drive into our dinner, the crime would not affect our project. Why bother with Quadrant? The goal recedes while we lose our way."

"You can't lose a way you're on," the commissaris said. "Besides, the road *is* the goal. Make that call, will you?"

20

MEANWHILE AND EVEN SO

Captain Noah remembered de Gier. De Gier was the foreigner who distributed hundred dollar bills. And the foreigner wanted information? As to where, in Key West, ex-military oddballs hang out when in the money? "A strange coincidence, Old Buddy." Right there, where else? In the girlie bar where the captain himself was spending de Gier's hundred dollar bills that very minute. In The Perfidious Parrot, where the captain, at this very same moment, spoke into his cellular phone, de Gier would find his quarry.

"Must take a sip from my freshly poured Budweiser, Bud Bud Buddieboy." Noah burped happily. He asked de Gier to come along to grab his very own Bud Bud Buddieboy in Key West's Number One Lapdancery. Bouncy bare bosoms, the captain explained, rhythmically a-shake between the clients' knees. "Listen." Captain Noah's raised phone filled de Gier's telephone cell with a seemingly random mixture of sound blasts: KeBUM, keBUM, kerrrr-*BUM*. Heeh Heeh Heeh

HEEH-heeh. Yaah Yaah Yaah *YAAH*. Turrr-*RATTEL* Turrr-*RATTEL*. KAHCHEE kah-*CHEE*. "Can you hear the bare bosoms?"

"Not really," de Gier said but the captain didn't hear him. "You hurry now," Captain Noah shouted. "I'll be here awaiting."

After the captain clicked off de Gier asked a passerby where The Perfidious Parrot bar might be. Near the Seaside Store? Marked by red/white divers's flags? Opposite Pelican Hospital? Behind the house-high wall painting of a parrot? "Thank you."

The passerby, a local man, seemed friendly. De Gier might as well pursue his luck. "What *is* lap dancing, sir?"

"Are you from out of town?"

"Holland," de Gier said.

"Holland, Michigan," the passerby said. "Always wondered what Michigan folks talk like. Amazing. It's like a foreign accent." The passerby said he had never been in Michigan. He had flown over it once. He had thought about what folks might be doing down there. Wasn't that where a good doctor helps the terminally ill finish themselves off a little early? Seemed like a good idea. Maybe Michigan hookers become intimate too? Not like in his home state (the passerby smiled self-consciously) "here in Florida Masturbiria."

De Gier looked surprised. "Prostitutes don't take clients upstairs here?"

"We keep things public." The passerby assured out-of-stater de Gier that a Floridian "upstairs" was a thing of the past. "Hookers wriggle on Johns's laps. Johns sit ve-ry quietly."

De Gier tried to visualize the procedure. "What if the danced-on one gets excited and touches the dancer?"

The passerby looked upset. "Don't even think about touching here."

De Gier bicycled past silver-gray weathered wooden houses facing a harbor quay. Sailboats were leaving the shore, fishing boats were approaching. Sailors with earrings and faded bandannas wrapped around shaven skulls sucked on curved pipe stems while they leaned against the bleached carcasses of beached boats. Beautiful young people raced about on ski jets. A rusted Chevrolet, coming from the opposite direction, passed de Gier's bicycle.

Tempting images flashed through de Gier's mind. Suppose he stayed here, bought one of the ramshackle buildings that displayed a FOR SALE sign, sat on a weathered gingerbread-decorated balcony sipping whiskey, playing the trumpet, living on lobsters, stonecrabs, and key lime pie? Watched the boats go by. Bought a boat himself. Sayukta could visit. Maybe have some Cuban or Haitian ladies for tea. Keep changing company. Admire Sergeant Symonds in her uniform hot pants while the Mynah bird whistled a waltz.

Sub-images flashed along. Home-cooked exotic dishes featuring the day's catch. His boat would be bizarre, maybe a Chinese type mini-junk like one he had seen in the harbor. Drinking coffee in the early morning, like the old Cuban gentlemen he saw everywhere, perhaps he could assume a similar persona, wear an immaculate straw hat and pressed white pants, a dress shirt, white and brown shoes, sip espresso, get energy, do nothing with it. The waitress was on her way already. "*Otro cafecito, señor* Rai-nus?" (she would recognize a good tipper)

"*Por favor, señorita.*"

Pornographing the evenings away, fill up the days with sailing and diving.

De Gier got off his bicycle in front of The Perfidious Parrot.

The bar's logo was drawn in a few ragged Zen-like lines on the gable of a former marine warehouse. The bird, wings half-spread cockily, looked aggressive.

"We like it," the doorman said, noting de Gier's interest in the logo. The doorman imitated the bird's arrogant stance. His hooked nose resembled the parrot's beak. His clothes looked feathery. The wide orange silk sash became the parrot's belly, the white jacket its breast. The doorman's tall boots changed into muscular bird legs.

"Impressive," de Gier said politely.

"The painting of the parrot is based on Mayan art," the doorman said. "Pre-Colombian Mexican, modelled on a sixth century cave painting, found it in the Chiapas mountains. Mayan priests, in return for gold coins, performed totem-animal dances. The parrot powered the cave-temple's door-man. I drew the damn bird from memory. It came out good. He and I welcome the likes of you." He pointed a thumb across his shoulder. "You do want to get in there?"

"If you please," de Gier said politely.

The doorman held up his. "Ten dollars entry-money."

De Gier pulled out his wallet.

"That's to bounce you out with," the doorman said, "in case you misbehave. You know enough to keep your paws off the flesh? No flirtatious attitude? No smoking, eating, sleeping?" He flexed muscles. "Any punishment will be painful."

De Gier stared at the doorman.

The doorman looked noncommittal.

"Fuck you," de Gier said, putting his wallet back into his jeans's rear pocket.

The doorman narrowed his eyes. "*What* did you say, sir?"

"Fuck you." De Gier looked noncommittal too.

The doorman was expensively dressed. It is tiring to roll about on crushed oyster shells at high noon under a hot sky. Does it really pay to engage in fisticuffs with a neatly attired tourist ready to spend money in a holiday setting?

"Welcome, Friend," the doorman said.

Inside, music rocked. Captain Noah waved from his high bar stool. Nude, almost nude, semi-nude, three quarters-nude, barely/flimsily/fully attired women walked between tables, stripped or dressed in the aisles, kneeled or squatted in front of clients, danced on tables, rolled on the stage, slid along bannisters, strode in and out of doors, stood on their heads for short moments, stood on their feet for long moments, smiled slavishly, glared domineeringly, raised the corners of their lips up like madonnas, turned them down like hellish whores, twisted their bodies as if in great pain, or great need perhaps. Of what? Of love? Love of de Gier's money? A bald host in a red silk cummerbund shook de Gier's hand. "You know our rules, sir?"

De Gier breathed in deeply. The doorman behind him waved at the host. The doorman made an O out of his bent index finger and thumb. His lips said "o-kay" silently. The host retreated. "Welcome, Friend. Our establishment is your establishment, sir."

"Budbuddyboy," Captain Noah said at the bar. "There he is. Join me, you well-funded foreigner, you."

The captain pointed at the dancers. "The olive-green beauty

in the black skinny dress with the thin shoulder strips is a Syrian national, and the black lady is Jewish, escaped the Sudan for Israel, escaped Israel for our Peace & Quiet. The white women on stage are Irish, the taller of the two is Nasty Nick's."

"Nasty who?" De Gier asked.

"The doorman." Captain Noah was happy, he said, that he could introduce this new world to a new arrival. "Nasty Nick is an anthropology university graduate."

"Changed his field?" de Gier asked.

"Adapted his field," Captain Noah said. "Nick specialized in pre-Columbian civilizations, paid for his studies by professional boxing, brilliant student, good degree, nobody wanted him when he was done."

"Too different?" de Gier asked.

"Those who are different stick out and get hammered down," Captain Noah whispered. "I am French Canadian—different. Do you know," the captain's elbow dug into de Gier's side, "that you are foreign-different? You know what that means? No?" The elbow dug harder. "That means that the non-different don't understand you too well so you get to play the bad guy in their movies."

The waitress was British, with an introverted ladylike expression. She was large breasted. She wore a tight jacket. The jacket's V was covered by a rose-colored scarf. De Gier ordered fruit juice. "Spiked?"

"No thank you."

She smiled. "You don't drink alcohol?"

"No longer," de Gier said.

"Admirable," the waitress said.

"Drunks drool on them," Captain Noah said, watching the

waitress walk away. "See those ladylike swaying hips? Wait till you see her ladylike thighs. Ahhh." The captain shook his head wildly. "We must be serious. You're here on business. The whereabouts of ex-military men. The crude oil business. I have some information there too. Which do you want first, oil or the bad soldier?"

"Is there a connection?" de Gier asked, much aware of femininity everywhere. He should be. It was expected, Captain Noah said. "Are Dutch ladies more attractive?"

"They aren't here," de Gier said.

The captain said he couldn't imagine more beautiful breasts than those of the British waitress, not even in unknown Holland. Could Dutch women have longer legs than the olive-green Syrian, who happened to be passing their table that moment? Were Dutch female hips more seductively smoothly oval than the Irish ones now on stage?

De Gier watched Nasty Nick's tall Irish girl friend dance with a black woman. The Irish girl wore ballet shoes only, the black woman seemed about to undress. The two dancers were kissing.

"Crude oil," the captain said.

De Gier kept watching.

Captain Noah's hands covered de Gier's eyes. "You gave me money up front for information on the Caribbean oil trade. The *Sibylle*. Piracy near St. Maarten, Netherlands Antilles. Remember?"

De Gier promised to listen, while watching.

The captain said he had asked around. There was an oil-transshipment facility on the Dutch island of St. Eustatius, one island south of St. Maarten. The facility belonged to a corporation that transferred supertanker cargoes to storage tanks, then transferred the product again to small tankers. A wholesale business—buy large quantities at a discount, sell small quantities at a mark-up. Buy when oil is cheap, sell when oil is dear. Play the market. Demand and supply. "You have that?" Captain Noah asked. "Or did it get mixed up with butts and boobs?"

De Gier tapped his right temple. The information was recorded, 100 percent error free. He said so.

The captain also reported that computerized supertankers are handled by small crews. Five, six men at most, including the captain. Tanker crews are almost always on board because their ships do not waste time in harbors. Being stuck in confined quarters causes depression. A negative state of mind leads to abuse of alcohol, drugs and porno on TV. It would not be difficult to take over a ship run by a sad and befuddled crew. Captain Noah had heard that insurance premiums on tanker cargoes were high and rising.

"Aha," de Gier said. The British waitress had returned with papaya juice on the house, compliments of Nasty Nick who could be seen smiling and waving in the doorway. De Gier smiled and waved back. The waitress made de Gier step off his barstool, sat on her heels, placed her tray on a low table, showed long smooth thighs. She settled him in a chair. She stepped out of her short skirt. She took her jacket off. She knelt between de Gier's knees and dropped her brassiere. Her breasts rubbed his thighs. She pouted. Her body followed, like the chassis of a well-sprung sportscar, the bouncing beat of the rocky blues thundering from loudspeakers placed in all the corners. She made her tongue pop from between tight lips, then let it slither about lasciviously. She removed her slip. She rubbed her pubic down against his knee. She leaned, turning, sideways, alternating breasts against alternating thighs. She got up and let her nipples caress de Gier's cheeks, get lost in his moustache. She got dressed. De Gier handed over a banknote. She raised her skirt and inserted the bill into her slip. He thanked her. She thanked him for thanking her. She walked away.

"Oil," the captain, still on his bar stool, said from above, "is a fascinating product."

"What?" de Gier asked.

"You seem fond of women," Captain Noah said. "I like that in a man. You're not overly fond of men?"

De Gier checked the captain's low brow, his ragged eyebrows growing into each other, the small squinting eyes, the earlobes grown into his neck, the jughead ears, the moth-eaten fluffy beard, the bent legs, the hairy toes showing in the captain's open sandals. "Men are okay," de Gier said politely.

"Men-liking men do have taste, though," Captain Noah said. Key West had been restored by them, gloriously, subtly. Tasteful restaurants, cozy bars, perfect Beds & Breakfasts, lovely gardens, all demonstrated good taste. He himself had none. When at home in inland Maine he drove a rusted-out pick-up, the back loaded with empty beer cans, a deer rifle clamped against the cabin's rear window. Noah, back home, slumped next to Suzie, an inflated life-sized doll strapped in her seat by the passenger's safety belt. Suzie wore a blond wig that Noah had found in a catalogue. He dressed her in tight jeans and a T-shirt that said GUANA-PARTY? under a picture of copulating reptiles. Suzie wore a bottle between her legs. Noah smiled sadly. "The way I live there."

"A bottle of alcohol between Suzie's legs?" de Gier asked.

"The bottle fits into her body, mouth facing out. It's a receptacle," the captain explained.

De Gier shook his head.

"Not good?"

"I never thought of any of that," de Gier said.

"And if you had?"

"But don't you have live women out there?" de Gier asked.

"Big babes," the captain said. "The frightening kind. Three sizes only. Regular big. Big big. Oh-my-God-it-is-coming-at-me big."

"I see," de Gier said.

He also saw dancers performing a parroty show, in feather costumes that were being unzipped. The dancers confronted the audience, they came down to touch clients. De Gier was danced on by the Syrian girl. When the music stopped she drank a Coca Cola. De Gier was served with more papaya juice, waved his way by the doorman.

De Gier made conversation. "What do you do when you're not working here?"

The Syrian studied at the University of Miami, spending her days off in Key West. She was about to take final exams. She was going to be a legal secretary. She said that the tall blond girl who had just come in attended medical school. "She is almost done too. We make good money here. The waitress will be a lawyer." Captain Noah invited the blonde girl over. She wore an evening dress, adorned with small oval mirrors for buttons that the Syrian undid. The blonde girl recognized de Gier's accent. She had Dutch parents who spoke American now, like herself, but she was born in Holland and remembered some words. "You like it here, darling?" she asked in Dutch.

De Gier said he did in Dutch.

She sat on his knee. She pulled his head down so that her bare breast brushed his cheek.

"You will be a general practitioner?" de Gier asked.

The blonde stripper didn't think so. She wanted to be a surgeon. Perhaps she could help now that breast cancer was becoming common. De Gier, nose in cleavage, shivered. He handed over a banknote. She thanked him. She also excused herself, it was her turn to perform on stage. She remembered more Dutch, wishing him a happy stay in the country, asking him to take greetings to her parents' hometown, *Schoonrewoerd*, meaning "beautiful land between dikes."

"All doctors and lawyers?" de Gier asked, pointing his nose at the moving display of firm flesh.

Some, Noah said, but most of the lapdancers just worked for the doorman, wasting their youth before a future of giving blowjobs for crack. Nick the Pimp drove a Ferrari and shared his penthouse with the employee of the week. The others lived in his ghetto-motel, with malfunctioning air conditioning. He insisted on collecting most of their money.

De Gier told the Sudanese Jewish woman, active on his lap, that he enjoyed his blissful situation. If only it would last.

The Sudanese comforted her client. "It will last as long as you can hold it."

Bouncing breasts made de Gier thirsty. Papaya juice kept flowing. De Gier got sleepy. The dancers kept coming, kneeling, separating his knees, pushing, touching.

"You do have quite a supply of twenty dollar bills," Captain Noah said. "You want to hear about your former Special Forces man?"

"My former what?" de Gier yawned. He wondered whether he was allergic to papaya.

"You phoned," the captain said. "Ex-military types. Well funded. Where they lose their loot. That's here, Old Buddy."

Right, right, de Gier remembered. He said he was looking for an ex-military man who looked like he did. "Mickey," the girl on de Gier's lap said. "Has to be Mickey. I did think you were he for a moment but that couldn't be for Nasty Nick just threw Mickey out." She nuzzled de Gier's cheek. "You are cuter."

"You looking for Mickey, Buddy Boy?" the captain asked. "How come you didn't say so?"

De Gier forced his mouth to talk. "Please tell me all about Mickey."

"A lush who comes here often," Captain Noah said. "Used to be a Green Beret. Squats in a camper in the William Street trailer-park. Drives a rusted-out open Chevy convertible. Just got his license back, police took it away for drunk driving, next time they'll keep it." Captain Noah pointed at an empty bar stool. "He was sitting right there, just before you came in. Squeezed the nipples of your medical countrywoman, got shown out by the skinheads."

Captain Noah's voice seemed to be coming from quite close. *"Hey, buddy boy, are you feeling okay down there?"*

De Gier saw how Nasty Nick hit Captain Noah and dragged him toward the exit. De Gier wanted to help the captain but couldn't get off the floor where he was resting. The music sounded much different and then suddenly dropped off, except for the drumbeat that throbbed on relentlessly. The women were tearing off their skins. They were only skeletons under-neath. Nasty Nick was a giant parrot whose hollow voice, within de Gier's skull, shouted threats. The parrot hopped closer, bent down and peeled de Gier out of his skin. Other parrots picked up de Gier's raw carcass, dragged it outside and ground it into the crushed oyster shell parking lot. "You really need to do this?" de Gier wanted to ask but a parrot squeezed de Gier's throat between its crooked toes and tore it to pieces with its sharp beak.

21

NUDE ON THE CEMETERY

The sea north of Cuba stayed rough, even though Skipper Peter said that that was unusual for the time of the year. No matter, said Ambagt Senior—all you had to do was drink more alcohol. The idea, like any idea by now, upset Grijpstra's stomach. The skipper drank on, alone in the barroom. The commissaris and Carl Ambagt were tied to their chairs on the *Rodney*'s rear deck. The servant brought them beakers filled with coffee, with lids through which plastic straws pointed upward. "Otherwise we'll have a mess here." He frowned at Carl. "And who cleans up?"

"Sometimes the wise-asses drive me crazy," Carl told the commissaris, while watching the servant departing abruptly. "They know exactly how far they can go, and that's where they're always going."

"I wish you a lot of employees," the commissaris said, winking, to show that he didn't mean the malediction.

Right, Carl said, but what could one do on a luxury yacht

without staff to keep the luxury going? The more desires are created the more servants are needed to keep them fulfilled. A demonic circle. Carl blew angry bubbles through his straw. "Dad likes to be waited on." He flicked his full coffee beaker across the railing. "I'd just as soon as get my coffee myself." Carl's voice squeaked. "It used to be Mom who never allowed Dad to leave the couch."

"Your mother is a caring lady?" the commissaris asked.

"My mother belongs on a cookie can label," Carl said. He raised eyebrows at motherly coziness. "Happy Ambagt family munches cookies in happy home. Happy Dad munches while he reads the paper. Happy Mom munches while she irons the laundry. Happy Carlie munches while he does his homework. Happy Dog begs for a cookie. Watch Stupido *sit*."

Carl threw the commissaris's coffee beaker into the Caribbean too. "Happy upstairs apartment at Bourgeois Alley in Rotterdam. Watch Ma cut rancid cheese with a blunt knife. Bend over dented cooking stove. Straighten plastic cover with Mondrian design on wobbly kitchen table." Carl glared furiously. "Are you analyzing my character? Want to know what makes me jump?"

"You interest me," the commissaris said. "Finding out about you saves me living your life." He smiled. "So you don't like Mondrian's art?"

"It's okay for decorating walls," Carl said. "Dad used to have a Mondrian, hung it in the bar, but we sold it in St. Maarten. It brought a pretty penny."

"All that money," the commissaris said. "I'm surprised you haven't hired some female company for your journey."

"Dad doesn't care for loose women," Carl said. "When I bring them aboard the crew tries to get them."

The commissaris seemed shocked. "You allow that?"

"I am the slave of slaves," Carl said sadly.

"Your life must be complicated."

Carl, touched by his interrogator's kind voice, admitted to a longing for simplicity. Like it used to be in Rotterdam. Without Ma's coziness of course. A simple Rotterdam upstairs flat, without a view. If he wanted a view he could read Carlos Fuentes or Mario Vargas Llosa—literature provided views no window could ever offer. In a simple two-room apartment Carl would have time to read again. On this damned ship there was never any. Not that he didn't appreciate his high-quality yacht, the envy of all other users of the high seas, but there was always some little thing or other. Carl gestured widely. Jeezz. But then, what could one expect for thirty million, eh? And then there was the staff. Good people, his sailors knew their jobs, not lazy either but always at you for this or that.

Carl imitated the servant's voice. "What would you require for dinner tonight, Master Carl?" All Carl ever wanted was simple soup, always simmering. Give it a stir once in a while maybe. Make it out of anything in season—carrots, potatoes—what did he care? Serve with noodles. Suck and gulp. Store-bought ice cream afterward. Catch a movie once a week. In a regular cinema, big screen. Who needs a mini screen at home, like they had on the *Rodney* here, with wraparound sound and whatnot? An ordinary ticket to look at a simple big screen. Who wants to fuss with expensive home equipment that breaks down once a month?

"Is there," the commissaris asked, "room for a simple companion in your simple fantasy?"

Carl shrugged. "Nah."

"No intimacy?" the commissaris asked.

"Please," Carl said. He thought. "Well, maybe. If she spoke Spanish. On a rainy afternoon. I could do that."

"You would work?"

"What *is* this?" Carl shouted. "You're Dr. Jan Freud?"

The commissaris said he liked to know who he was dealing with.

"Not who,"Carl said in his normal voice. "*What* you are dealing with." He grimaced. "We're dealing with oil here."

The commissaris looked serious. "But what are we really dealing with here? You want your oil back and you will get your oil back, and I want a million for getting you your oil back and I will get that million, just to show some legal income for G&G, but what do you think we're really after, Mr. Ambagt?"

"What?" Carl asked tonelessly.

The commissaris looked expectant.

"Profit," Carl said. "Got to make profits. Got to make damn profits forever."

The silence grew. The wind had died down. The *Rodney*'s engines murmured quietly. "Something to do with Spanish." Carl said, "I could work in something to do with Spanish."

The commissaris didn't react.

"When I'm back in Rotterdam?" Carl asked. "You ever read Manuel Vazquez Montalban? Or Pablo Ignacio Taibo Dos?" He shook his head in wonder. "What those fellows can do with the language. That is beau-ti-ful, sir."

"Will you have a pet?" the commissaris asked.

"A crow," Carl answered promptly. "I'll find it in the Harbor Park."

The commissaris laughed. "What makes you long for a crow, Carl?"

Carl had a connection with crows. They pointed the way. He dreamed about them.

"The way to where, Mr. Ambagt?"

Carl described the path the dream crows showed him. The path was in a forest, sun-dappled, pine needles glowing. It led to a glade, with silver moss on weathered rocks, and golden lichens.

"Do you reach that goal?"

Carl sighed. He had only seen it. From afar. He would like to reach it.

The commissaris pointed at the helicopter that was clamped to the deck, at the solid golden ashtray, the aft deck's teak floor, the spotless white uniforms of the sailors on the *Rodney*'s bridge, the marble nude woman holding up the glass tabletop, the Liberian flag flying about the azure sea. "You could do without this?"

"This was mostly Dad's idea," Carl said.

"Wealth doesn't really concern you?"

"Sure it does," Carl gestured. "If only to show off." He wiggled a convincing finger. "Do you have any idea of how many people live like me and Dad? How many can actually make use of the vicissitudes of life? Do you know the ratio of those who do to and those who are done to?"

A sailor reported that something was wrong with the plumbing. "Meaning what?" Carl asked.

"Meaning no drinking water for awhile, Master Carl." The sailor, already on his way back, turned around and smiled.

The water problem brought another problem to mind. Carl asked the commissaris how the enquiry was going. "Any progress?"

The ship changed direction and was hit sideways by swell. A wave broke and water splashed on the commissaris's glasses. He rubbed them dry. "Which enquiry, Mr. Ambagt?"

Carl pushed his face close to that of the commissaris. "What was that?"

They both got splashed now. The commissaris dried his glasses again.

"We are expecting to be recompensed for our lost cargo," Carl shouted. "You were in Aruba. You said so. You must have talked to Captain Guzberto Souza.

The commissaris shook his head.

Carl seemed outraged. "No? So what were you doing there? And what does your fat friend do except puke all the time?" Carl almost wrung his hands. "You have two experienced detectives on the job. I want you to catch the pirates, force them to repay us. Why did you leave de Gier in Key West? What has *he* come up with?"

"Nobody plans to come up with anything," the commissaris said. "As you haven't paid us we're in our vacation mode now. We're waiting, Mr. Ambagt."

Carl, holding on to the helicopter's side, faced the commissaris. "What about the hundred thousand we paid up front?"

The commissaris spread his hands. "We haven't seen your money, Mr. Ambagt."

Carl let go of the helicopter, slid across the deck, disappeared down the stairs, was back in his chair within minutes, ballpoint and notebook at the ready. "Could I have the number of your bank account please?" The commissaris checked a card in his wallet, recited the figures. Carl disappeared again, returned promptly. "Dad is transmitting your hundred thou as we speak, sir."

"He forgot?" the commissaris asked.

Carl said that Skipper Peter tended to be slow in paying out moneys.

"Aha." The commissaris studied the Liberian flag fluttering just beyond his outstretched legs.

"So what are you staring at?" Carl asked. "Phone your bank. The money should be there by now."

The commissaris checked the date and time on his watch. "The weekend is about to start in Europe. Tomorrow is Saturday. I won't know until next week whether your father has paid us." He looked at the clearing sky and asked what the green lines were on the horizon. "The last of the Bahamas," Carl said. "The beginning of Haiti." It would be better to steer somewhat north now. Cuba was still close. Although you had armed activity between drug runners there, the sea near the Bahamas was considerably safer than Cuban waters. Cuba liked to confiscate luxury yachts straying within her territorial waters. You could buy yourself out of course but there would be delays, jail time, extra fines just before leaving, all kinds of trouble.

"The Cuban Navy is the enemy here?"

"Right." Carl laughed. "Castro went broke, Castro became a pirate."

The commissaris enquired as to why that was funny.

"The more chaos the better," Carl said happily. "That's what me and Dad like about the Caribbean. No safety. Once things are safe we can forget our profits. More trouble, more money."

"Muddy water?"

"Good fishing," Carl agreed. "Piracy. Wreckery. Do-as-you-pleasery. Going back to true motives. Taking care of Number One."

"Egotism," the commissaris agreed.

Carl grinned. "Serving the needs of the One and Only."

"But," the commissaris asked, "given your self-serving natures, how do you obtain cooperation from others?"

"We dangle money in front of them."

The commissaris spread a hand and looked at nothing lying on its palm.

"One hundred thousand has just been electronically conveyed into your account," Carl pleaded. "True. I swear by all that is holy."

"By your own greediness?" the commissaris asked.

The commissaris and Carl looked out from the ship's stern. The FEADship followed calm seas along a long reef. Dolphins gamboled. The setting sun illuminated their gleaming grey-green bodies. An albatross planed on a parallel course, effortlessly aloft on its seven-feet wingspan. Islands showed as emerald lines on the horizon.

Grijpstra appeared and lowered his heavy body painfully into a deckchair. "Are you going to do something now?" Carl asked the commissaris.

"You didn't stick to your side of the bargain," the commissaris said sternly. "The deal is off. We'll negotiate afresh. Another hundred thousand up front if you please."

"Never." Carl snarled. "You'll have to deliver."

"De Gier phoned," Grijpstra said. "The Key West sergeant let him go and he is on his way to St. Eustatius. He'll stay at Old Rum House. There were some problems but it worked out in the end."

Carl, mumbling furiously, walked out of earshot.

"Bad problems?" the commissaris asked.

"Ant bites, sir. He needed injections."

"Oh dear." The commissaris looked worried.

"Mosquitoes too, flies, anything," Grijpstra said. "He woke up naked in the Key West Cemetery."

"Drinking?" the commissaris asked.

"Papaya juice," Grijpstra said.

Carl waved at bikini-clad girls on a sailboat. "Helllooooh." The girls ignored the towering yacht.

"And de Gier found out something," Grijpstra said. "He has a plan."

"Stupid bitches." Carl had come back. "Rattling about on that plastic shoe box." He turned his back to the railing. "What plan would that be?"

"If de Gier's plan fits in with mine, as I'm sure it will, and you will pay that second hundred thousand, as I am sure you will," the commissaris said, "you will recoup your loss."

"I did pay," Carl said.

"Half." The commissaris smiled, "Or so you say."

"Toast," Grijpstra told the servant. "No butter. Tea without sugar. Tepid. Nothing special."

The servant noted the order. Grijpstra said that a slice of smoked salmon, thinly cut, just a sliver, might be added. Maybe a pickled pepper.

"Okay," Carl said after the servant had left. "You're right. The money will go via Veracruz in Mexico and Mexico is slow." He looked sad. "Petty bank clerks have to prove their power at the expense of us real people."

"You have any cash on board?" the commissaris asked.

"Do I have cash on board?" Carl asked. "With these retard islands around us? Say something goes wrong. You think they have ever heard of credit cards here?"

"Pay us that second hundred thousand in cash." The commissaris pointed at an approaching green line. "That must be Haiti." He unfolded his map. "Maybe not such a good place for cash transactions, but here, next stop, that would be the Dominican Republic. How about this Puerto Plata? That means "money harbor," does it not? There should be a bank there. Suppose you give me the cash here and drop me off in Puerto Plata tomorrow. I can have your cash transferred to our Amsterdam account."

Carl complained. Why should they pay double? The commissaris comforted him, it all came out of the same million due to them later, did it not?

Yes, if the stolen cargo was recovered.

It would be, the commissaris assured him, but not if the cash wasn't provided right now.

"It hasn't been earned," Carl wailed.

"Nobody gets what is earned," the commissaris said. "You get what you have negotiated for." He had read that in a magazine in the airplane flying to Miami.

The next morning the ship's drinking water problem hadn't yet been solved. The cook used bottled water to cook breakfast.

The ship was out of milk and eggs Benedict had to be made with nondairy creamer. After brushing his teeth again, the commissaris was helicoptered ashore by Carl.

"And?" Carl asked when they left the Dominican bank, "What do I get now for my two hundred thousand dollars?"

"Once we get down to work," the commissaris said, "we tend to work quickly. More or less have to, you know. It's like the murder cases we used to solve. Delays wipe out tracks."

The commissaris hummed and grinned after the helicopter had landed on the *Rodney*'s rear deck once again.

"Glad to see that you feel better now." Carl switched off the chopper's engine. "I bet you can see some tracks now, right?"

"The world is an open book," the commissaris said.

"But you have to able to read it," Grijpstra said after Carl returned from a briefing with his father. "We all have our special skills. You slip up with yours . . ."

". . . we repair the damage," the commissaris concluded. He looked concerned. "How is your father?"

His father was worried, Carl said. Skipper Peter was watching his online computer's monitors suspended from his cabin's ceiling. The monitors showed the world's fluctuating markets. Ambagt Senior had been speculating of late, while concentrating on so-called "turn-around" stocks, buying at what he hoped were lows. "Bad for his heart. Too much tension."

Speaking of tension, the commissaris said, it was about time for him to take a nap.

Grijpstra joined him.

"What does de Gier know now?" Grijpstra asked when they were back in their cabin.

"What we know, Henk."

"What do we know, sir?"

The commissaris indicated the bathroom. Grijpstra opened the taps. The commissaris whispered into Grijpstra's ear.

"Frogs?" Grijpstra asked.

"Shshsh," the commissaris said. "Souza was frightened by frogs, remember? And the other thing de Gier will have found out about is that Quadrant Bank is also an insurer."

"Thomas Stewart-Wynne's employer? That sent him out here?"

"Since you couldn't get through to Quadrant from here," the commissaris whispered, "I tried in Puerto Plata. I spoke to Stewart-Wynne's chief. Our dead man in the Key West jeep specialized in checking cargo claims."

"So the *Sibylle* was insured after all?" Grijpstra winked slyly. "So what do you think happened?"

"The piracy happened," the commissaris said.

Grijpstra's smile widened.

22

A Plucked Parrot

De Gier met Karate at Key West Airport. De Gier didn't ask but Karate told him anyway, he wasn't doing too well. Karate had been squeezed by a fat man who overflowed his seat in the Amsterdam-Miami airplane. "A giant condom filled with yogurt." The stewardess had been old and ugly. Karate did not demand fawning servility but just a little common pleasant behavior, when a passenger asks for another mini-bag of stale peanuts and another can of lukewarm juice from concentrate, was that too much? Karate indicated his moist crotch. "Happened when the mummy flight-attendant poured coffee. The plane fell into an air pocket. She was in league with the pilot. The pilot had aimed for the air pocket. Coffee time? Into the air pocket, hoho." The plane's movie was bad. Ketchup would be on the next flight. He had finked out, offering excuses: his passport had to be renewed, his tropical costume was still at the cleaners. Ketchup had found a new pal to sleep over with. Fine. Okay. It wasn't that Karate insisted on faithfulness, no sir, he knew full well that loyalty to a pal wasn't "being in with the crowd anymore," but, hear here, when you're working on a project you make time to be together—or was he being old-fashioned now?

And what was all this wetness in Florida? "Since when does it pour in this tropical super swamp?"

And why did Karate have to sit on the luggage carrier of a rental bicycle? What was wrong with hiring a Mercedes or a Ferrari? "Damn it all, I got mud on my pants now." If de Gier wouldn't mind could he perhaps avoid the next puddle? "Oh, please! Again!"

And what kind of birds were flying above them? Not vultures, were they?

And why were de Gier's face and hands all puffy? Bug bites? Woke up in the cemetery? This very cemetery they were passing? Woke up in the nude? Had been lucky that he hadn't been eaten by the cemetery's crocodiles slithering from the swampy area over there? Crocodiles dig up graves to get at the corpses? But what was a nude de Gier waking in the Key West cemetery for?

Papaya juice in a lap dance bar? Been taken out to the cemetery by pernicious parrots? Hahaha.

No, no, Karate wasn't laughing, he was just clearing his throat. Karate had caught a bad cold in the airplane, been infected by a circulating virus. "Same air keeps coming by. Same virus gets you good each time." Karate was still coughing when de Gier, in a suite in the Eggemoggin Hotel, explained what Karate, and Ketchup who was about to arrive, had to do that night. All the main points were repeated clearly.

Subject is Mickey Donegan. William Street trailer camp. A

degenerate de Gier look-alike, complete with ridiculous mustache. The Perfidious Parrot. Old convertible Chevy in bad shape. No alcohol for him and Ketchup while the project was on. No papaya juice either. Bottled sodas only, to be opened in their presence. A map of Key West. Yes, Karate would study same with attention. The black cross was William Street, the red cross, The Perfidious Parrot.

"Got it?" de Gier asked.

Karate had gotten most if it. He didn't get why de Gier wasn't doing this himself, why he, Karate, and Ketchup, the treacherous fink, had to come all the way from Amsterdam at their own expense—okay, they did have that free pass on Royal Dutch Airlines—all the way to sopping-wet swampy Florida to arrange a "situation." Surely this wasn't because of the fee Ambagt & Son was paying Karate and Ketchup for finding Grijpstra and de Gier a million dollar job, was it? Surely not. This couldn't be some type of revenge, could it? Really. Petty. Did de Gier have any idea how tired Karate was? Ever heard of jet lag? Plus lack of sleep because of some stupid movie that just missed being bad enough to make him switch off the earphones?

Karate's indignation interfered with his breathing. He became red in the face. De Gier had to slap the little man's cheeks to bring him to reason.

"Rest," de Gier said. "Set your alarm so that you can meet Ketchup's plane. Remember to pay for this hotel suite yourselves. A mere thousand a day. Small change for you carpetbaggers."

"And where will you be when we get all this going?" Karate asked.

"Around," de Gier said, "around and around. Not to worry."

"And how do we know what happens in the end?"

De Gier promised that he, at a future meeting, probably in the billiards-café of the stripping lady in Amsterdam, would report in detail, submitting newspaper cuttings, for there might be a few.

"*Will* be a few," Karate laughed. "This should indeed hit the papers. Leave it to us, Mr. Former Sergeant, sir. Hahaha."

Former Special Forces Specialist Michael C. Donegan, presently self-employed, promised himself that, starting probably today, he would go easy on his daily intake of alcohol. Two wake-up demons were too many wake-up demons. He was used to facing one hangover demon. Mickey could ignore it. He would just swing his long legs off the orange-crate bed in the plywood camper parked on the worst corner lot of the Williams Street Trailer Park, and simply walk through the apparently solid image. The demon always just stood there. Sometimes it was in drag, pretending to be Mickey's deceased mother, sometimes it amused itself by being a zombie with the body of a human corpse and the head of a parrot. On mornings following official holidays it might resemble a regular devil, complete with horns and fangs, waving a red hot poker. One wake-up demon was nothing special. It might follow him outside but would waft away if hit by spray from Mickey's showerhead, attached to a garden hose dangling from a fig tree's air root. Or maybe it was the light that made the hangover demon fade. Once the demon was dealt with Mickey was free to figure out some scheme to provide himself with beer money. The hangover demon was irritating but could be dealt with, but now there were two demons, and he couldn't walk through them. He had tried but they pushed him back on the bed, gently, while politely addressing him in some European version of English. The Euro-speak sounded as if its practitioners had flies stuck in their throats and were trying to get rid of the bothersome insects. "Chchchch-chuh, how are you doing, Mickey?"

"Hey!" Mickey said.

"Beer?" one demon asked. It offered a cold can of Heineken. It seemed to say "Heineken" too but the vowels were all wrong and it snarled as it pronounced them, showing its upper teeth as a dog will do when it welcomes its master after mistaking him for an intruder. A friendly embarrassed snarl.

The other demon was smiling too, offering another tasty can, rivulets of thawing dew running down its gleaming sides. "Proast," the other demon said.

Mickey, sipping from the can, peering through a dirty window, saw an orange glow through the twisted fig tree's roots outside. Sunrise? Demons double in the early morning, but the window faced west. Maybe the intruders were regularly human. Repo men? But he owed no money on his car and owned nothing else. He realized he had slept all day. Pictures put themselves together in his slowly booting-up brain. Nasty Nick. Female chests. Nasty Nick's partner, Bad Baldy. Showing Mickey the door. Things hadn't gone too well. He focused on his visitors, who were filling up most of the spare room in the tiny camper. Two almost identical short men in clean jeans, polished half-high boots, ironed shirts, new-looking baseball hats with the same text ("Sounds like bullshit to me") were smiling and emitting the weird sounding vowels that were part of their speech. Mickey got up slowly, smiling too, as if welcoming the unknown parties. He touched one. Yes. Solid.

"Hi," one visitor said. "You are Mickey? Show us girlie bar? Hello? Eat somezing first? Stone kreps?"

"Fried fishes?" the other visitor asked. "Squid soup?"

Mickey, although mostly living on alcohol now, still ate sometimes and seafood seemed like a good idea. "Who . . ." he croaked, rubbing his throat, ". . . *are* you?"

"Vriends," both short men said simultaneously. They introduced themselves. Cornelius offered a cigarette protruding from a crumpled blue pack. "French, very koot." Fernandus flicked his lighter.

Mickey inhaled deeply, then coughed. His friends patted his back affectionately. The sudden and powerful intake of nicotine cleared Mickey's brain. Mickey sucked more smoke from the black smoldering tobacco. "Yes, good." He put on his jeans and T-shirt. "You do have money, have you?"

"Plentie of munnie," Cornelius said. "We haf," Fernandus said. They showed handfuls of bills, twenties and fifties. "Enuf?"

Mickey thought so. Taking a cold shower outside helped to clear his brain further. It produced a theory that would explain the two little men who were now sitting on the steps of the camper, slapping at mosquitos, blowing smoke at flies. "You're from a ship?" Mickey asked. "Crew? Someone gave you my name and address? I'm to be your guide?"

"Sure," Cornelius said, smiling. "Datsit," Fernandus said, "cruise ship. The *Statendam*."

"Pursers," Cornelius said. "Smuggled dope. Made munnie. Now spend it. You show where. Girlies."

"First eat fishes," Fernandus said.

The three ate in a garden restaurant, specializing in seafood, off Whitehead Street. No liquor was served but Cornelius and Fernandus had dropped six-packs into Mickey's trunk and now retrieved them. Broiled fresh snapper came within an oval of lemon slices, stone crab was served with its own hot sauce, the frozen lemon pie with freshly whipped cream. "Ahhhhh," the foreigners kept saying, "Koot." They also kept raising their cans. "Proast."

"Proast," Mickey toasted. This was all all right. Lady Luck had shown up again to repay him for expert services rendered. His tolerance for alcohol had gone down steeply lately and even though he hadn't had more than four of five beers Mickey was drunk. He was telling his sympathetic hosts about the beautiful and pure Christina, who had once shared his camper. How this good woman had been seduced by the island's worst pimp. How Nasty Nick made the innocent Christina work in a bad place, The Perfidious Parrot. How he couldn't visit Christina there anymore. His audience listened spellbound. "Main Chott," Cornelius growled. Fernandus merely gasped. How could such injustice be? It could, Mickey assured them. Mickey picked a frangipani flower off a bush next to his chair, compared the white flower to his beloved Christina, made his hosts smell her subtle fragrance, then scowled, then crushed the flower. "Nasty Nick did that."

"Say no more," the avenging spirits told their protegée. They paid the bill, leaving the smiling waitress with a large tip. They hopped into Mickey's car. The chariot, with Mickey at the wheel, roared off.

Not ten minutes later, after speeding through red lights, across sidewalks, parks and parking lots, careening on the wrong sides of streets, its horn blaring, its driver and passengers shouting, the Chevy had traversed the city, and slid sideways across The Perfidious Parrot's parking lot, where it braked abruptly. Doorman Nasty Nick was hit by a shower of crushed oyster shells, plowed up by the Chevy's wheels.

"That's him?" Karate asked Mickey.

"He's mine," Mickey screamed but the two Dutchmen, standing on the car's back seat had jumped out of the car and assaulted their temporarily blinded opponent before Mickey had even opened his door. Karate went for Nick's head, Ketchup for Nick's knees. The victim had been a semiprofessional boxer and was ready to throw some punches but his attention was distracted by a new threat looming up. A tall hooded human shape, riding a pink bicycle, entered the scene via a sidewalk and now circled Nick. De Gier, wearing a black cape with glowing bones painted on it, pulled off his hood. A skull grinned, deep-set red eyes glowed from ivory sockets.

"What . . . ?" Nasty Nick screamed before Karate hit him on the temple and Ketchup pummeled him under the belt. Mickey, professionally trained to take pleasure in painful destruction, kicked Nick between the legs.

Mickey, delirious with alcohol and rage, took the cyclist for his own wake-up demon, arriving late. He waved at the spook and ran inside, following his mates who had already rushed into the nightclub's hall. Bad Baldy, Nasty Nick's partner, a huge man, backed by a muscular wide-shouldered bouncer, blocked the way. Baldy was about to reach for a shotgun hidden behind a counter. Ketchup whistled on his fingers and Karate pointed at something above Baldy's head. The big man looked at the hall's ceiling. Ketchup jumped and slid across the counter, swiveling as he moved. His feet kicked Bad Baldy in the belly. Baldy slumped forward. Mickey's clasped hands thumped Baldy's shaven skull. Karate grabbed the shotgun, hit the remaining bouncer on the chin with its butt, aimed the weapon at the ceiling and fired both barrels. Then the three attackers invaded the main room. The DJ, another big man, joined the melee while the raucous rock music kept playing and women kept stripping and contorting their bodies. Some clients joined the intruders, others chose to assist the DJ. Baldy reappeared. Mickey caught a flying chair and broke it on the big man's head. Baldy went down again.

"CHRISTINA!" Mickey shouted. The name became a battle-cry. Christina, a petite redhead who was trying to leave through a broken window, was pulled back by the legs by Mickey. She had no desire to be saved but was picked up anyway, bundled in a torn-down curtain and carried outside. A falling candle set a tablecloth on fire and soon flames were licking at the walls, igniting wooden furniture, crackling along the seams between dry floor boards.

While the building burned Ketchup and Karate made sure the still defensive Christina was tied up in Mickey's backseat. Passing cars, attracted by the fire, drove onto the parking lot. Other cars were frantically trying to leave. Sirens were heard in the distance. Ketchup and Karate directed traffic so that the Chevy could get away. The two little men stepped into shadows and disappeared. The spooky cyclist was long gone.

* * *

Newspaper cuttings, faxed by Sergeant Ramona Symonds to Rinus de Gier c/o *The Old Rum House* in St. Eustatius, Netherlands Antilles:

Cutting # 1 (*Key West Police* Daily Report)

Today, 3.30 A.M., a white male known as Michael C. Donegan (33), residing in Camper # 3, William Street Trailer Park, unemployed, was arrested by me, Policeman Albert B. Paton, (strained wrist, medical report attached), driving patrol car 1, with the help of colleagues driving patrol cars 7 and 3, respectively Samuel "Piggy" Jones (broken eyeglasses, damage report attached), and Carl Opken (dislocated shoulder, medical report attached), at the crossing of White Street and Truman Avenue where his vehicle hit a tree. Subject appeared to be inebriated (slurred speech, unsteady gait, strong smell of alcohol). Subject refused breath test. Subject resisted arrest. After being handcuffed, Subject kicked and broke a side window of patrol car 1 (damage report attached). Subject was accompanied by Christina "Chesty" Fetcher (26), residing at the Happy End Motel (Terry Lane). Fetcher is an exotic dancer performing at The Perfidious Parrot striptease bar (Greene & Williams Streets) who accused subject of kidnapping and assault (signed and witnessed complaint attached). After my arrival at Simonton Precinct, dispatcher J. Dembska reported a telephone call by Nicholas "Nasty" Silsby, doorman and part proprietor at/of aforementioned strip-bar, clocked at 3.20 A.M. Silsby told Dembska that aforementioned Michael Donegan, recently barred from The Perfidious Parrot, forced entry into the strip-bar, and assaulted him, Silsby, and kidnapped the aforementioned Christina C. Fetcher. Donegan was assisted by two unknown subjects. The three of them, allegedly, also set fire to the building housing The Perfidious Parrot. Subject Donegan, pending further investigation, is being held at the Simonton Street Precinct. His two accessories were not apprehended. Silsby described subjects as white males, 30+, small of stature, who spoke German.

Newspaper cutting 2
(*Miami Daily Messenger*)

VIOLENCE IN KEY WEST

An escaped prisoner was shot to death last night in Key West. Michael "Mickey" C. Donegan (31), being held on suspicion of assault on a nightclub doorman, kidnapping of an exotic dancer, arson, DWI, avoiding arrest, resisting arrest and assault on three policemen, managed, last night, to climb a twenty foot brick wall behind the Simonton Street Jail in Key West. Warden Tim Jones stated that Donegan had asked him for cigarettes but was informed that the jail had been declared "smoke free" recently. Donegan, the warden said, thereupon announced that he would obtain his nicotine "some other way." No one suspected that the prisoner would be able to scale a twenty foot wall topped by a roll of barbed wire. The prisoner was, however, a former Green Beret, and had been decorated in the Gulf War. The jail's wall had previously been repaired leaving small projecting wires in the plaster. Donegan used the projections to support his bare toes and rolled across the barbed wire on top of the wall. The prisoner, dressed in bright orange jail garb, jogging along, reached Fleming Street. The warden had meanwhile alerted all police patrols in the city. A bicycle constable ordered the fugitive to stop. Donegan shouted that he was on his way to get cigarettes at Fausto Supermarket and would return soon. At that moment a shot was fired and Donegan dropped to the pavement. According to the witnesses the policeman had not drawn his gun. The identity of the killer is, as yet, unknown. Only one shot was fired. It may have been a drive-by shooting. The bullet hit Donegan in the heart. Military precision?

23

BOUNTY HUNTERS

St. Eustatius, one of the three northern Netherlands Antilles, is barely six miles long and two miles across. Facing Oranjestad, St. Eustatius's capital and port, a hamlet with some few hundred inhabitants, the *Admiraal Rodney* had dropped her anchor and swayed quietly on a calm sea.

Grijpstra and Carl Ambagt, aboard the *Rodney*'s sloop, were being rowed ashore. De Gier waved at them from the balcony of his second story hotel room. The Old Rum House, built centuries ago from the island's sandstone and local lumber, topped by roofs of imported Dutch tiles, stood on a cliff commanding views of the ocean and neighboring islands. The commissaris and the skipper watched what was going on from the *Rodney*'s sundeck. Ambagt Senior was on his second sherry ("Laying out my daily schedule in an orderly fashion," he had just said), the commissaris was on his first double espresso. The skipper was spilling sherry on a freshly laundered admiral's uniform, the commissaris's shantung suit was crumpled from its many ocean splashings. A folded face towel placed inside his pith helmet by the ever-thoughtful servant kept it from sagging over the commissaris's eyes.

"Looks like a little bit of heaven," the commissaris said, pointing his cane at St. Eustatius.

Skipper Peter snorted. "For rugheads only." His hand swept in a halfcircle indicating the entire crescent of the Antilles. "You know what is out here? Nothing but nasty niggers." The skipper looked at the island morosely. "There, on 'Statia' as they call it, is a hotel on the other side, called *Beachcastle* or somesuch. Me and Carl stayed there some years back and we were robbed."

"By black people?" The commissaris shook his head. "How unfortunate. At gun point?"

"Burglars," Skipper Peter barked.

"You caught the criminals in the act?"

Skipper Peter said he had not, but his luggage was stolen.

The commissaris looked stern. "So how do you know the culprits were black?"

Ambagt Senior grimaced. "Carl and I had been out for a walk, or been trying to. There is a lot of litter piled up on the beach here. We were worn out by having to step over broken buckets, torn ropes, bottles and what have you and were looking forward to a rest, but back in our room all our clothes and gear were gone." Skipper Peter mimed the sad surprise of that fateful moment. "Your stuff is gone. You ever had that happen to you? Makes you feel naked?"

The commissaris said yes. Luggage fails to arrive at airports. Kind of pleasant. You don't have to carry what isn't there. Lightening of the daily load. Less to worry about.

"Yes," Ambagt Senior said sadly. "Worry. Most annoying. Objects change into empty space. Nothing to hold on to. But they had left us something, my new camera, a thirty-five millimeter Nikon. The damn thing sat there, staring at us from the table."

"Your burglars had no interest in photography?" the commissaris suggested.

"Not that so much," the skipper said. "There was film in the camera which I had developed much later. There were our own snapshots and two clear pictures of big black backsides."

"You think that is funny?" Skipper Peter asked.

The commissaris excused his sudden hooting. He pointed at a small mountain with a jagged peak on the south side of the island. "A volcano? Active, you think?"

"Dormant," Ambagt Senior said. "But the Antilles are treacherous, you can't count on anything. Same with the natives. And to think we set them such good examples." He carefully felt his nose which looked more swollen than usual. "Do you know that St. Eustatius used to be known as the 'Golden Rock'? Dutch merchants used to make big bucks here."

The commissaris showed interest. "Two hundred years ago, up to fifty ocean-going ships *a day* used to anchor here," he was told. "Benjamin Franklin himself kept a mailbox on St. Eustatius."

"Here, eh?" The commissaris contemplated the silent inactivity ashore. A mini volcano to the south, a narrow valley straight ahead, five molehills to the north. Behind the narrow beach a bit of a boulevard with a few trees here and there, vainly trying to cover up a dull dry yellow inland. The village consisted of crumbling walls and some sagging tiled roofs. There were no other ships in sight. Oranjestad reached into the water with a single short pier, a few hundred feet long. At the far left end of the island there was a far more imposing structure built out into the ocean, a giant quay where two supertankers were being pumped dry of their cargo. Between the low hills large aluminum storage tanks gleamed.

"Billions were earned here," Peter Ambagt croaked, "measured in today's values. Billions, dear sir. All made by smart thinking. Golden British pounds, yessir." He held up index finger and thumb, some two inches apart. "Solid. The Golden Age, the era when America was still a colony and Britain made it illegal for her American subjects to trade with anybody but the homeland. Colonists sold their raw materials cheap and had to pay top dollar for finished British goods."

"So there was smuggling," the commissaris said cheerfully. "I like restrictive laws." He nodded approval. "Invite illegal business so we can all have adventures. Cops and robbers forever, Skipper Peter. British cops, eh? American free men?" He rubbed his small slender hands. "A splendid conflict. So deals with America were made through our merchants here?"

So it was, Skipper Peter said. Smuggling between the Netherlands and America was channeled through Statia where large cargo vessels kept coming and going. Gigantic craft in those days, three stories high, filled to capacity with high-margin products. Why this particular island when there are so many? Because St. Eustatius had a perfect anchorage on its leeside. "Right where we are now," Peter said. He raised his glass to toast the location.

The commissaris visualized the scene. Wooden frigates and

galleons, hoisting or striking thousands of square feet of complicated sails. The Netherlands tricolor flying, ashore and on many mast tops. Melodious shouts in many tongues as multiracial crews loaded or warehoused cargo. Rowboats manned by boisterous sailors skimming underneath bowsprits adorned with barebreasted figureheads of mermaids, courtesans, even noblewomen. Live women on the beach, posturing to attract potential clients' attention. Gurgling jars filling pewter mugs with rum or jenever in cool basements or under quayside sunscreens.

Statia's commerce, Skipper Peter related, doubled as soon as America prepared for her own liberation.

"Weapons," whispered the old man greedily. "Gun powder. The never ending need for ammo. Uniforms. Food. Transport. The military is a money hole." The mercantile fleets kept coming, protected by Dutch warships. It was the time of the great Dutch admirals. Old Ambagt pronounced their names with reverence: Heyn, Tromp, the redoubtable Michiel de Ruyter.

"Pete Heyn," Ambagt Senior sang in an off-key treble, "his name was sma-all."

"Big were his ba-alls," sang the commissaris, remembering the lines of a patriotic school song.

"His dee-eeds were fi-ne," sang Skipper Peter. "His name still shi-nes."

"Wasn't Admiral Heyn the man who seized the Spanish silver fleet?" the commissaris asked. "Much earlier on, in the sixteen hundreds?

Yes. No matter. Profit is profit. Skipper Peter's long spidery fingers trembled with greedy tension. Those were the days, he told the commissaris. The Spanish fleet was anchored off the

Cuban coast. They had been through a bit of a storm and, stupidly, were sleeping in. The Dutch vessels anchored behind a wooded island, invisible, masts mingled with the silhouettes of tall trees. Admiral Heyn had his crews board sloops and row quietly toward the enemy. The small boats were shrouded by early morning fog. When Spanish guards raised the alarm they were already being shot at by marksmen using long barreled matchlock rifles.

"Buena Guerra," shouted the Dutch officers, "good war", indicating that the enemy would not be harmed upon surrender. *"Buena guerra, amigos queridos."* The beloved friends promptly surrendered. Shiploads of silver treasure taken from Inca temples changed hands once again.

An example of profitable warfare, Skipper Peter explained, but there were also Dutch privateers, and there was always the slave trade. All business was transacted via Statia. Sugar plantations flourished on the tiny island, some coffee was grown, there were extensive vegetable gardens, cattle was grazed, there was an abundance of poultry.

"Free black labor," Skipper Peter squeaked, "a blessing for free white spirits. The Golden Rock, my friend." His dentures clicked as he laughed. "Check the public library in Oranjestad. Nice etchings." The excitement made old Ambagt squeeze his nose too hard. Blood seeped between his fingers and stained his gold-buttoned whites. "The ugly ones worked in the fields, the beautiful ones were kept around the villas. Handsome slaves walked naked. Free labor." He wiggled his bloody fingers while tittering dementedly, *"Mhree mhree."*

"Free labor for free spirits?" the commissaris asked.

There were stupid people, Skipper Peter explained, spilling

liquor and catching his upper denture, snapping it back smartly. There were also clever people. The stupid are doomed. The clever are blessed. The doomed are to be ruled by the blessed. Ah, the blessed merchants of St. Eustatius.

"That was then," the commissaris said, watching the quiet coastline ahead. "What happens now?"

Now little happens, Skipper Peter said sadly. Statia dozes like her volcano Mazinga. Mazinga, an old Indian word, means "Eater of Men," but at present Statians were just sitting around, waiting to be eaten later. He himself would never put another foot on the damned island. It wasn't worth the trouble to risk heart and lungs to climb the steep Slave Path up to the village. "They don't have to carry me, slaves are out of fashion for the moment, I know, I know . . ." he was whining again, ". . . but they could install an elevator if they want to attract big spenders like me."

"Pity I don't feel up to walking up steep heights right now," the commissaris said, rubbing his painful thighs.

Skipper Peter looked at the commissaris's legs. He laughed.

"I limp better than you," he said, banging his stick on the deck. "You got nothing on me. I am the Eternal Winner." He emptied his glass and held it up for the servant to fill. "You know that winning never bores me?"

"Even now?" the commissaris asked, winking. "Do you really not mind losing that uninsured *Sibylle* cargo? Or do you have something up your sleeve perhaps?"

Skipper Peter winked back. *"Heheheheh."*

Commissaris and skipper watched Statia's shore through powerful binoculars, handed them respectfully by the servant. They saw how burly Grijpstra and tiny Carl climbed the path that twisted between cliffs and trees. The narrow coastal strip, crossed by the path, looked like a green belt around the island. "Behind it there is nothing but misery," Peter Ambagt squeaked. "Those few palm trees don't fool me. I'll stay right here."

De Gier, from his balcony, watched Grijpstra and Carl approach. The hotel was within the island's narrow green zone. Mauve bougainvillea and white oleander blossomed alongside the Slave Path. Cocos and royal palms waved their fronds above hibiscus and frangipani bushes. Red brick walls and blue roof tiles reminded him of Holland.

Meanwhile, on the *Rodney*, the commissaris told Skipper Peter that the island looked pleasant. "The previous splendor could be brought back, don't you think? Fix up the cottages, plant flower and fruit gardens. Invite a jazz combo to play under the palm trees. Go for quiet walks in the early mornings. I'm sure the islanders could be manipulated into cleaning the place up. Figure out what the locals are good at, have them do that, shower them with praise. Flatter the island's government, make it believe that all the changes are its own work. Wouldn't you like to do that, Skipper? A project for your old age? You, being a genius, might enjoy restoring St. Eustatius to its former glory." The commissaris, energized by his own eloquent salesmanship, waved enthusiastic hands. "I might help you. Have a beauty contest, a music festival, a beach cleaning race, get the kids to draw or sculpt examples of local wildlife, rediscover popular dishes and make the grannies proud of their cooking. Play on their religion. Get priests and parsons involved, the governor, elders. Give them all the credit."

"Sounds like work," Skipper Peter said moodily.

The commissaris didn't think so. "All you do is initiate the project. If it works out, okay, you leave it to them and tell them it's their own doing. Then we sit back and get them to pick their beauty queen. You get to pin on the medal." He pointed at the mountain. "You'll be beloved."

Skipper Peter contemplated the idea. He admitted that it might provide some pleasure. His drunkenness ebbed as he talked about a descent into Mazinga's crater some time back. There had been songbirds and giant lizards, an authentic rain forest, Statia's own species of giant fern. He mentioned archaeologists, who found imprints of Carib Indian dwellings, similar to Venezuelan native housing that still exists, a type of pagoda with triple roofs. The Statian villa would have had walls of woven rushes, removable, so that seasonal sea breezes could cool the rooms. Old Ambagt's thin arm swept toward Mazinga's silhouette. "A clear view of forest and sea. The place was different then. Lots of tall trees, plenty of ponds in the valley."

"The present ecology could be improved," the commissaris said. "A worthy experiment maybe. Have clever students figure out a way to use solar energy to distill sea water. Once you have irrigation get everyone to plant a hundred trees."

Skipper Peter shook his head. "I'm a scavenger, not an improver. The planet is going down. I'm after the final pickings."

The commissaris was quiet.

"There are better spots," Skipper Peter said gruffly, "where everything is in place already, like on Bora Bora, Fiji, the southern Solomons. But wherever I go ashore they'll make me pay taxes." He pointed at cannon barrels peeking out of Statia's ancient fortress, then shook his fist at the Dutch flag flying over the ancient battery. "They'd squeeze my bank account dry."

"Quadrant Bank," the commissaris said, "employed that British fellow, Stewart-Wynne, who broke his neck driving a jeep through Duval Street. You didn't know the man, did you?"

"Who?" Skipper Peter asked.

"Insurance inspector Thomas Stewart-Wynne," the commissaris said.

"*Bank* inspector," old Ambagt said triumphantly, squinting at the commissaris across the rim of his glass. "Quadrant is a bank." He gingerly touched his nose. "Nothing to do with insurance."

The commissaris shrugged. "You know how it is with these big companies nowadays, they like to branch out. I hear Quadrant has been in freight insurance for a while now. Specialized in tanker cargos, so I am told."

Skipper Peter's eyelids fluttered uncontrollably.

"Hire a cop to do dirty work," the commissaris said. "and you face the curiosity that police training breeds." He smiled at his host. "And now that you admit to having insured the *Sibylle*'s cargo would you mind filling me in on its worth?"

Skipper Ambagt nodded. "That would be the exact amount I expect you to recover." He gestured for a refill. "Half, dear boy."

"You're sure you don't want a full glass, Skipper Peter?"

Ambagt Senior watched his glass fill up. He sipped, then squinted at the commissaris. "The cargo's value? Twelve million gallons of crude in the *Sibylle*. Forty-two gallons to the barrel. Say twenty dollars value to the barrel. Lemmesee. Twelve million divided by forty-two, that would be around, mhree, two-hundred-and-eighty-thousand barrels? Times, whaddeewesaynow? Twenty? Yes? Okay. That would be, eehrm, five-and-a-half million dollars worth." He showed his fist. "That isn't cat piss."

The commissaris tsked compassionately.

"It's the complete cat," Skipper Peter yelled. "And you'll skin it for me Mr. Fuzz, you and old Fatso and Master Movie Mustache." He banged his glass on the upturned nude woman table. "If you know so much, eh, do you know that Quadrant has not paid me yet?"

"Is the insurer denying your claim?" the commissaris asked pleasantly.

"Delaying the claim pending a routine investigation." Ambagt Senior was squeezing his nose again. "And because that insurance inspector, that faggoty storefront cowboy, couldn't drive a recreational vehicle through Key West without killing himself, the delay keeps on." Old Ambagt smashed his glass on the table. "That's why Carl told you the cargo wasn't insured. As long as we haven't been paid, that statement is true." The skipper's nose seemed ready to burst now. "You know what money *costs* these days?"

"Seven percent?" the commissaris asked.

"For risk-taking entrepreneurs like me?" Ambagt's polished boots stamped on the teak deck. "Eighteen-and-a-half percent, and that's with the *Rodney* as collateral." The boots stamped faster. "Anything goes wrong and I lose my vessel."

"How," the commissaris asked, "did you come to know that

the Quadrant inspector was gay, dressed like a cowboy, and lost his life driving a jeep in Key West?"

Skipper Peter grinned. "Because Stewy phoned us daily and then he suddenly didn't. Because we read the newspapers when we were docked in Key West. Because we watched local TV." The skipper's grin widened. "Okay? Mr.-Know-it-all-but-not-quite?"

The commissaris remained unperturbed. "And why did you tell me you never heard of Quadrant Bank while you were doing business with their insurance department?"

"Because it has nothing to do with why I hired you clowns." Skipper Peter looked at the island's denuded hills. He toasted the commissaris with his shaking glass. "Ketchup and Karate recommended you as all-out go-getters. One cargo lost, *two* cargos recovered." He gestured for a new glass. "I hired you clowns as bounty hunters."

The expression made the commissaris think of action films that he saw on the VCR in his study, while Katrien watched the romance channel in the bedroom. Bounty hunting was for tough guys. This was to be for real. Double Caribbean piracy. Recovered treasure. A tale to take home to Turtle.

Skipper Peter, exhausted, and the commissaris, bemused, watched schoolgirls swim between ship and beach. A puff of cloud made its leisurely way to the top of dormant Mazinga. The commissaris thought it was a pity his legs were hurting. He would like to look down into the volcano's crater, hear finches warble amid banana leaves, hear giant lizards rustle between fern trees.

"One loss that leads to double profits," Skipper Ambagt said, "but so far I'm the fisherman on the bridge in front of our house in Rotterdam, in the old days, when I was a kid, and there were still canals like you guys have in Amsterdam and the Germans hadn't bombed the city and filled in all the water with our own rubble."

"Hmm?" the commissaris asked dreamily.

"I used to ask that fisherman," Skipper Peter said, "whether he had caught something yet and he'd say: 'If the one that is nibbling bites and I catch another I will have caught two fishes, sonny.' "

"The insurance will be paid and we will deliver," the commissaris said. "Not to worry, sir."

Peter Ambagt's rubbing caused his tortured nose to bleed profusely. He kept talking while applying Band-Aids handed to him by the servile servant. "Doubling your return on investment is what makes business go round. The first principle of business, sell at double your cost." He laughed. "The only useful thing Carl learned at school. Buy for a guilder, sell for two, so you can pay a little commission to associates who do the work. Keep everyone happy."

"My father was a trader," the commissaris said. "*He* said the principle of business was continuity. Keep profits modest. Don't just go for one trade, consider the next one. Enjoy yourself quietly while the profits flow in."

"Continuity?" Ambagt Senior asked. "But we have that too, my man. You really think I had just one tanker coming? There's also the *Rebecca*. Another supercargo on its way from Iran, due within ten days now." The skipper smiled. His hands trembled and his knees shook but he looked excited. "Again bound for Havana. Cuba still won't pay. Same thing all over."

"All this time you've been scheming for a repeat?" The commissaris moved forward on his seat, clasped his hands around his cane, stared intently at the skipper's face. "*Two* cargos lost, *four* cargos recovered?"

"Me?" Skipper Peter asked, sipping sherry.

24

A WARRIOR'S REWARD

Carl Ambagt, in a spotless off-white linen suit, wearing a white-brimmed matching hat, followed by little kids who had been playing on the pier, observed how Grijpstra and de Gier greeted each other with formal hellos. "No hugging and backslapping?" Carl asked. "Aren't you two pals?" Carl embraced then patted air, to show how energy passes between close friends. "Or are you blaming each other for not doing your job?"

"Runt." Grijpstra shook a hairy fist under Carl's red face.

"Fisticuffs, Fatso?" Carl did a boxer's dance, his hands balled into fists.

De Gier pushed Grijpstra aside so he could face the opponent. "My dear chap," de Gier said sweetly, looking at Carl kindly, "fine friend, little buddy." He bent an arm, as if to invite Carl to lean into it. Carl relaxed. De Gier's hand darted forward and pulled Carl's wide-brimmed hat down. De Gier's foot tripped Carl's leg. Carl fell over backward. Grijpstra caught

Carl, set him upright, spun him around. Carl, blinded by his hat, became a spinning top on the quayside. The Statia kids cheered, and Grijpstra and de Gier walked along the coastal footpath.

Grijpstra was still upset. "Pushy little scumbag, isn't he?"

"Now," de Gier said, "is that nice? You were Carl's guest on that beautiful boat."

"On that tub?" Grijpstra bellowed that nobody would ever get him to put one foot on the *Admiraal Rodney* again.

"You're safely ashore now, Henk."

Grijpstra stamped on flagstones. "Bah."

"You're on a tropical island. Every bourgeois dreams of this." De Gier shook Grijpstra by the shoulders. "Enjoy your bourgeois dream."

The coastal route, designed and kept up to lure cruiseships, was shadowed by palm trees. Low brick walls supported concrete planters filled with lobelia, impatiens and juanitas, mingling their prettily colored flowers. A skinny old donkey, loaded with baskets partly filled with sickly looking fish, overtook them. The donkey's mistress, an old woman in dark clothes said Good Day in Dutch. The detectives lifted their hats. Grijpstra stopped to study the outline of de Gier's hotel. "This joint okay?"

"Bankrupt." De Gier pushed Grijpstra into a cobblestoned front yard. Rusted deckchairs were stacked between tree stumps. Wildflowers grew from cracks. "I'm the only guest here. The place is to be auctioned off. A maid is supposed to make beds and sweep but I haven't seen her yet. The phone and fax work. A manager comes in later in the morning, she lets me do my own cooking."

Grijpstra checked his watch. Time to eat? He noted that the ground didn't sway and that he wasn't feeling nauseous either. He suggested breakfast.

"Fried fish with a slice of lemon?" de Gier asked. "I can bake biscuits too."

Grijpstra preferred a steak, or some sausage maybe.

De Gier had found goat meat at Oranjestad's farmers market. "Maybe okay for stew. Fish is less hairy."

Grijpstra chose eggs. De Gier cooked on flickering gas flames, in dented pots, using instruments that he had derusted by rubbing them on bricks. A large omelet rose slowly. He picked thyme and parsley from what was left of a kitchen garden in the yard and cut the herbs with an axe that he had sharpened on a grindstone. He toasted bread above the stove's flames, manufactured milk from powder and tap water that he filtered through a clean handkerchief and boiled before mixing. He smashed coffee beans, using the axe's backside after wrapping the beans in a tea cloth he had found.

He let the coffee boil briefly. "Never too long, Henk. I'm using grandmother Sarah's formula. Watch this." He spoke melodiously. "Twen-ty *one* twen-ty *two* twen-ty *three*, rea-*DEEE*, off the flame the pot goes-EEEE."

De Gier served brunch outside, on cracked but clean plates, arranged on a rock wall protecting the hotel yard from a steep drop down to the beach. Grijpstra was told to pick a bouquet of poinciana flowers and find a vase in the hotel lobby. De Gier spread paper napkins and pulled up chairs.

"I don't dislike this," Grijpstra said, enjoying omelet and tasty trimmings, fresh coffee, cool sea breeze and view.

"We get twenty percent off," de Gier said, "for lack of service."

"Why pick St. Eustatius?" Grijpstra asked. "Wouldn't the tourist haven of St. Maarten be more convenient? The *Rodney* crew claims this place is a pain."

"Work," de Gier said.

"?"

"You look stupid like that," de Gier said. "Please. We have a job to do. We're being paid. Crude oil. Supertanker. Piracy. A dead man. Two dead man, counting the cowboy driving through our Key West dinner. We're supposed to arrange a happy ending."

Grijpstra grunted.

De Gier patted Grijpstra's cheek. "It'll be all right. Now think along with me. Twelve million gallons of oil were pumped out of the pirated *Sibylle*. Where? At sea? Are you kidding? Into what? Into another supertanker? Never. Two metal whales wallowing next to each other, one spewing, one sucking. And nobody notices?" He pointed at the ocean. A yacht sailed by, her skipper alert at the rudder, his girlfriend showing herself off on the foredeck. The *Rodney* was at anchor, with crew members moving about on her decks. The ferry plane to St. Maarten had just taken off from Statia's airstrip. The plane banked giving pilots and passengers plenty of opportunity to see the ocean below. A tanker and a cruiseship moved slowly on the horizon.

"I know," Grijpstra said. "I have been thinking about that. A lot of traffic even further along, on the open ocean. I asked the boatswain on the *Rodney*. There are busy shipping routes all through the Caribbean, plus random boats. American war planes keep an eye out too."

"So don't you think anything unusual, such as two super-tankers in intimate contact, would be seen, talked about?"

Grijpstra acknowledged the possibility.

So that didn't happen, de Gier said. "The *Sibylle* was entered from some fast small vessel that then disappeared. The tanker was hijacked and taken to a place where she could be off-loaded. There were only a handful of pirates. You don't need an invading army to subdue a small crew."

"Certainly not at night." Grijpstra nodded. "The *Sibylle* crew is drunk. Asleep. Watching skin-flicks. One man on the bridge, that young fellow they did away with. The ship would have been on automatic pilot. Then what happened?"

"Tell me," de Gier said.

Grijpstra thought.

"Where would pirates aiming to exchange crude for cash take a tanker?" de Gier asked. "To a transfer station, maybe?" De Gier pointed to the north side of St. Eustatius. "To a nice long pier with equipment that drains the oil from the holds and pumps the cargo into storage tanks?"

"Why here?" Grijpstra asked. "There may be many transfer stations around here. The map shows lots of islands." He pointed both ways. "All the way northwest to Florida. All the way down south to Venezuela."

De Gier shook his head. "The empty *Sibylle* was found float-ing in this area, near the only island that sports an oil terminal that does not belong to one of the big brand names." He pointed at the pier again, at the far side of the island. A supertanker was moored on one side, another was maneuvering close by.

"They do seem to ripen faster in the tropics," Grijpstra said, admiring schoolgirls running about on the beach below. "Would that be a dance class? What gracious young ladies." He looked at de Gier sternly. "How come you know so much? And how come that beautiful Key West sergeant didn't keep you as a pet? Did she catch Stewart-Wynne's killer already?" He made an effort not to look at the dancing girls. "Why was the insurance cowboy killed anyway? Did he figure out what was going on down here?"

"What else?" de Gier asked. "The fool identified the pirates and then hung around so that these pirates could get themselves a hit man who arranged an accident. We watched the outcome while we were trying to crack lobster tails."

"Pirates are professionals." Grijpstra shook his head. "They shot up that poor sailor boy on the *Sibylle*, why not shoot up the cowboy too? Who needs a hit man?"

"Simple," de Gier said. "You're the senior detective. You tell me."

Grijpstra, applying experience, identified with the criminal minds.

"Yes?" de Gier asked patiently.

"Our pirates must be American," Grijpstra said grudgingly. "They can misbehave here in this lawless territory, but they better behave at home."

"What American pirates live in Key West?" de Gier asked.

"No prompting." Grijpstra held up a defensive hand. "The pirates must be members of the U.S. military who were moonlighting here. We saw them in action when you got me out on that leaky schooner. By the time they learned that the Englishman was on to them they were back at their home base. And then he turned up there too."

De Gier nodded.

Grijpstra thumped de Gier's shoulder. "Special Forces couldn't take a risk, right? Not on U.S. territory, in Key West. So who was their hitman?"

"Mickey," de Gier said. "A former Green Beret, a specialist in assassination whom they could trust. But Mickey got himself arrested by the Key West Police. So the moonlighters had to take Mickey out."

De Gier went to his room and came back with the cuttings Sergeant Ramona Symonds had faxed him.

Grijpstra grunted and mumbled while reading. He thumped de Gier again. "You know this is about puppets manipulating puppets? Pirates unmasked by the English inspector, who is hit by Mickey. You arrested by Sergeant Ramona because you're in the way and she figures you'll save her trouble. You using Ketchup and Karate so that Ramona gets Mickey. But Mickey gets hit by pirates?" Grijpstra laughed out loud, hitting his thighs. "Ketchup and Karate who tried to play *us* for puppets. On behalf of the Ambagts, our ultimate puppeteers. Nice. Were K&K hurt badly, the little rascals?"

"You bet," de Gier said happily.

"And that nice police sergeant?" Grijpstra asked timidly. "She rewarded you?"

"Some woman," de Gier said happily.

Grijpstra wasn't interested in details, he proclaimed. Whether de Gier had been properly rewarded for his services made no difference to Grijpstra. What can you expect from a woman

JANWILLEM VAN DE WETERING

who cohabits with a bird? "I suppose you just had coffee?" Grijpstra asked.

"No," de Gier said.

"Is that so?" Grijpstra asked. He didn't want to pry. But one abstract aspect interested him a little. Grijpstra, since the advent of Nellie some years ago back, hadn't been "in practice" so to speak. Not in "playing the field." He had heard, however, that things were rather different now. It wasn't so much that the female, innocently falling backwards, pulled the male, by happenstance as it were, into a close relationship. Females, the true dominants in human sex, had come out in the open. Males, Grijpstra had heard, were supposed to be shy now. "Or not?"

"Ramona was shy," de Gier said.

"And you?"

"I'm always shy."

"So? You both managed?" Grijpstra tried not to raise his voice. "What happened?"

De Gier scratched his left buttock. "The usual, I guess."

"What's usual," Grijpstra asked, "about a beautiful black bisexual woman with a bird as a roommate?"

De Gier said that Ramona had been quite usual about the whole thing.

"And you?"

"The same with me."

What had really impressed him, de Gier reported, was Ramona's apartment, which he thought to be artistic, a study in yellows, oranges and some reds, cushions, carpets, a couch, a painted table, the furniture dominated by a wall-sized wooden collage. Ramona's ancestors, she had told de Gier, were West African. Her original tribe had a custom. All members, when

entering adulthood, had to put together decorative arrangements that symbolized their spiritual path and aspirations. The
collage then served as an inspiration for daily life. Ramona had
chosen stylized bird heads on a sheet of weathered plywood
that she found on a beach. The bird heads, that she had sculpted
from dried mangrove roots and sun-bleached seashells, formed
the outline of a crocodile's body. "Symbolic," de Gier said.

"Of sex?" Grijpstra asked.

"No. Of a course of life that she had chosen." You know
what was funny, de Gier asked Grijpstra, the collage had
reminded him of the symbolism of Grijpstra's series of *Dead
Duck on Amsterdam Canal* paintings.

"My dead ducks," Grijpstra said crossly, "are just goddamn
dead ducks."

De Gier said that Ramona said that her bird heads were symbolic of petty ego-aspects becoming part of the universal spirit,
and that the crocodile, in West African art, signifies enlighten-
ment. The birds having been eaten by the crocodile, and then,
together, becoming the crocodile are "like your ducks slowly
dissolving into an Amsterdam canal." De Gier tried to explain a
little further. Grijpstra's obsession with showing dead ducks
could symbolize Grijpstra's wish to do away with his customary
stupidity, greed (of adding to Grijpstra-ness), jealousy, fear (of
losing Grijpstra-ness). "We all get tired of our ego-cling-
ing. . . ." De Gier paused for dramatic effect. "Once we've
pierced the veils, Ramona's beautiful African crocodile will
swim in your purified Amsterdam canal. You see that? Don't
you?"

"So the sex you two enjoyed was mutually helpful?" Grijpstra asked hopefully.

De Gier said he sincerely hoped so. He folded the newspaper cuttings and the police report and put them in his shirt pocket. There wasn't much to add. Happenstance, once again, was a factor. The Key West Police didn't think that the military had posted sharpshooters all over the city and arranged for Mickey's escape so that they could get at their target. Of course, anyone involved in the raid of the *Sibylle* would have been prepared to kill Mickey before he could betray them, but with the man in jail . . . who would have supposed that he would escape to rob a supermarket of some tobacco?

"Happenstance," de Gier said. "The ultimate puppeteer, isn't that what the commissaris called it?"

"And Mickey presented a nice target," Grijpstra said. "Wearing one of those orange jail suits, running toward them. All they had to do was point and squeeze the trigger."

De Gier agreed. A pity in a way. According to Captain Noah, Mickey was a good sort, intelligent, witty, creative. But what can you expect from a drunk? Once alcohol is involved. . . . De Gier shrugged sadly.

Grijpstra took offense. Was this another message paid for by Caring Mothers? What was so great about the sober life? Ah, the days, one wife having left, the next wife not having arrived yet, that Grijpstra painted in an empty apartment. The nights in cafés where he played billiards, drums, told jokes, drank jenever. A time of insights.

"You could be boring," de Gier remembered. "Repetitive. Sentimental. Querulous. Hard to put up with."

"Not to me," Grijpstra said gruffly.

What the hell? De Gier, admiring the dancing schoolgirls on the Statia beach below, said that since his abstaining, he missed those days too. He told Grijpstra about possible plans for a life in Key West. Face doom and damnation, cigar in mouth, double bourbon in hand. Recreate The Perfidious Parrot again, play the trumpet, consort with wild women.

Grijpstra shifted moods abruptly. "None of that." He reminded the wayward dreamer of Sayukta, back home, watering de Gier's plantation of weeds. He scanned his friend's cozy future. "A couch, a screen, a four-door Honda." And as for now, dammit, there was work to do. How were they to find a cargo equalling the lost Sibylle cargo? How could they hijack same? How to sell the loot to a fence? He pointed at the oil tanks ahead, describing the buyer of stolen crude. The fence, Grijpstra surmised, would be a sleazy type.

De Gier said "Sure. A fat guy in a pin stripe suit. Big jowls. Watery blue eyes. Bad disposition. Gets sick a lot."

The fence could look like the commissaris for all Grijpstra cared. Ever since he and de Gier had kept the drug dealers's stash, ever since the commissaris had invested the money, all three of them had become bad guys.

De Gier walked about the hotel's courtyard, arguing excitedly that Grijpstra was taking a petty view of liberty indeed. By holding onto their prize he and Grijpstra had placed themselves beyond good and evil. They were supermen now, working in Nietzsche-esque spheres of freedom. They were Bodhisatvas helping to wake up mankind. Had Grijpstra ever seen Tibetan drawings of free spirits? Often the arhats, gnanis, gurus, etc., wore necklaces of skulls, had mouths filled with fangs, were shown as skeletons moving about fires of ego-destruction. They just looked evil, but were not. He and Grijpstra were out of the good/evil confusion, but still functioning to assist the slow and stupid.

Grijpstra thought he and de Gier were just being bad. Besides, de Gier shouldn't think he was clever on the lower level either. This amazing insight, that the *Sibylle* pirates were American soldiers? The commissaris had found out on Aruba, when visiting Sister Meshti's clinic, who the pirates were. Captain Souza thought he had seen giant black frogs during a delirium. "Frogmen," Grijpstra said. "U.S. Military types. As soon as I told the commissaris about our sail on the *Berrydore* we put it together. Me and the commissaris. Frogmen—frogs." He smiled sarcastically. "Simple. . . ."

De Gier suggested a walk around the island. If Grijpstra, because of weight/age, became exhausted they could rent a car. Statia might be a wasteland ravaged by goats but there had to be something good to see somewhere. Something to tell Nellie about.

"Please," Grijpstra said, observing the mature schoolgirls cavorting in the ocean below him.

25

Looking For Little Abner

They walked.

"Did the entire island go bust?" Grijpstra asked, pointing at deserted cabins that leaned against each other or had crumbled into themselves. Weeds grew wild in empty rooms, vines covered cars discarded at street corners, changing them into bizarre and dusty flower baskets. Statians walked along in silence.

"Handsome people," Grijpstra said. "Well dressed too. Where do they get the money?"

Not by working, de Gier thought. This seemed to be a non-working island. During the two days before the *Rodney* arrived the only people de Gier had seen who were active were children. Adults rocked in chairs on balconies, nodding greetings at passers-by. The island's religion still seemed active, for de Gier had walked by a church filled with singing voices. There were parties: he saw women in semi-transparent dresses waving fans on a lawn. He noticed a garage where dying cars resisted repairs, a bakery offering one kind of bread, used clothes sold out of a shack, a government building where silent officials sat quietly behind empty tables. A restaurant was, according to a handwritten note taped to its window, "Closed for Season." Another shack offered picture postcards of scenes on neighboring islands. De Gier told Grijpstra about a fish market he had discovered, open from 8 to 9 A.M.

"A lot of fish?" Grijpstra asked.

"Very few fish."

"So what do they eat here?"

Roadkill, de Gier thought.

Grijpstra tried to ignore the plaintive wail of unmilked goats, skin-and-bone cows breathing hoarsely, donkeys with open wounds, madly scratching dogs, starved cats coughing. De Gier, to cheer Grijpstra up, pointed at curiosities. They passed a cistern built out of huge rocks, dragged up a hill by slaves, later decorated with the sculpted heads of slave masters, chalked a deadly white. A rusted moped, ridden by a boy in a jockey outfit, raced by. Water leaked from casks on an overloaded donkey cart. An otherwise bare field displayed a heap of garbage around a lopsided sign saying NO LITTER. A deserted factory had lost its roof.

To divert themselves the sweating detectives discussed clients. "You believe there are evil assholes?" Grijpstra asked.

"Only ignorant assholes," de Gier answered.

They discussed Ketchup and Karate's possible future. "So Nasty Nick did manage to hurt them," Grijpstra said gratefully. "Serves them right. Shooting a rifle near a helpless old man."

De Gier thought that frightening the commissaris was not altogether such a bad idea. A cure for conceit?

Grijpstra didn't totally disagree. The chief did, perhaps, tend to exaggerate his eternal right-ness. It was amazing that hubris didn't push him over at times. "You know what I mean?"

De Gier knew exactly what Grijpstra meant. They were walking on the beach by then, kicking cans and containers deposited by the surf. The commissaris had a downside. Admiring the man was silly, to follow him could be madness.

They discussed the case in hand. "How did your Special Forces know that Stewart-Wynne was wise to their piracy?" Grijpstra asked.

They knew, de Gier told him, because Stewart-Wynne had asked too many questions on the islands and swaggered about too much on Key West. Sergeant Ramona Symonds questioned the Eggemoggin Hotel chamberboy as to who he had let into the insurance inspector's room.

The chamberboy had shown Stewart-Wynne's suite to two big bad men. He broke down when Ramona grilled him. It wasn't his fault that the big bad men were overwhelming. Military types—short hair/tight jeans/T-shirts/muscles. The one with the mirrored-sunglasses was addressed by the one with the hairy wrists as "Captain." They found nothing, the chamberboy said, sobbing.

"Nothing to find?" Grijpstra asked.

There was a mini-cassette, sewn into the inside of Stewart-Wynne's cowboy hat, found by Harry the bicycle cop when he searched the corpse.

"Good," Grijpstra said. "Proves cops are better than soldiers." But de Gier still disliked Harry. "Luck comes to the lucky."

"You listened to the tape?" Grijpstra asked.

Sure. Fine testimonial material. Drunken dialogues conducted by privateering U.S. military men, all easily recognizable

voices. Voices of black bartenders. Voice of a Swedish prostitute, well known in St. Maarten and Key West. Boastful swash-
buckling talk. Played back for de Gier as a reward for his
brilliantly staged apprehension of the hit man Mickey.

Grijpstra asked, "Did these clearly recognizable American
military voices, that can be checked against voices of suspects in
the Key West barracks, mention the killing of the young blond
sailor by gunfire?"

Yes. Regrets had been expressed. There had been no need
for murder. But what with all the adrenaline going, the activity,
the haste—shit happens. Besides, the sailor had gestured in a
threatening manner. Maybe the boy had been armed.

Grijpstra frowned sadly, then gazed irritably at his shoes,
smeared with St. Eustatius beach tar. "But if the pirates suspected
that Stewart-Wynne had managed to collect incriminating material, why didn't they get rid of him here? In the Antilles?"

De Gier pointed at little boys that had been following them
all the way from Old Rum House and were now peeking out
from between thorn bushes. Statia was too small. Foreigners
were too visible. If they killed each other there would be
dozens of witnesses. Besides, the military had to return to their
Key West base after successfully completing their exercises in
the area.

"You're perfectly sure of all that?" Grijpstra asked.

De Gier didn't have to be perfectly sure of anything. To
have an idea that surmounted reasonable doubt—that was what
was needed now. They weren't playing cops anymore, they
were just in it for the money. No suspects to be dragged to
court. No analysis of elements that would add up to grounds for

an arrest. No trouble. Nice work, if you cared to think about it, after all. Plus one million U.S. dollars, the world's most acceptable currency. De Gier smiled.

Grijpstra looked at the litter, pushed by the surf to the far side of the beach. "Why don't they clean up here?"

"They don't do anything here," de Gier said. "What is it to us? We eat the last fish sprinkled with the last parsley chopped by the last serviceable knife in a bankrupt hotel, we take the last plane home and are happy ever after."

Grijpstra shook his head. "Right." He frowned. "It's the same ocean though. Our home is on it too."

De Gier tried to keep smiling.

Grijpstra wondered what happened to the remainder of the *Sibylle*'s crew. The young blond sailor got pecked by seagulls. The captain died of loss of his legs. What about the others? The first mate? Engineer? Communications officer? Another sailor? Were they hit on the head and heave-ho'd across a railing?

"The voices on Stewart-Wynne's tapes mentioned them," de Gier said. "The surviving crew was needed to get the tanker to the transfer pier. Afterward the crew sailed the tanker back to the ocean, and were picked up by helicopter and dropped off at another island. De Gier thought that island was St. Kitts, formerly British. The *Sibylle*'s crew members were given money enough to buy tickets out and to spare and were happy and thankful."

"They were threatened too?"

"Of course," de Gier said.

"And they'll be crewing on some other tanker now?"

De Gier shrugged. "Maybe later. First they'll have to get high on the payoff money. It may take a while."

"You're sure they weren't fish food?"

De Gier was *not* sure of anything, he had said so before.

"Don't get nasty," Grijpstra said.

If de Gier wanted to get nasty he would do just that.

"You know what *I* think," Grijpstra said, "*I* think that our theorizing is incomplete. What if the soldiers were in cahoots with the Ambagts."

"To steal their own cargo so they could collect the insurance?"

"Of course," Grijpstra said. "Castro wasn't paying. I say the soldiers may have been hired to work for a fee but it's more likely they were told they could keep whatever the fence paid them when they brought him the *Sibylle*."

De Gier danced around Grijpstra. "And then the Ambagts hired *us* to catch the soldiers they'd hired?"

Grijpstra stamped around de Gier. "And to make them pay back the entire value of the cargo they'd sold off to a fence?"

Walking along they agreed there was only one course of action left open. See the fence. There he was, they told each other, pointing at the hills ahead, at parked tankers, at gleaming storage tanks, at buildings shadowed by palm trees. They would just walk into the oil fortress, threaten to expose the boss as a buyer of stolen goods, make him transfer the value of twelve million gallons of crude at current prices to their account in Amsterdam, go home and repay the Ambagts, less eight-hundred thousand dollars, the balance of their fee.

"Right?" Grijpstra shouted.

"Right," de Gier shouted.

They marched on, in step, swinging their arms, one-TWO, one-TWO. It was a hot day getting hotter. They slowed down, passing ruined warehouses where merchants once made fortunes. A guide, in a beige uniform with a badge, offered to show the two tourists around. She led them to a slave house where people had been stored for export. The tourists were shown the fortress's cannons where sleeping Dutch marines were woken by French marines, advancing in stocking feet. But free America was no longer buying smuggled goods but buying directly. No need for middlemen on little islands. The disappointed French left, the Dutch raised their flag again, but Statia's bankrupt merchants went back to Holland and the former slaves were free to apply for Dutch social assistance. "Which is where we are now," the guide said, finishing her tour and refusing a tip.

Grijpstra was sweating. De Gier knocked on the door of Tulip's Rental. Tulip herself, a shiny giant behind an oak desk that, she said, had served Admiral Rodney once, had her husband show them her passenger car. It came with a taped voice that talked to the renters. "Your right front door is not closed." "You're low on fuel." "Your oil is leaking." "All your systems are dwindling." The voice spoke with a Chicago accent.

"What is *dwindling*?" Grijpstra asked.

"To become less," de Gier said.

A small boy, hiding behind bushes, pushed a black goat into the road. De Gier braked. The goat, unhurt, began bleating. "You hit my goat," the boy shrieked. De Gier got out and paid him five dollars.

Grijpstra petted the animal. "Nice goat you have there, friend." The boy handed out two large glass blue beads. He explained his gift. "Delft blue" beads were valuable in the slave trade. Winners of African tribal wars exchanged their prisoners for beads. When the slave trade was abolished hundreds of cases of beads were emptied out onto St. Eustatius's beaches. The beads disappeared in the sand but sometimes turned up again, were picked up by kids and sold to tourists. "Treat them good and they'll bring you luck," the goat owner said.

De Gier folded his bead into a handkerchief. Grijpstra dropped his in his jacket's breast pocket. Boy and goat went back to their station behind the bush.

The car wouldn't start. Carl Ambagt came by in a fenderless jeep, Tulip's other rental. He stopped when he saw de Gier's and Grijpstra's raised thumbs.

Carl was no longer mad at his detectives. He did get irritated again when, half a mile further along, he had to wait. Two municipal pick-ups had stopped alongside each other, facing in opposite directions. The vehicles blocked the narrow shoulderless road. The drivers were deep in conversation. Carl honked impatiently. The drivers retaliated by lengthening their islandic get-together.

Like all tribulations this one ended too. The jeep drove on and passed stables and fenced off fields where two horses scratched around between withered weeds. There was a handwritten FOR SALE sign. Stores and cafés stood empty behind open doors hanging forlornly from single hinges: sinister black holes containing lukewarm still air.

Grijpstra found a map in the jeep's glove compartment and called off road names: *Jeems, Paramira, Zeelandia,* the names of bankrupt plantations. There were no street signs on the narrow potholed roads. A disheveled white woman on large bare feet, black with dust and beach tar, smiled distractedly around broken teeth. "Transfer Station?" She tried her smile again. "Better go home, dearies." She shuffled off.

"Life in the Caribbean," Carl said. "Maybe it is too easy, right?"

The ever present small black boys pointed the way to the transfer station. The road was closed off by barbed-wire fencing, tall and forbidding looking. Behind the open gate were men armed with long rubber truncheons. The men, imposing like wrestlers, or professional boxers, wore camouflage uniforms above spit-and-polish ankle high boots. The visors of their hats pointed straight ahead.

"Are you men soldiers?" Carl asked.

The men shook their heads.

"Security guards of the oil company?"

The men nodded.

"Can we come in?"

The men shook their heads.

"We wanted to ask a few questions about the *Sibylle*," de Gier said. "A tanker. Whether she off-loaded here. Can we talk to your chief?"

The men shook their heads.

"We don't really know what his name is," Grijpstra said. "Your manager, the boss."

The man raised their truncheons, then brought them down on the palms of their free hands. The slapping was rhythmical. It looked like the men were about to walk through the gate and beat up their unwelcome visitors.

Carl turned the jeep slowly and carefully.

"Bye," Carl said.

The men presented their truncheons.

"You call him the chief fence?" Carl asked Grijpstra, as he drove around potholes, pointing the vehicle at Oranjestad, four miles down the road. "Dad calls him Little Abner. That's what the buyer looks like. Like in the cartoon?"

26

A HISTORICAL ENQUIRY

"Puzzle?" the commissaris asked. "Missing piece?"

"Sir," de Gier said. "Where exactly do we fit into the plans of the firm Ambagt & Son?"

"Look at it this way," the commissaris said. "Skipper Peter finally told me that another supertanker, also chartered by Ambagt & Son, the *Rebecca*, is on her way here. The same song again. The *Rebecca* carries a full load of Iranian crude destined for Cuba. The idea is not to let her pursue her itinerary, for Cuba won't pay Ambagt & Son."

Grijpstra and de Gier, considering the new information, and remembering that Skipper Peter was a genius in arranging connections, and what else is business other than the arranging of connections, saw a connection.

The commissaris guided their line of consideration. "Think of the business Ambagt & Son conducted with Soviet oil sold to a previous pariah, South Africa. The difference here is that

South Africa paid Ambagt & Son and Ambagt & Son didn't pay the Soviets and that Ambagt & Son did pay the Iranians and won't be paid by Cuba. Times change. Methods change. Greed remains."

De Gier saw where he and Grijpstra might fit in. Grijpstra saw it too. A little later. "Piracy," de Gier said. "Not by the military this time."

"How so?" the commissaris asked kindly.

"Military personnel are only free agents in their time off," de Gier said. "They happened to be having time off here in the Antilles when the *Sibylle* came by but they're having their time off in Key West right now."

"And their equipment," Grijpstra added.

"The military were too violent for our simple merchants," the commissaris said. "There is not all that much money in murder. Besides, murder severs connections."

De Gier agreed. "Let the suckers go so that they can come back to be cheated all over again."

"Continuity," Grijpstra remembered, "a principle of profit."

The commissaris was pleased that his pupils had been learning. The Law Enforcement industry, forever financed by unavoidable taxation, is always ready to arrest, incarcerate and kill, but a commercial enterprise has to be wary of displeasing its clients.

"So," de Gier theorized. "Our client is out of pirates but then Karate and Ketchup pop up in St. Maarten and recommend Detection G&G Incorporated as just the ticket."

"But we are set up from the start," Grijpstra theorized along. "Not told what we are really in for. Led by the nose, manipulated, egged on, cajoled . . ."

"Carrot-ted, stick-ed," the commissaris added.

"Pure genius," de Gier said. "Carl had the top score on the exam he took for admission to Holland's first school of business while he was stealing super Fords for sly Pa Peter . . ."

"Gradually," the commissaris said, "subtly, we were puppeteered by this cute little fellow and his bloody-nosed pater toward the pending arrival of the *Rebecca*. Exact timing was, of course, essential. When, in the beginning, we resisted, Ketchup and Karate were told to become forceful, there was the beating, the drowning, the amusing little interplay with the feather on my hat but . . ."

". . . we gave in too quickly? Is that why we had our days off in Key West?" De Gier was astounded. He became indignant. "But I must have felt that, sir. I tried to slow us down." De Gier pointed accusingly at Grijpstra. "I did something right. Remember, in the Amsterdam café, I said we shouldn't do this?"

"The rush was my fault," the commissaris said. "I was getting bored watching your investments double. I was so eager that the Ambagts had to slow their ocean passage."

"There was nothing wrong with the *Rodney*?" Grijpstra asked.

"Probably not," the commissaris said smoothly. "In a way I am glad we're in this. Amsterdam is too friendly." He beamed at his pupils. "There is deliberate nastiness out here. Showing us up as simpletons." He raised a finger. "Conscious evil, not the wishy-washy tolerance we got used to."

Grijpstra saw no conscious evil intent. "The Ambagts happened to be greedy. The frog-fellows happened to be violent.

We happened to be silly. The *Rebecca* happens to be on the way."

The commissaris, enjoying the view from his room at the Old Rum House, sipped a drink that de Gier, self-taught herb-ologist, had brewed from wild lemon verbena. "Sure this won't kill me, Rinus?"

"Mildly euphoric. Peps you up so to speak. Sorry about the jam jar, sir. All I could find in the kitchen.

"Happenstance," de Gier said now. "That trouble with the FEADship was real. The boatswain told me when I ran across him on the beach early this morning. Normally the ship runs smoothly. Grijpstra was right, sir. It all just happened."

The commissaris objected that conscious effort can turn bad means to good ends but got twisted in his argument. He gave in. "All right then, we do happen to be here on time."

Grijpstra held his jam jar against the light, frowning at the pale green liquid. He shrugged and sipped, then shook his head, surprised at the fresh taste. "Are we really going to be pirates now and help the Ambagts in their deals with the fence?"

"Who?" The commissaris sat up, spilling his liquid. "A player I am not aware of?"

"The oil buyer at the St. Eustatius international oil terminal," Grijpstra said. "Alias Little Abner."

"We couldn't get into the transfer station," de Gier said. "Uniforms guard the gate."

"Just phone the buyers," the commissaris said. "They'll be in the Statia phone book. I'll do it for you." He winked slyly.

De Gier scratched his bottom nervously. "Uh. Sir?"

"Rinus?"

"Can't we drop out at this point?" de Gier asked. "You got

us the two hundred thousand up front. Grijpstra can have it if he likes, become legitimate again by declaring income and be happy with Nellie."

Grijpstra jumped up. "Whoa. What about you?"

"I was thinking of trying out Key West," de Gier said.

The commissaris could see that. "You might be happy there, Rinus."

"See if I care," Grijpstra said, shaking both fists in de Gier's face.

"You could stay here on Statia," the commissaris told Grijpstra. "You like church music. Play drums in the church de Gier was telling me about, with the see-through ladies singing. But first we deliver. We did take the Ambagts's money you know."

"No honor among thieves, sir," de Gier said. "Old Peachnose and Little Diddums lied to us."

The commissaris faced his own temptation. There was Aruba, the saintly cat-man, the practice of Sisters Meshti and Johanna, the broiled fish at the everything café. Meanwhile Turtle waited in the Amsterdam garden. And Katrien. "First we'll be pirates." He limped about enthusiastically. "Another childhood wish fulfilled. Do you know that I secretly wore an eye patch as a kid and waved my grandfather's army saber? And I called myself Francis Drake."

The commissaris, whose legs felt better and who had been able to manage the steep Slave Path stayed at Old Rum House with Grijpstra and de Gier. De Gier was experimenting with ragout of goat over rice. Grijpstra made salads.

The receptionist, a white-haired white lady, came to work more often, mostly to help the commissaris make sculptures out of litter on the beach.

A gardener, claiming to have been fathered by Haile Selassie, the emperor of Abyssinia, who he physically resembled, showed up to place flamboyant flower arrangements in the guest rooms and on the dining table.

"Can't you stay on the yacht?"

The commissaris told Haile, Junior he couldn't do that. An hour a day was all he could manage. He had himself rowed out in the *Rodney*'s sloop together with a nurse who treated Skipper Peter's nose. Skipper Peter, facing a drop in the stock market, wasn't happy.

Even so, the commissaris felt some sympathy. "If I had been born in Rotterdam," he told Grijpstra and de Gier, "and contracted polio at an early age, and was a practicing alcoholic, and had a son like Carl, and knew about nothing but the art of car theft and how to commit fraudulent acts with crude oil, and if I hadn't had the fortune to meet with you chaps, and hadn't been influenced by Turtle's attitude, and if Katrien hadn't grabbed me when the grabbing was good, I might, most likely, have ended up just like Skipper Peter, don't you think?"

Grijpstra and de Gier nodded politely.

"How is work?" the commissaris asked.

De Gier and Carl exercised every morning with a rented Zodiac rubberboat, equipped with twin outboard engines. The ship's helicopter was too flimsy to carry cargo, so Grijpstra took the ferry plane to St. Maarten once a day to shop. The commissaris visited Statia's library where a quiet young woman in a flowerprint dress helped out with his research on Admiral Rodney, made tea and shared the Dutch canned cookies he presented her with.

"Dear," the commissaris said. "That Admiral Rodney who

confiscated everything here is a scoundrel who interests me. Why would my Dutch clients name their yacht after a British seafarer? And why does Skipper Peter dress up like an admiral?" The librarian told the commissaris that Admiral Rodney had been a winner. "But who won from Admiral Rodney, dear?" The librarian brought the commissaris books on the admiral's life, illustrated with etchings, and took him to the little museum to show off the island's valuable collection of original documents, and had photocopies of other papers faxed in from the State Archives in faraway, never-seen Holland. "Oh, isn't this *int*eresting, dear?" the commissaris kept saying. He snapped his fingers. "Before I forget. Would you have an envelope? I have to send a check to one Maurice Maslof, my cabdriver friend on Aruba. Do you think you could find Maurice's correct address?"

"How could you forget to pay an Aruban cab driver?" The librarian had been to Aruba. She knew how tough things could get on the real islands. "Didn't the cabbie pull a knife on you?"

The commissaris hung his head. "I was the bad guy, dear. I paid the poor man with toilet paper and got away in a jet plane."

The commissaris telephoned Inspector Simon Cardozo of the Amsterdam Municipal Police and asked for some days-off for the inspector's subordinates Ketchup and Karate. As a favor to a helpless old man. Cardozo said both constables were on sick leave: Ketchup, in their apartment overlooking the Amstel; Karate, in their Caribbean holiday house. The commissaris put in a conference call. "Let bygones be bygones, come out here or I'll send de Gier after you."

* * *

De Gier fetched the volunteers from St. Eustatius airstrip. Both men still functioned. Ketchup's dislocated vertebra had slipped back into place and Karate's ankle wasn't as swollen as it had been.

Grijpstra and Carl Ambagt learned to shoot grappling hooks and lines out of a mortarlike contraption the *Rodney*'s engineer constructed. The *Rodney* herself served as a practice target. Ketchup, Karate and Carl, dangling from a smoothly hoisted harness, made their way up to overwhelm unsuspecting sailors. Grijpstra skippered the twin-engined rubberboat used as an assault-craft. It wasn't easy to avoid the obstacles presented by Cutthroat Ledge, Dead Man Coral, Gallows Rock, a pair of hard to see sandbanks known as The Graves, Wreckers' Shoals and reef-surrounded, tiny, Smutty Nose Island. Carl liked the names. "We're not doing anything new, right?"

Grijpstra flew in and out of St. Maarten's airport. He fetched wetsuits, goggles, black paint, balsa wood, chisels, power tools, fireworks, freshly baked muffins and biscuits, frozen veal croquettes, cookies for the commissaris's library lady-friend, pickled herrings, a wheel of Gouda cheese, oversized candy bars and other delicacies and staples to satisfy the needs and cravings of the attack group, no longer content with roadkill-stew on stale bread.

"Don't you just love this kind of friendly cooperation?" de Gier asked the constables, waking them in an Old Rum House back room.

"Remember how you like us being your role models," Grijpstra told the fatigued constables.

"Where would you be without us?" de Gier asked.

"Home," Ketchup said, "Switching between the porno and

soccer channels on the dish. Tell me why I am climbing ropes at midnight dangling over sharkfins cutting through riptides?"

"Not for the money," Karate said. "We have everything money can buy. I've got everything money can buy up to *HERE*."

"Yes," Ketchup said, "but why be abused?" He rubbed his aching body. "Why not just *leave*?"

Grijpstra wasn't sure whether the constables were still needed. Maybe he, Carl and de Gier could do the job. Too many bodies might get in the way. De Gier thought so too. He was checking the ferry plane's schedule to St. Maarten airport.

"You could have your next meal in Amsterdam, boys."

The constables said they were kidding, they really liked this job. They were having fun. Truly.

27

The Road Is The Goal

"One should," skipper Peter Ambagt said, "put one's goal as far away as humanly possible, it should be almost unattainable." The commissaris, visiting his client on board of the *Rodney* asked why so.

"I am quoting my father," the skipper said. "He drove a number 10 streetcar, Rotterdam Center to Rotterdam North, always to and fro. He wasn't happy. He set his sights higher. He wanted to be a streetcar inspector. That happened. Dad was promoted—different uniform, stripes, chevrons, nice hat. Streetcar drivers saluted Dad. He didn't go any higher for he never aimed to go any higher. Was Dad happy? He was not. City Transport retired him early, to be rid of his complaining. Did retirement make him happy? Never. The pay was too little and TV was boring and Dad had all these aches and pains. He solved his problem by crossing the street in front of trucks. Too close, so the first time his leg was broken, but the doctor fixed that and then it got smashed again. The doctor couldn't fix that too well and his third accident brought on a heart attack. That did it."

"Dead?"

"Yep," Skipper Peter said. "One unhappy, dead Dad."

The commissaris was intrigued. "But you're aiming higher. You'd like to be City Transport Director?"

"Federal Minister of Transport?" Skipper Peter asked. "Maximal state pay plus a little squeeze here and there? But would that be enough?" He squinted at the commissaris, lowering his head so he could look across his bulbous nose. "What did you set yourself as a goal in life?"

"Nothing," the commissaris said.

"Beg pardon?"

"Not-something," the commissaris said. "Because if it was something I would get it and then what. Right?"

"Your target is Nothing?"

"That's correct."

"Nothing can't be," Skipper Peter said. "Oh. I see." He smiled wistfully. "The ever-receding? Like love or something?"

"Nothing," the commissaris said firmly.

"Right." Skipper Peter held his head to the side, as if he were trying to look around the commissaris. He touched his nose carefully. "Good idea, maybe. I've thought of that too. It's logical in a way. Put off your goal to where there's no way of getting to it ever. That way there'll never be disappointment." He tittered. "Mhree mhree. Further and further. All the way to Zero?"

"Zero is still something," the commissaris said seriously. "It has a rim." His finger drew an oval. "You'll want to get rid of that."

"Take the rim off Zero," Skipper Peter said, leaning further out of his chair, about to fall out altogether, but the servant set him upright again. "Then what?"

The commissaris changed his tone from didactic to respectful. "And your goal, sir?"

Skipper Peter straightened his admiral's hat, put his hands on his knees. His voice suddenly boomed. "Three hundred million dollars. I tripled my goal last year. It used to be a hundred but times change, sirrah."

"Things certainly aren't getting any cheaper," the commissaris said understandingly. The commiseration pleased Skipper Peter. He now felt free to complain, between thoughtful sips, that that one hundred million dollars, for which he and little Carl had been working themselves to the bone all these years, was required for daily needs. In order to be quite free of any worry the target had to be adjusted. Ambagt Senior held up three fingers. "One third of a billion."

"You're close?" the commissaris asked.

"Not quite." Skipper Peter pushed out his lips and half closed his eyes. "I'm prepared to take a calculated risk that will close the gap."

"Amazing." The commissaris raised his voice and slapped both thighs. "Amazing, Skipper. I am the man you need at this very moment. Calculated risk. Yes." He stared at the skipper in utter amazement. "A coincidence. Heaven smiles!"

"You're into taking a calculated risk yourself?" the skipper quavered.

"Am I ever." The commissaris moved up his chair and bent lovingly toward his host. "And I am . . . ," he whispered, indicating a distance of a millimeter between the tips of his index fingers, ". . . I am *this* close to reaching that goal, of making my fortune, Peter."

"Yes?" Skipper Peter asked hoarsely. "What makes you think you're going to be that lucky?"

"Lucky?" the commissaris asked. "Who trusts Luck? Good Fortune eats you so Misfortune can throw you up." He carefully tapped the glass tabletop supported by the upturned nude. He raised his voice. "What I trust is Certainty only." He shouted. "BULLSEYE, Peter!" He dropped his voice. "I go by totally reliable inside knowledge only. You know what?"

"What?" whispered Skipper Peter.

"My wife's brothers are directors of banks *and* of a certain corporation." The commissaris clapped his hands. "One thousand percent sure. The stock is down to its lowest possible level. It's poised to go to its highest. A phenomenal turnabout." He slapped the least painful of his thighs. "The opportunity of the century, my dear friend Peter. I'm going all out." His glasses slipped off his nose but the servant managed to catch them. "Thank you, my dear," the commissaris sighed, leaning back exhausted. He addressed his host again. "All my speculating life I waited for this. I will wager my wad, sir. Borrow another. Call in all favors, mortgage my property, scrape up every last cent." He got so excited he had to pat his chest to release some air. "This is *It*. Afterward I retire." He smiled weakly. "Nobody will see me again. I will roam about freely." He waved at the environment. "Live off the fat of land and sea."

Skipper Peter raised a warning finger. "You said you were after Nothing just now."

The commissaris laughed. "I lied."

The skipper's face came closer. "Count me in, Jan."

The commissaris got up with some difficulty and shuffled around the skipper's deck chair. He was half speaking, half chanting. Certainly he would count the skipper in but first the *Rebecca* job would have to be done, and the remaining eight hundred thousand dollars paid into the account of Detection G&G in Amsterdam.

"Why worry about peanuts?" Skipper Peter asked.

"Peanuts matter," the commissaris explained. He hadn't gotten where he was today by ignoring peanuts.

"Your men know?" the skipper asked hoarsely.

The commissaris sat down, smiling wisely. His disciples weren't ready yet. The concept of *haute finance* hadn't even occurred to Grijpstra and de Gier as yet. The commissaris nodded to add emphasis. "My project, dear Peter, is for the initiated only." He was nodding again. "For those who have proved themselves in every possible way." The ship, moved by the ocean's swell, changed position. The commissaris's face was no longer in the shadow. Sun rays illuminated his smiling countenance. "For the elite, Peter." He pointed at Ambagt Senior. "For *you*." He pointed at himself. "For *me*."

Skipper and commissaris seemed at rest, eyes closed in meditation, hands folded devoutly on the tops of their canes. Communication, however, seemed to flow at its highest level.

"Why did you join Grijpstra and de Gier in this adventure?" Skipper Peter asked after their meditation had ended. "I didn't frighten you, Jan, into that decision, did I?"

The commissaris congratulated his friend on the astute nature of that question. He saw no point in using half truths, considering the elevated nature of their togetherness at this moment.

The cruel beating that de Gier suffered, the immersion of Grijpstra in foul waters, the whistling bullets in the Silent Zone north of Amsterdam that had broken his pheasant feather, yes, certainly, the commissaris's *persona* had definitely been shocked. But—the commissaris leaned forward confidentially—were they dealing with *personas* here? What were personas but masks, to be worn during certain episodes only. The present project had to do with *essence*. Essence is pure being. Pure being knows no fear.

The skipper spoke solemnly too. He agreed but preferred to highlight a different aspect of human endeavor. There was the idea of challenge. Having accepted, and eventually mastered, challenges all his life he was now prepared to accept the final challenge. Now what was the name of the fund the commissaris had in mind?

The commissaris apologized. He could not say the magic word just yet. The present project had neither been completed nor paid for. But weren't he and his pal Peter sharing a special moment here, against a backdrop of the most beautiful land and seascape of their planet? Moved by the moment the commissaris could now only gesture. Once he had found his voice again, the commissaris said, "I saw that advertisement for FEADships in *Time* magazine. 'Only a few of you readers can afford the luxury of the vessel shown.' Do you know that within days I may have the honor of being your equal?"

"Share the *Rodney* with me," Skipper Peter said. "Maybe I'll move ashore altogether. Maybe here. Do the things you said. If I don't establish an official residence I may still be tax-free."

The commissaris beamed. "We will be friends."

28

Admiral George Brydges Rodney (1718–1792)

It was party time on board. To please Skipper Peter, Rotterdam cuisine, early fifties style, was served, prepared from foodstuffs the cook had helicoptered out of the St. Maarten Dutch deli.

The servant displayed an alabaster dish filled with glassy overboiled potatoes. He fetched its twin holding slimy endives. There were also mashed beets. Dessert was custard, crumbly at the edges. Coffee was weak, with milk skin floating in it. The alcohol was a brandless chemical Dutch gin, "young jenever," poured from a label-free glass jar.

The skipper raised his shot glass. "Rotterdam backstreet moonshine. Teehee." He winked. The commissaris winked back. The time had come. Both men left the room.

Once on deck, shielded from immature hostile ears by the raucous calls of gulls, friend Jan told friend Peter that he was buying Fokker Aircraft shares, a company about to be taken over by Koreans. Skipper Peter rushed to his cabin to E-mail his brokers. He came back exhausted, drank too much too quickly, passed out and was put to bed by boatswain and servant.

That he was getting so drunk now, Carl meanwhile told de Gier, was caused by surprise. The boarding and subsequent conquest of the supertanker *Rebecca* had been so easy. To think that Grijpstra's crew had used fake weapons, imitation pistols and carbines made out of stained balsa wood. To think that constables Ketchup and Karate, both in pain, and tired, nevertheless acted convincingly as fierce buccaneers. That the Pirate Air Force was no more than the *Rodney*'s mini-chopper, that Fatso Grijpstra had swaggered about as the Pirate Captain, that he, little Carl, and de Gier, hardly in the prime of life, or even in first-class condition, had shouted and snarled and jumped about and managed to be so *bad*.

"Not to forget Admiral Sir Francis Drake on our flagship," de Gier said grimly, thinking of how the commissaris had insisted on wearing a black eye patch and had been seen by the servant strutting about the *Rodney*'s decks, while being kept informed by cell-phone by his crew of the boarding of the *Rebecca*.

Yes, Carl said, to think that all members of the expedition had been made unrecognizable by Calvin and Hobbes made-in-China masks, on sale in St. Maarten. How willing the *Rebecca*'s captain had been to take his ship to the Statia pier. To think how easily the Calvins and Hobbeses had disposed of the *Rebecca*'s crew on the island of St. Kitts afterward, presenting the crew members with reasonable amounts of money. How the abused crew showed genuine smiles when the rubber boat took off. "Have a nice day Calvin, thank you Hobbes." How easy negotiations had been between Carl Ambagt and the fence, alias "Little Abner," Statia's oil buyer, escorted by burly guards dressed in army fatigues, who each carried a suitcase filled with crispy greenbacks, soon to be deposited into an Ambagt account with a Statia bank.

"Any more supertankers on the way?" Little Abner asked. "Won't your insurers refuse to meet a second claim?"

Carl Ambagt didn't think so.

To think that the only mishap was a serious rupture of Skipper Peter's delicate nasal skin.

"It all went so smoothly," Carl sighed. "You guys proved there was no need for those damned Special Forces to waste that poor young *Sibylle* sailor."

Grijpstra, who didn't care for Rotterdam food, called Carl names.

Carl was unhappily surprised. "Beg pardon?"

"No need for you to use violence back in Amsterdam on us either," Grijpstra growled. "On *us*. Remember the skeletons, the mucky water, the pheasant feather? Amsterdam is supposed to be a pleasant town."

Carl, spilling young jenever, admitted to a burden of guilt. He knew now that the set-up could have been carried out by gentler means. "Respect For The Other." Carl thumped the table. "Love your neighbor. Don't do onto your fellow suckers ... you are right, you are *right*." But he had learned. He stood corrected. He thanked his teachers. If only he could have come out of denial earlier. If only he had known G&G before. He would have hired them to hijack the *Sibylle* as well. *Without* bloodshed. Happy folks all around. One tanker a week. Think of the money they could have made. He slapped his forehead.

"You had your father hire Captain Souza because he was incapable and that young fellow because he was an innocent, to make things easier for the Special Forces," de Gier said. "Go on. Admit it. We're friends now. Remember?"

Carl looked unhappy. Did they really think he was that bad? Even after all they had lived through together? Couldn't they understand that Carl's only mistake had been that he hired human dogs who went out of control once he and his father let them off their leashes?

"The young sailor died," de Gier said grimly.

And Carl *was* sorry. Really. Things will go wrong sometimes. But he was basically a good guy. Not a drug dealer like Detection G&G had been thinking all along. Cars and crude oil are legitimate products. He was a Rotterdam gentleman/privateer, belonging to a time-honored honorable profession. Carl kept saying that, long after Skipper Peter had been carried to bed by the staff and long after Ketchup and Karate had demonstrated new attack-grips that went wrong somehow and put them both out so that the staff had to carry and row them ashore and bed them down in their back room in Old Rum House.

"And don't call me names, Fats," Carl told Grijpstra. "You have your million. We kept our word. Dad had it wired into your account. Your chief checked that by phone. It's all there now."

"Just a moment," de Gier said. "What about the death of Thomas Stewart-Wynne, friend?"

Carl swore neither he nor his father were involved. He read the news in the Key West papers: *Tourist in rental jeep enters*

restaurant and breaks neck. Carl couldn't believe de Gier's attitude. "Jeezus H. Kur-rist. Stewy got killed by the Special
Forces."

De Gier asked the servant for another soda.

Carl, about to reach a zebra-skin covered couch, was disturbed by the can popping open. He tripped on the corner of a
Tibetan rug. Boatswain and servant carried off his limp body.

All this kept the commissaris from reporting on the life of
George Brydges Rodney (1718–1792) but once he stood over
them, holding his cane, Grijpstra and de Gier agreed to listen.
The infamous admiral managed, the commissaris told his students, to loot St. Eustatius itself, or rather, its complete wealth,
for the Golden Rock itself was left by the scoundrel.

"Admiral (First Baron) Sir George Brydges Rodney, reached
the age of seventy-four. He was brilliant. I know now why the
Ambagts used his name for this vessel.

"February 3, 1781, a mere two centuries ago. Rodney,
British mariner and warrior, took St. Eustatius by complete surprise. King George III's personal friend, First Baron Admiral
Rodney, was delighted to receive orders to devastatingly
punish the isle of St. Eustatius.

"Why?"

Because, the commissaris explained, as he strutted about the
Rodney's spacious bar room, because of jealousy. The merchants
of St. Eustatius made fortunes while supplying Washington's
armies, and assisted the rebel general to win his war against his
British overlords. But that wasn't all that enraged George III.
What really got the royal ruler upset was that, once the Ameri-
cans had won their fight for freedom, the Dutch governor of
Statia was the first international dignitary to acknowledge the

Stars and Stripes, with an eleven gun salute fired from Fort
Orange. Greeting the U.S. flag that was carried by a mere sloop
of war, that happened to cruise by the island.

"Can you imagine?" the commissaris asked, pointing at the
sea ahead? Albion had lost. America was free. Little Holland
cheered. The commissaris raised his ginger ale. "To America,
gentlemen, land of Mulligan and Monk." Grijpstra and de Gier
raised their Cokes. "To W.S. Fields," Grijpstra said. De Gier
hesitated. "To George Carlin?"

The report on the admiral continued. How did Rodney
punish the Dutch merchants for saluting America? He landed at
the port of Oranjestad. "Right here." The commissaris pointed
at lights flickering ashore. "After dinner, at dusk, and because
the Dutch soldiers were carousing and the Dutch merchants
were counting coins, British marines could escort Rodney
straight to the governor's mansion. Without a shot fired everything of value was confiscated. Jewish merchants were shipped
to the neighboring British island of St. Kitts, the remaining
businessmen had to help figure out what was worth what. The
British admiral kept the Dutch flag flying. Incoming vessels
were promptly boarded and confiscated. The small British naval
force was kept busy and amused. "The loot . . ."

"Right, right, right," Grijpstra said. There had to be a happy
ending or the commissaris wouldn't be smiling and strutting
so. The Ambagt vessel was called *Admiraal Rodney*. Bad Rodney, like the bad Ambagts, was a winner. As they should not
be. And as, in the end, they wouldn't.

De Gier, arguing along the same lines, tried not to anticipate
a happy ending. Neither Nietzsche nor any good contemporary
guru would approve of de Gier's need to make things come out

right. There was no right. Right and wrong are egotistic and therefore momentary interpretations. And as things keep going, there is no end anyway. So what was he doing here? Just watching, de Gier told de Gier. He did hope the admiral would fall on his face though.

The commissaris intuited Grijpstra's and de Gier's reflections. "Are you with me?"

Grijpstra heh-heh-heh-ed in anticipation. "This is going to be good, sir."

De Gier heh-heh-heh-ed along.

"The loot," the commissaris continued, "was enormous." If his audience took into account that England was deeply in debt, and that Rodney organized an auction and collected five million British pounds sterling, in gold, in return for the confiscated stores, cargoes and vessels, they should be able to share King George's joy.

"I'm against sharing," Grijpstra said.

De Gier, his brief insight long forgotten, didn't like the idea of sharing joy with British royalty either. A scoundrel and bluffer like this pompous admiral, an anti-Semite, plucking a fortune from a defenseless group of hard working merchants?

"You know," the commissaris said confidentionally, standing between de Gier and Grijpstra, speaking in a low voice, "What we got ourselves caught up in here is a direct continuation of what happened then?"

"Rodney's loot?" Grijpstra asked.

"Ambagts's loot?" de Gier asked.

Five million solid gold coins were loaded into the bad admiral's flagship. And a beautiful ship she was, a glorious three-decker, over one hundred guns, several of the guns capable of shooting seventy pound projectiles, so-called "caron-nades." Carrion-cannon. Able to cause havoc, especially at short range. "Golden age hi-tech," the commissaris said.

"Yes yes yes?" asked Grijpstra and de Gier.

Rodney's ship *Victory*, the commissaris said, accompanied by two slender but heavily armed frigates, sailed proudly for England but the flotilla happened, near Ireland, to be struck by a sudden windstorm. The frigates got lost and the tattered *Victory* sailed alone.

"Yoho," Grijpstra and de Gier shouted.

The lonely flagship heeled over dismally. Half the crew was swept overboard. The remaining sick and wounded sailors tried to push heavy guns back to their stations. Gold coins from broken chests hurt their bare feet. The gunpowder was wet through. Sails were torn and useless. The ship, about to flounder on Irish shoals, was to be saved by a Dutch privateer.

"There we go," de Gier said.

The privateer's captain, leading a boarding party that swung across on cables connected to grappling hooks, was happily surprised when he inspected the *Victory*'s holds. Five million golden pounds were brought to Holland and surrendered to the Dutch authorities who had signed the captain's Permit to Plunder.

"Authorities," Grijpstra said. "We know what they do with found treasure."

"Take it to Fiji," de Gier said. "St. Maarten. The Florida Keys. Party it all away in Las Vegas. That captain was just paid his wages."

The commissaris begged to differ. His research at the St. Eustatius Public Library proved that, although some of Statia's recaptured money was spent on elegant gable houses on the Gentleman's Canal, the bulk of the money was invested in sea-dikes, creating more farmland by draining lakes, and building faster frigates that would bring in more loot. A few coins had even been paid to the Statia merchants as recompense for their losses. The commissaris nodded. "Yes, and the privateer's captain was pensioned off handsomely and lived on a small farm North of Amsterdam for some twenty more years."

"With a buxom blonde wife?" Grijpstra asked.

The commissaris smiled affirmatively.

"With a lithe golden-skinned oriental lady?" de Gier asked.

The commissaris smiled affirmatively.

"And Admiral Rodney?" Grijpstra asked.

"Admiral First Baron Sir Brydges Rodney was jailed, by his former friend King George III, in the Tower of London."

Grijpstra cheered. De Gier applauded. "Hurrah," the boatswain, who had been listening in, said respectfully. "Great work," the servant said kindly. An older Chinese, a quiet man, who normally working as assistant-cook but that evening helped out with serving, kept on polishing glasses.

"Hurrah?" Grijpstra suggested.

"Things often work out different," the assistant cook said.

29

Things Often Work Out Different

Skipper Peter spent the morning handling telephones, faxing handwritten notes and working his E-mail keyboard. He bought Fokker Aircraft shares with savings and on margin. He bought at going prices. The share price was dropping and his brokers urged caution but he shouted them down. "Buy buy buy, you hear me?"

Buy, buy, buy, it was. Brokers like commissions.

So he was losing some money, Fokker Aircraft would soon pick up again. "Right?"

"Right," the commissaris said, smoking his very last cigar on the poop deck. "Right you are, dear Peter."

Hot tip, Fokker Aircraft. The Koreans were just waiting to take the ailing company over. Shares were down to eight guilders, but about to double, and double again. How much had Skipper Peter invested? Two hundred mill? Double that once and he had already overshot his target.

★ ★ ★

Grijpstra shook his head when, one lazy morning at home in Amsterdam, in bed, not two weeks later, Nellie gave him the paper. There she was, front page, color, the *Admiraal Rodney* seized by creditors, being chained to a mooring in St. Maarten's port.

That evening de Gier and Sayukta were invited to dinner at the commissaris's home. De Gier refused second servings of Javanese rice with shrimp crackers on the side. "Your favorite dish," Katrien said indignantly. "Are you ill?"

"Rinus groans all night," Sayukta complained. "I can't stand it. I thought I had found my true hero and he keeps breaking out in a sweat and trembling." Her wide eyes became wider. "Sometimes he cries."

"He hasn't heard the good news yet," the commissaris whispered to his wife, winking. "He doesn't know it's all over. For Grijpstra too. Grijpstra doesn't know either."

The commissaris, in his weathered cane chair, between the weeds in his rear garden, about to light up his very last afterdinner cigar, asked de Gier how he felt now that the Ambagts no longer carried their burden.

"Nothing changed for me," de Gier said sadly. "Those growing numbers in Luxembourg, they're in my dreams."

"No more," the commissaris said. "They're back to zero, dear."

De Gier didn't get that.

"Your loot is gone," the commissaris said helpfully. "And the account is closed. You recall that you and Grijpstra gave me a power of attorney?"

De Gier laughed.

"Are you all right?" Katrien asked indignantly.

De Gier was about to leap about the garden when a thought struck. Had the commissaris invested his and Grijpstra's money in Fokker Aircraft? That would have been stupid. But there was a flipside to that option. Stupidity in a teacher releases the smart pupil. Could de Gier now return to Key West and be bad there?

There was no need. "I invested in Meshti," the commissaris told him, "and in the good sister Johanna, who take care of the destitute terminally ill."

"That was a lot of money, Jan," Katrien said. "Aren't you overloading the dear sisters?"

The commissaris was hopeful. "They're kind of special. They'll take care of the money."

"What money?" Sayukta asked.

"It's a long story," the commissaris said.

De Gier was sent to tell Grijpstra the good news.

"Good," Grijpstra said.

"We still have that honestly earned Ambagt million," de Gier said.

Grijpstra shrugged. "That'll go to taxes."

His prediction proved to be 63 percent true. There was still some left, to be invested in bonds by Nellie. The bonds's guaranteed income wasn't enough to support G&G's lifestyle, not with Sayukta refusing to have de Gier live off her wages and de Gier having to pay rent for the loft. "To work," Grijpstra said happily. G&G advertised. Clients came. By that time Grijpstra had news about Skipper Peter Ambagt. According to the boatswain who Grijpstra met in the jazz café Endless Blues, the old man dropped dead after the servant brought him the paper with the Fokker Failure headline. "He wasn't too healthy anyway," the boatswain said. "His nose. Incontinent. Cirrhosis. Mood shifts. Not a happy man at all."

"And the *Admiraal Rodney*?"

The FEADship, sold by auction and renamed *General Schwarzkopf*, was now anchored in the Gulf of Bahrain, facing Qatar. A sheik was the lucky bidder. The sheik, easy to get along with now that oil prices are rising again, and not really a Fundamentalist although he prays on the poop deck a lot, likes to dally. The boatswain dallied along but had overdone it a little, so he was given one week off.

And Carl?

The boatswain hadn't seen Carl since Fokker Aircraft's sudden nosedive.

A few weeks passed. De Gier, visiting Rotterdam to have dinner out with his sister, a once-a-year ritual, saw Carl at the next table in a medium-priced restaurant.

"How're you doing?"

Carl said he was doing fine, thank you. Although the prediction by a certain Jonathan—Carl had once stayed at Jonathan's Inn, more like a Bed & Breakfast, Jonathan was recommended once by Stewart-Wynne, remember Stewy, the guy in the jeep, right? Key West, right?—Well, Jonathan, a priest in his off time, voodoo, a seer, that sort of thing, on the Antillian island of Anguilla, had de Gier been to Anguilla? Well, Jonathan had "seen" Carl living in poorly furnished rooms, lino floors, bare minimum sort of thing, right? Okay, that had actually happened now, but Carl had found pleasing work.

"In the automotive business?" de Gier asked.

"Try again," laughed Carl.

"Crude oil perhaps?"

"Once more," laughed Carl.

De Gier raised his hands.

"Teaching Spanish," Carl said.

"Teaching who?"

"Anyone who answers my ad in the *Rotterdam Herald*."

"You like that?"

Carl said he loved that. He loved his lifestyle too. No nose-bleeding daddy-o, no endives or smashed beets, no nonpaying Cuban clients, no finance calculations that wouldn't fit onto the screen of his pocket calculator, no tubes clogged by rats, or fuel lines by microbes, no helicopter that was allergic to sea-air, nobody to put up with but a baby crow he had found in the park the other day and who had the run of his rooms. Carl addressed de Gier's sister, a quiet woman who knew what was what. "Whatever you do, ma'am, stay away from FEADships, and if you can't do that, don't equip them with choppers." He turned to de Gier. "Right?"

"That little fellow was rich once?" de Gier's sister asked after Carl rushed off to make his appointment with his next Spanish language pupil.

"He had enough," de Gier said. "Enough is too much, you know that? Poor is better. *No* always outweighs *Yes*." He patted his sister's hand. "Not to be what we think we are, Catoh, is the key that unlocks the mystery."

Catoh hated that. She had hoped that, now that her brother was forced to work again at last, and courted a sensible woman, and talked about buying a four-door car, he would be done with all that negative thinking.